HOW THE WIRED WEEP

IAN PATRICK

To [illegible],
Best wishes.

COPYRIGHT

First edition printed in 2020

DEDICATION

TO DAVID SHEPHARD.

A man, who saw decency in those rejected by society and provided wisdom to many in times of doubt.
You will never be forgotten.
Ian.

1

ED

'Where is he?' Sienna asks, as she turns her wrist to observe a watch that isn't there. Commuters depart for their destinations and stragglers now rush for the Tube and bus.

'He'll be here,' I tell her.

I know he'll be here. I relax with the vibration of the engine. Bide my time, observe and remain alert. It's at times like these things can go wrong.

'Ed, he was always late. I don't know why you kept him on the books.'

I've no idea what's eating her today but a big part of me hopes she'll relax.

'Because he's the best we have, that's why,' I remind her.

'Get out! He's been inside for six months,' she jokes but makes a fair point.

'That's right and the figures, since his incarceration, reflect his holiday. When you get more experience in this role, you'll understand,' I tell her, in a light-hearted way.

It has only been thirty minutes since the agreed meet time. Some cops just don't have the patience. DC Sienna Myles, aka Smiles does, even if she lets her guard down every now and then. She's sat in the back of our covert vehicle. The blacked-out rear and side windows shield her from outside observation. I'm at point in the driver's seat.

A phone in the central console vibrates. I move the other phones aside and select the one that displays the name, Ben, on the small screen.

'Yes.' I want to hear the voice before I say more.

'It's Ben. Look, man, I know I'm late, yeah. I had no money, but I've got a lift. Should be with you in about...' His voice becomes faint. There's another voice in the background. It's a male relaying the expected time of arrival.

'Five minutes, yeah?' His voice is louder. I listen and end the call.

'Was that Ben?' Sienna asks.

'He'll be at the drop point in five minutes. Time to get out. He's in a motor. It could be a cab or a mate, I don't know. If it looks dodgy just text me and I'll meet you in Danvers Street,' I tell her.

'Sure.'

Sienna takes one last look through the side mirror before getting out of the car and walks away from our vehicle and into the unknown.

2

ED

Five minutes to a source is more like twenty. I use the term source because that's what Ben is. I'm his handler, along with Sienna who co-handles him.

I have one other team member already deployed. DC John Heddon. He's in his twenty-ninth year. One more then his police career's done. The street's quiet. A postman goes about his routine. My work phone goes off. It's Sienna.

'He's out, alone, heading towards where you should be now. Dark hoody, black baseball cap and a bandana pulled up over his lower face,' she informs me.

'I'll get into the meet venue and wait for him.' I hang up, grab my coat and head towards the library, remote locking our car as I leave. There are thieves about. It's a Monday and, as we expected, the library is occupied but not excessively so.

I head towards the back. I see an unoccupied table and claim it as mine.

I display my intention of residence by opening a Metro newspaper across the table's surface. The Olympic games and the challenges of policing it will bring to London dominate the first three pages. The pressure's on. Reduce gang crime for a safer London. London can't be seen to acquiesce to violent crime when millions of eyes will be upon us. I can see the main door. Ben enters. Sienna follows shortly after. He takes off his hat and pulls down his bandana. He's lost weight but looks healthier for his spell inside. He's certainly been hitting the weights. He nods at me. He walks with a composed shuffle and sits down.

Sienna joins us. She takes the paper.

'Good to see you again my man! It's been too long. Why didn't you come and visit me inside on more than the one occasion you did, bruv? Forget how to arrange a Visiting Order?' Ben laughs at his own joke.

'You're looking good. Obviously been eating well,' I tell him.

'This is muscle not fat!' he responds at a volume not considered appropriate for the setting. Others turn our way.

'Try to keep your voice down. If we're approached by someone you know we're a charity here to offer ex-offenders recruitment.' I gently remind him of our tradecraft agreement.

'Sweet. I know the drill, you don't have to worry about me. No one knows that I'm out of prison.'

Sienna remains silent but observant of our surroundings. She doesn't pay us any attention. To anyone coming in she's in her own world reading the paper at the same table as two guys.

'What's your plans now you're out?' I ask him. It's good to establish if we have a working life left.

Ben looks around then leans in. 'I've got something for you. I heard about it when I was inside. A robbery gonna happen in the next two weeks on a jeweller's up West. All gonna be tooled up on bikes. That's what I heard.' He leans back in his seat and scans the room.

'Who told you?' I ask him.

'A fella who I was in prison with. He wants me to get a message out to one of them on the job. A guy called Troy. I'm to meet him tonight and tell him Fat John says, 'do it'. That's all I know. I'm gonna need cash to meet this guy though as I'm broke.'

'Do you know this Troy? Where are you meeting him?' I need more than he's choosing to give me.

'I know he'll be at a house party in Hackney tonight. Fat John says turn up and I'll be shown to Troy.'

'Who's Fat John?' I ask.

'Big lump, he is. I don't know him that well. He just heard I was getting out and wanted a favour doin',' he says.

'How long have you known about this robbery?'

'Before I was leaving. Came into my cell and gave his instructions.' Ben looks over his shoulder. The comfort of the library is slowly becoming a tomb. I need to spell something out to him. A reminder about how we work.

'I can't tell you to do that, you know that don't you? You've just got out and we've not done the paperwork to get you authorised to work for us. You'll have to give it a miss tonight.'

Ben waves his hands above his head and rocks back in his seat.

'If I don't show up I'm a dead man. It's all been set up.' He's not happy.

'All he's asked you to do is pass a message on. He could have done that by phone or got Troy or one of his cronies to visit him,' I inform him.

'Look it ain't that simple,' Ben states as he leans back in.

'Go on.' I need him to see I'm interested.

'I've got to collect a parcel first and deliver it to Troy at this party. The parcel is at Fat John's bird's house. I swear I don't know what's in it. He needs it taking over tonight with that message. If I don't then he says he knows where my mum lives and she'll suffer,' he replies as he scratches what appears to be four days worth of stubble.

'You do what you have to but you're not acting on any authority, from police or me as your handler. You do it and it all goes wrong then you're on your own. I need to arrange another meeting with you and my boss. We've got a new DI. It won't be until tomorrow before he can see you.'

Ben lowers his head, turns away from me, sucking his lower lip and rubbing his hands.

I'm conscious of the predicament he's been put in but he needs to know his place in the pecking order out here. Loose cannons only waste balls. I try to placate him.

'Look, you know how these things usually work. They come to nothing or the guy who needs the parcel isn't where he's meant to be. How would anyone know you didn't try to get the parcel or go to the party to deliver it?' I tell him. Ben isn't convinced. I press the message some more.

'Trust me. Tonight can wait. If they're serious about the job they'll work with you if they know you're not messing them about. You've just got out. They'd expect you to be off your head tonight,' I explain, hoping he'll see sense.

Ben turns towards me and nods his disappointment. He scrapes his hands through his dark, lank, greasy hair.

'Look, here's twenty quid. Get your phone topped up and call me again tomorrow. We'll get things officially sorted out, OK? Go and have a night out,' I instruct him. Ben's face says it all.

'On twenty quid? You lot are a fuckin' joke, bruv.' Ben takes the money and grabs his hat. He gets up and leaves, pulling the scarf over his lower face as he hits the streets. Sienna looks up from her magazine.

'Well, that went well,' she says. I add nothing. She's right; it wasn't how I'd hoped the reunion would play out.

A male now appears from behind the bookshelves and walks over. We both turn towards him as he takes a seat at our table.

'I'd say it was a right car crash.' I look at DC Heddon.

'Let's grab a coffee,' I tell them.

We leave separately. I get Sienna to collect the car while I get some fresh air and head towards our usual coffee place. The other two will meet me there via their own routes. We never leave as a group.

I pull up the collar on my coat as I exit the library.

I'm conscious of another meeting later. Not work-related. This one is set in stone and I can't afford to miss it. A bus draws up and I jump on. I pay the fare and take the upper deck. I feel safer up high. If anyone's followed me from the library I'll get a better look at them coming up the stairs. I feel blocked in but the risk of follow was low on this occasion. That includes from police as well as criminal; police follow people away from prison who are of interest, as do criminals. All risks must be minimised.

The journey is brief. The Costa coffee a welcome sight as I alight the bus and enter.

3

BEN

What a waste of time. I should have known when he finally turned up at prison on some kind of bullshit visit that he'd be bad news. Fooled me again into working with him. I'm nothing to him, just a mouthpiece for information. He calls me his source. He doesn't care. I mean, twenty quid? Twenty quid won't get me a draw and credit for a phone! The man's a fool. He's got his priorities up his arse. I told him I didn't want to meet no one else too. Now he tells me there's a new man in charge who I *have* to meet before I get to see the real money.

Ed has proper mugged me off and now I can't get home. I need to eat. I can see a KFC and look at the twenty. I need a smoke more than that type of food. The food I want needs prior arrangement. I have some credit left on my Nokia that I got back from the screws when I left prison. Fool Five-O never took it. I try the best number for weed in north London. I wait for a connection. The doorway I'm hidden in is good to chill. The line's dead.

I see a guy I used to roll with, he's heading for Angel Tube.

'Yo, Curtis! What's up, bruv? I'm back out.' I move towards him waving my hands. He stops and comes back, eyes about. He must be carryin'. He moves in and gives me a man hug.

'You buying?' he asks me.

'Do I look like I'm makin' money? I ain't got anything yet. I've just got out,' I say. I feel my coat pocket move.

'I've had a decent morning. You don't forget my generosity now.' The man's good.

He breaks away, we fist bump as we separate.

'So, what's happenin' with you? You lookin' fit as fuck since you been inside,' he tells me.

I smile at the compliment.

'What else am I gonna do banged up? We've gotta be fit for the battle. It's a brutal place, the street, so I'm hearin' right now.'

I'm always fishing for what's going down. I make money off other people's loose talk. No one suspects me of talking to the police. Never have.

Curtis wouldn't be talking to me if he knew I'd had him lifted once. Five months he got off the back of my information and two hundred notes for me, courtesy of the filth. Way I seen it was he was wanted by police and would have been nicked anyway, so I might as well profit from his sorry fix.

I remember getting the reward money from my man, Ed. It was the last I saw of him before I got sent down. I blew the cash on gear and drink in one night.

Sweet as until the next day Five-O picked me up for something I didn't do but got sent down anyway. DNA, they said. Bollocks to that. Fit-up, I say. They came early in the mornin' and staved my mate's front door in. Took the frame out and everythin' with huge door spreaders. I was out of it and woken up to loads of shoutin'. I got dragged out of bed, put face down on the floor and handcuffed. Proper ragged me about.

Ed's different from that lot, though. He's been my go-to man ever since. Go-to for cash. He's a decent guy for a plod. He does what he says he will and pays me quick. So he should! I don't take kindly to non-payment. Last guy who owed me lost fingers.

Curtis is chillin' now he's got rid of the last wrap. We take a seat and watch the world go by. Most watch for the fun of it, but not us. I watch for the next rich opportunity to rob while he waits for the next opportunity to deal.

'You comin' to Hackney tonight?' he asks.

'What's goin' on?' I ask him.

'Troy's throwin' a party,' he replies.

'Who's Troy? I've not heard of him.' I throw that out. See what gives.

'Not heard of him? How long have you been away? Anyway, no matter. He's coming up in the ranks since he knifed one of the elders over here. That's why I'm on this corner doing what I do. No one wanted all-out war, just a corner to work from. Troy insisted on Angel and he got it.'

Sounds legit. I explore some more though.

'Why Hackney?'

Curtis looks about and lights up a spliff. He offers me a draw.

'He's got a bird there. It's her house he's trashin' not his. Tonight. Go to London Fields, you'll hear it. Be there. You need to get to know him, he'll be big here, trust me.' He gets up and takes his draw with him towards Chapel Market. Now I know I've got to go, no matter what Ed says.

There's only one word I respect and that's the word on the street. Ed's got his firm and I've got mine. What Ed doesn't know won't hurt him. I always keep my powder dry.

I check my phone and feel my stomach turn.

I pat my pocket and feel a small bag of weed. Looks like I'm good for the other food after all.

My guts feel rough after that burger. I'm too used to prison food, not the crap you get out here. I told them I was Muslim when I got sent down. See, Muslims get better food inside, all fresh and halal. None of the slop the others get served up. Plus, you get let out more for prayin' an' that. I ain't no Muslim, but the brotherhood was good to me in there.

They looked after me. I've never believed in a god. Why would I? What kind of god would create this fucked-up world, man? But they was cool.

I ain't been home yet. I need to get this parcel before I get to my place, as I know the bag of weed's callin' me. I want to chill in my own space. That's what I love about the YMCA. They give you a room and, as long as you ain't any trouble and pay your rent, they leave you alone. I lost my last room, obviously, but I was given another try now I'm out. Right now, it's all I've got. I ain't sleepin' rough again. I've run out of mates' couches to crash on.

They're all banged up for madness and their birds have moved on to the next prospect. So, the Y is it. Thing is, the women are in for a heap of shit when their fellas get out.

I've never hit a woman and don't agree with it, but my mates see things different.

I'm outside the door to Fat John's bird's flat. I pull up my hood and move my bandana up my face and ring the bell. All I can hear is barking.

Loud, deep barks. There's a woman's voice shoutin' at them to 'shut up'. I look about the street. No one's interested. I hear a chain go. The door opens a bit.

'Who is it?' Her voice sounds like she's swallowed gravel.

'I 'ave business,' I say.

'What? You ain't got none here, pal, now do one before I let the dogs see ya.' Charming. I try again.

'A guy called Fat John says I do.' There's a brief silence, then the door chain slides off. The door opens, lettin' out a smell of death. A skinny crack head lookin' girl in a long white T-shirt and black shorts is standin' there. Her hair's a mess and her eyes are red and squintin'. Her nails have old chipped varnish on. She's like a bat. Only comes out at night.

'Come in,' she says. I take another look, then step inside. I've been in some shit-holes, but this place takes the piss. My feet stick to the vinyl floor tiles the moment they touch the surface as I walk.

God knows what's sticking to my Converse shoes.

I swear I'll need to wipe my feet before I leave.

She sways through to a back room. She looks like the dog's eaten her skin and ignored the bones. I follow but keep my face scarf up. I have a blade in my pocket and put my gloved hand in and feel the comfort the shank gives me. I can see a kid's clothes are chucked about everywhere, but no kid.

The tops look small and most of the clothes are dirty and stink. Used nappies are littered among spent works and empty takeout containers. It's like walkin' through a skip. She sees me lookin'.

'Yeah? Gotta problem? Girl gotta live, ya know. I ain't got time for housework and shit.' She sits down and lights up.

I stay where I am in the middle of the room, looking out the back window at the park below. No one's playin'. I turn to her.

'So, where's it at? I ain't got all day.' She says nothing, just takes a draw.

A large mountain of clothes is stacked up in the corner. I can see a buggy wheel underneath it all, and then the clothes move.

I move back. My hand drops to my pocket. 'What's under there? You got rats?' I ask her. She throws her head back, cackling as she does. Her taut skin pulls tighter on her gaunt face.

'It's me kid, you dopey sod. He's just waking up.'

She gets up and moves clothes away. Under the ton of cotton is a kid in a buggy. He's just got a nappy on, nothing else. He's sucking a dummy and looks wasted. His eyes are as large as planets and he just stares at me. She picks him up and he flops over her shoulder. He's only four or five years old.

'How long 'as he been like that? He needs an ambulance,' I tell her. She puts him on the sofa and gets a towel from the floor and puts it on him. He stays motionless, but I can see he's breathing.

'He'll be all right. He got me methadone and took a bit. He's done it before, the little shit, but he always comes round. Right, let me get that parcel – it's in here.' She goes into the back room. I wait. He's still staring at me. Poor kid. I survived, but I don't know about him. She's off her head and he ain't getting anything from her other than gear and a screwed-up life. She comes back in carrying a JD Sports bag with a drawstring top.

'It's all here. Take it to Troy tonight. I'll be there too. I've been told to make sure you deliver and to tell Fat John if you don't turn up. Get to Archway and bell this number. You'll be told where to drop it. Party was in Hackney but he's moved it as the filth are all over his bird's estate on some knife sweep so he's havin' it at another mate's. You'll get the address when you call.'

I take the bag and look inside. It's a good weight and it ain't drugs. The twat's fitted me up with a piece to deliver and I can't refuse now. I step back and hit an open dog food can on the floor. There's a small scoop out the top and it's rotten. Even the flies are done feasting on it.

My nose has got used to the smell, now I'm about to leave. I see the open toilet door where she'd removed the bath panel to get the piece.

The toilet's blocked and spilled out everywhere. She moves the kid's feet and flops back on the sofa. I turn and let myself out. Some people don't know how to live or just don't care. Me? I'm living the dream. One thing prison taught me was how to stay clean. Shame it didn't mean clean of crime or drugs.

I take the bag and stuff it in my coat and head for the bus home. Before I go, I note the flat number in my head, and bell Ed.

4

ED

My desk phone is ringing. I reluctantly answer.

'Hunter.'

'Ed, come into my office, will you?' The line goes dead. It's my new Detective Inspector. Apparently, he's done an intelligence job before but never covert work. My ears in the job say he's an all right guy, but no backbone. All he wants is promotion and that involves gathering his own personal evidence for advancement. He hasn't overseen a unit like this one. He's here for the experience. He'll definitely have an experience he'll never forget.

I've seen this before on other squads outside of the covert world. People come in wanting to change everything but end up alienating staff, then leave. They promise much but deliver little.

I get up, exit the office, and shut the secure door to the unit. I knock twice as is customary.

I hear a chair scrape back and footsteps approach the door. He opens it. He's on an active call. He motions for me to come in and sit down. I do as he asks. He's settled in quickly. Family photo on the desk, congratulations on your promotion card next to it, probably from the wife or partner. Commendations adorn the wall. A mug claiming he's the *world's best boss* is sat proudly on a 'covert policing' mouse mat. He sits down and kills the phone call.

'Colin Ashworth, it's good to meet you. I've been sent here on promotion so I'll be grateful for any steer you can give me while I get settled in. First thing I'd like to do is organise an office meeting. Meet the team and then the Covert Human Intelligence Sources.' We shake hands across his desk.

'We call them CHIS, guv. I'll set up an office meeting for later this week,' I reply.

'Today would be good, Ed. I'm keen to get things off the ground and meet everyone as quickly as I can.' He takes a sip out of his Best Boss mug. I take a breath.

'Today it is then. It will be after five though as the team are deployed,' I add, knowing he won't want to be here past four.

This time he's the one to take a breath.

'Call them in now. I'm sure what they're doing can wait. Oh, and there's another DI outside the main office who wants to see you about a health and safety matter. That's who was on the phone. Can you meet him?'

'Of course. Will that be all, sir?' I add, giving the impression I'm a busy man.

'Yes – and call me Colin, no need for formality between DI and DS.'

I get up and leave. Sure enough, outside in the corridor is another DI. I approach our door where he's patiently waiting.

'DS Hunter?' he enquires, waving his clipboard to get my attention.

'Who's asking?' I reply.

'DI Bridges. I need access to your office to discuss a health and safety issue that's been brought to my attention. I understand you have a fish tank in there. You can't have one, I'm afraid. I also believe it's plugged into an extension socket situated adjacent to the tank. Is that correct?'

'Yes,' I reply. Honesty is always the best policy.

'Well, what's it doing in there?' he demands.

'Keeping the fish alive. They couldn't survive without water, sir.'

'There's no need for the sarcasm, Sergeant. It has to be moved. Water and electricity don't mix or wasn't that something you knew?'

'I did know, yes. I have a mate who's an electrician. It's impossible to move them at present. A number of the guppies are pregnant. I'll rewire the lead direct into the wall socket if that's what you wish?' I answer and wait.

'Now look, they shouldn't be in there. It's a covert office not a fish farm. Any electrical work *must* be done by Property Services Department and not by a have-a-go electrician with a *Wiring for Dummies* manual.'

'As I said, sir, there are pregnant fish in there. To move them now would 'cause unnecessary stress and suffering. Every fish matters, guv. Can't be done. Also, the team love them. Brings down stress. An essential management tool, wouldn't you say? Maybe you could use that for your promotion application to DCI? Now, if you'll excuse me, I've work to do.'

He's having none of it.

'Let me in now, Hunter, and that's an order.' He moves towards the door to our office.

'No can do I'm afraid. It's a covert unit. You don't have the vetting level to access it. I'm surprised you got past the front entrance. Now go do some police work.' I swipe the keycard and enter, shutting the door on him.

I walk over to the fish tank and peer through the glass. A purposeful banging can be heard on the office door. The fish remain calm, huddled in their shoal. The plants sway with the force of the air pump. I crack open the lid to the fish food, take a pinch, and watch it spread across the water. The fish rise as one to the surface and take their feed. Stragglers wait in the middle for the spoils to drop.

The rest of the team look aghast. Sienna looks up from her computer screen.

'Who have you upset?' she enquires over the banging.

'A pond life inspector and our new boss. Our boss wants an office meeting today. I told him you were all out as that's where you should be. So, keep quiet. He doesn't know the code to get in here and his keycard isn't activated yet. I'm on the phone if you need me and I have a car if there's anything active. Make sure you lock everything up before you leave. Clear desks please while the new one settles in.'

The banging persists. I grab the car keys, unlock the interconnecting door to our storage unit and emerge further up the corridor. I exit the building and find the covert car I'd left in a surrounding street. As I reach the car my phone goes. It's Ben. I wait until I'm safely in the car.

'Ed, it's Ben. What's up?' he asks not out of genuine interest.

'Nothing much. You?' I respond.

'I've got something for you but it ain't what I usually bring,' he says. He sounds keen but troubled.

'Go on?' I tell him.

'I've got a mate who's friends with this bird. He was at her house today and the place was a right kip, shit and piss coming out the toilet, old food over the floor and get this, open tins of dog food with scoops out. Oh, yeah and she's got a kid. Kid don't look too good either and it's been botherin' me, like, so thought I'd tell youse lot. The kid looked off his head like he'd taken summat he shouldn't have. Know what I mean?' Ben asks.

I look out of the car window as the phone connects to the hands-free in the covert car. I see our new DI approaching. He's established where I am very quickly. I'm impressed. He doesn't look happy though. I unlock the back doors. He gets in. Before he can speak, I put my finger to my lips.

'When were you there?' I ask Ben.

'I ain't been there! Like I said, my mate was. He told me in conversation. I don't know the woman,' Ben replies.

I've worked with him long enough to know when to press

and when to leave it. I have the DI in the car and he's listening. First time he's heard an informant.

'Have you got an address?' I ask Ben.

'Yeah, yeah, he told me where she lived an' that. Flat 2c Lavender Rd, Hackney. The two dogs are staffies, bruv. Nasty looking bitches. Could be one of them pitbill things.'

'Pitbull you mean?' I correct him to make sure I've got the right breed of dog and he isn't mentioning one I haven't heard of.

'Get you with your fancy language. What are you, my English teacher now?' he says and starts laughing. He's stoned. I get out a notepad and record the address and what he's told me.

'Leave it with me and tell your 'mate' not to go back.' I inform him.

'Sweet. When am I meeting this new fella you were speaking about? I hope he isn't like the other tosser you had,' Ben says as the DI looks at me. I shrug.

'Tomorrow. You'll meet him tomorrow. I'll let you know where and when. Keep your phone on and don't be late.'

'Cool. Bell me later.'

The line goes dead. The DI sits forward in the seat and I lean into the driver's door to see him.

'I don't want to get off on the wrong foot, Ed. I didn't expect to be dealing with an irate colleague on my first day over an insolent officer and a row over a fish tank,' he tells me, obviously not happy.

'Welcome to Covert Policing, Colin.' Is the best reply I can muster.

'I'm not green, Ed. I have a decent track record. Let's not fall out too early, eh?'

'Fair enough. I've been a dick, I'm sorry. There's been so much change for the unit recently. They're tired of the lack of support despite the constant demands for more intelligence. The fish? They love them.' It's all the truth.

'The other DI has deferred the issue to me to manage. The

fish are of little concern to me. Just move the extension away from the tank. I can see you're busy as are the other two in the locked office…I have an active swipe card now and the code. It came with my welcome package from the Detective Superintendent three floors up,' he says smiling. 'What will you do about that last call? Sounds like a child at risk of significant harm,' he adds.

'I have a mate on a Dog Unit. I'll get her to do a visit RE the dangerous dogs. If she sees the kid, then she'll make an assessment at the same time. That way the CHIS will be protected. The complaint will appear to be about the dogs. Could have come from a neighbour or anyone. Sounds to me like the kid's been eating out of the dog food cans. Small scoops have been taken off the top. Any dog that was hungry enough would have packed that away and eaten the tin too,' I tell him by way of reminding him I'm still a detective and to leave me to get on with my job. He gets the message.

'I'll leave it in your capable hands. Update me after the visit. I'm interested to see how it resolves itself. I have kids too. You?' he asks.

'No. We're trying but no luck so far,' I reply as he pats my shoulder and gets out of the vehicle.

I re-dial Ben. He answers. I recognise his voice.

'Free to speak?' I ask him.

'Yeah, cool.'

'Don't go back to that address.'

'Like I said, I ain't been there.'

'Get off you haven't.' He's laughing now. We have a good understanding. We should do. I removed him from his family home when he was left in the kind of surroundings he's just described. He was ten years old. Little did I know I'd be meeting him again when he was eighteen. He doesn't remember me. Why should he? If I were in his shoes, my memory would have blanked that day out too.

Our office is in New Scotland Yard, Victoria. Rumour has it the building is costing too much and will have to go. It has a wonderful view of St James's Park station. I start the car's engine and decide to head towards home. After the usual battle across London, I finally arrive at the first junction of the M1. Anti-surveillance is a constant facet of travel. Necessary but becomes a drag when you're in a rush. I take the first junction. First gear becomes fourth. I hit the slip road and check my mirrors. We always leave any stationary position like a soldier leaves a compound in wartime. Evasive and always on the move.

In my world you're always looking over your shoulder. Evade and escape is the game. To remain still makes you a target. A sitting or standing one doesn't matter. Always be on the move until you're sure it's safe to stop. The training I've had was for a reason: survival.

London is a war zone. My battleground is the street. My unit is on a hearts and minds campaign to keep control and maintain law and order through gathering intelligence.

5

BEN

I put on some gloves from the cleaner's room. They're the type the filth put on when they search me. Seems strange wearing them when that lot do. The JD Sports bag is on my bed. Ed always says touch nothin' but if you have to, wear gloves. I can't have my prints on this baby. I pull the neck scarf over my mouth as I've got a feelin' I could drool. I open the bag. At the bottom is an old T-shirt. That's how I knew it were a shooter and not drugs. I ain't been called to move laundry. I take it out and roll it open on my bed. I just look at first. I've seen a few tools in my time but this is special.

A MAC-10 machine pistol with a full mag of 9mm rounds plus a spare. A 'Spray 'n' Pray' as it's known on the street. It's got a suppressor too. I've heard of them but never seen one up close. A guy was convertin' these from his shed. Trident boys are offering a ten-thousand-pound reward for information about where some of the guns are now. I ain't heard nothin' on that score, but now I have one. It looks like the real deal to me. It could be worth big money either way and it's right here in my room.

I'm sweatin' at the sight. What the hell Troy is gonna do with this toy I don't know but need to find out. I know I could out this on the street for good money or give it up to

Ed, but the risk's way too high for me to hang on to it. Ed can wait. He told me not to do anything, anyway. He wouldn't be happy if I turned up with this either. He's told me he don't like gifts of any kind.

I take a drag of skunk and stare at the piece. It's a thing of beauty. Ain't no one gonna fuck with you if you was strapped with that. No one. The smoke drifts to the ceiling as I lay back and imagine a life with cash. Instagram uploads of me lyin' on a bed of twenties. No Ed. I need this. I need this so bad. Problem is Troy ain't no fool and he'll kill me if I don't deliver. If he don't kill me, then Fat John will arrange it.

These boys don't mess around. Whatever Troy's doin' must be heavy shit to have this about him. I know I told Ed I didn't know 'em but, of course, I do. Fat John ain't gonna have anyone pick up a prize like this unless he knows and trusts them. What Ed don't know won't hurt him. There's a knock on my door.

'Wait up,' I shout. I roll up the piece and put it back in the bag and shove it under my bed. I knock out the spliff and bung it in a drawer.

'Hurry up, man!' says a voice I know.

'I'm comin', wait up,' I tell 'im.

I check around, then see the gloves on my hands. I rip them off and throw them out the window. All's good. I open the door. It's Ghost.

'What you want?' I say. I'm agitated and wasn't expectin' no visitors.

'Chill. We've got a ride, you comin',' he asks me.

'Can't, bruv. I'm on a promise.'

'Screw that. I've got you a lid and everything. We ain't workin', just going on a burn up.' Ghost shows me my old crash helmet from behind his back. Black it is, with a red devil sticker on it.

'I've got a couple of hours,' I say. I shut the door and go.

Outside the low sun is busting through the smog and damaging eyes. I put on my lid and see the rest of the crew across the road, waiting. The old team back together. I'm out and ready to rip up the Barbican. I get back slaps all round and punches to the lid. I can see the smiles. It's good to return to my family, my brothers, my crew. I get on the back of the bike and Ghost pulls a wheelie as he shoots ahead. The others follow, flipping the finger at mad drivers slamming their horns. We own the road.

See the streets you walk on? You walk with our permission. We have rules. One is, if you're out on your phone, head down, with your music going then you're fair game when we ride up alongside you and rob it. If you don't resist, we'll take your cash too. We know our art and practice good. We get decent money for them items, good money. Way I see it is that you'll have insurance. You can claim and get another, so we're all sweet. I wish there was another way I could earn but there ain't any hope out there for a young guy fresh out of Pentonville.

It's all about survival out here and I intend to survive the only way I know. Now, Ed. Ed, thinks I ain't involved in nothin'. Ed thinks I'm on the outside lookin' in, hearing and seeing shit and telling him so he can do something about it then pay me off if it all works out good.

Screw him. I'd never eat if it were down to him. He's still Five-O even though he's one of the better ones. I'd rather have the Sienna girl, but he's havin' none of that. I still don't know how he recruited me into this snitching game, but he did. How he convinced me to talk, but he did.

I've been with him a few years now even though I've been inside. He waited and stuck by his word that he'd be there when I got out. Time I showed him what I'm about and where I see him fitting in with my future. Like I said, I have rules and he's gonna have to bend if he wants to work with me.

I've got a woman to support too. I'll see her later once I've chilled out for a bit. She doesn't know I'm out, so it'll be a nice surprise for her.

Man, it's good to be back with the guys hitting the streets, back on the road. Muppets everywhere lookin' at us as we ride along in a formation that says, 'don't fuck with us'. We've been all over the news, YouTube, Facebook and Twitter. We rule the streets. Ghost sees a marked scrambler up ahead with a yellow jacket sat on it. White helmet and knock-off Ray Bans. He's sat there looking at traffic.

I tap Ghost on the shoulder, and he sees the cop. The cop's seen us too. Ghost goes straight. The cop's taken the bait. He sets off slow into the traffic. My crew make like shrapnel and scatter. The cop stays on us. Ghost is a great rider. The others are carrying pills an' that. We never carry nothin' as we're the decoy.

The bike's legit too so fuzz ain't got nothing on us. Ghost's up for some fun though and he banks right at a set of lights, then right again into an estate. The cop sees this. I look over my shoulder as he moves up in the traffic, trying to get closer. Then he hits the light and noise and Ghost pulls the throttle. Cars try to shift out the way, but they can't due to all the cars an' that. Screw the road, that's what the pavement is for.

People get out the way as Ghost weaves through them. He knows the roads and alleys good. Better than any cop. It comes with livin' and breathin' the streets all day. He keeps to the pavements and people get out the way then get back on so the cop can't follow. He's seen an alleyway and he banks the bike in. I lean with him as we move. There are steps ahead. I lean back to put pressure on the rear wheel as we bounce down each step and out the other side and away.

We lost the cop. This time. The buzz is still there. The cops love a chase, as do we. I know because one of them told me. 'It's just a game of cat and mouse,' he said. 'Sometimes the mouse wins, sometimes he doesn't.' I said nothin' as the cop ain't no cat! He's a fuckin' pussy though.

Ghost sees a possible up ahead. She's on a pavement, no parked cars to get in our way. She's facetiming on her phone and no clue what's going on around her. She's dressed well in the latest designer gear. She looks the type to have her own little flat in the city and eats out every night at the best places. Not like me. A dive of a room and getting what I can blag to eat each day. Ghost nods over at her. I freeze. I've just got out, I've got a delivery tonight and the filth will be all over this area now one lost us. The temptation's still there though.

Ghost starts off slow and makes out that he's going in the opposite direction to her. She still doesn't know we're about to pounce. He swings the bike round, turns and nods at me. I pull my gloves tighter and tap the top of my helmet. Sign to go. He opens up the throttle. I hang on with my right hand on the bike and get ready to lean out at the bitch with the designer bag, all the sway but no clue. I feel like I can get the bag and phone on this hit. We're nearly on top of her now. He smashes the front wheel up the kerb to the pavement. We're ten feet behind her as he gets alongside. Then he slows.

I can hear what he's hearing too. Copter blades. Sirens get close. I tap his shoulder and make a slashing sign with my hand across my neck. He opens up the throttle as we pass her, and she falls into a hedge as we get off the pavement and do one. She'll have to wait for another day. We do a couple of side streets then stop. I get off; give him my lid to take.

'I'm on my toes, bruv. Laters,' I say as he puts his hands up in despair and I make off towards the bus. She's gone now, anyway. One thing I did learn inside is to weigh up the risk. I was too impulsive before and would have just taken her phone and bag. Not today though. Prison did me some good but not in the way society wants. I see a bus and get on. As I do, another police scrambler rips past and I can hear the copter above.

The bus pulls away and I flop back in the seat and stare out the window smiling.

6

ED

I secure the job car in a garage block away from my house. I rent the garage myself. The job wouldn't fund it but insisted we take a car home as the role's twenty-four-seven and the car must be off-road and away from my home. Our safety is paramount as long as it costs the police nothing. No one's been compromised at home. Yet. The garage is on an estate. The youngsters know that I'm Old Bill but not what I do in the police. I grew up and went to school with most of their parents. The walk home is brief and a welcome reprieve from being sat in the car for the two-hour journey home. We couldn't afford to live in London so chose the suburbs to live and sleep.

I climb the few steps to the modern two-bed semi and turn the key in the lock. I step straight into the lounge and shut the door. Dinner's on and has have been for some time. It's eight o'clock in the evening. I dump my bag on the sofa.

'I'm home,' I announce to the void that is my living room.

'I'm in here.' The response is from Lucy, my wife. She's in the ground floor bathroom off the kitchen. I touch the kettle. It's still hot so I pour two teas. No alcohol right now. We've been off it for two years since we started IVF. I take the drinks through to the bathroom where I find Lucy, adorned by bubbles, candles glowing and reading a book. I put the teas down, lean over and kiss her. She responds in a way that's indicative of being game on tonight.

It's that active time of the month where every opportunity mustn't be wasted.

'How was your day?' she asks.

'The usual with the sources; met the new boss and annoyed another,' I tell her.

'I see. Well, you'll need to microwave your dinner. You spend more time talking to criminals than you do to me.' She ducks under the water. I drink some tea. It's tepid. Foreplay over, I head for the living room and put on the TV. My work, personal and source phones are balanced on the arm of the seat. None are on silent. All of them are on the maximum ringtone. My work phone goes.

'Hunter,' I say.

'Ed? It's Fiona from the Dog Section.'

'Hi, Fiona. What's happening? Everything all right?'

'I'm just out of the address you gave me earlier. Thanks for sending me into such a desirable place, much appreciated. Even Monty didn't want to put his paws down in that house,' she says as we laugh reciprocally.

'The dogs have been taken away by the RSPCA. The child was there. He's now in police protection. He had to be taken away by ambulance the poor little sod. He really wasn't in a good way. He'll survive but he was lucky we got there when we did. You get sent to dangerous dogs and end up dealing with something way more serious. The ambulance crew reckon he may have taken something Mum was on. There were empty bottles of methadone everywhere and spent works all over the house. I looked in the dog food cans. You could see finger marks where the child had been scooping it out to eat. Some people need shooting. How they have kids is beyond me,' she finishes and I remain listening.

'I ran Monty through the house to see if there were any other drugs. It was clean, apart from the bathroom. He indicated under the bath where a panel had been removed. I wanted to double check. A mate, who was on duty, brought up their spaniel who's a firearm trained search dog. He went straight where Monty had been and froze. Whatever was in there has gone. Thought you should know. Result for the kid. Call me again if you get anything else.'

'Will do. Thanks for responding so quickly. Dogs sorted and as a bonus you've saved a kid's life, well done.' I end the call and turn up the TV. Lucy is in the room now, enveloped in a white towelling robe and balancing her nail varnish on the sofa as she spreads her toes.

'Don't forget we've got an appointment in Harley Street tomorrow with Doctor Burton. No wanking or sex tonight for you, sorry. You've got to provide a sample. I want strong swimmers tomorrow and loads of them.' She kisses me on the cheek and carries on painting her nails. I had forgotten. Our bank hadn't. The loan transferred only yesterday. It's not that I don't want kids, I do. But I know I won't be about much the way work is right now.

I reflect on the last call. It never ceases to amaze me what can come out of a chance conversation. I've no doubt Ben was there, and this 'mate' is a figment of his imagination. But that's the nature of informant and handler. One never truly trusts the other. I couldn't give Fiona the full story as she may say something that the woman would pick up and link to Ben. Dogs are part of Fiona's line of business and fitted perfectly.

Lucy finishes her beauty routine. I try calling the DI to tell him the result from the address, but his phone goes straight to answering machine. Lucy gets up and brings in the food.

'That sounded awful on the phone. That poor child,' she says.

'It's terrible isn't it? Here we are trying our best to have children and not having much luck and then there's people like her who just seem to find it easy to conceive then treat their kids like dirt.'

'What support does she have?'

'I don't imagine she has any. I'm sorry. I just find it tough to deal with sometimes, the unjustness of it. I know it's ridiculous and she's just as entitled as we are, but it doesn't seem right. I think you'll make a great mum and can't wait to see you with our baby,' I tell her as I reach for her hand. She smiles at me.

'I think you'll be a great dad too,' she says. I'm not so sure on that count. I wonder how I'll cope with work and home. I know I'll want to be about as much as possible but know how tough that will be as there's no downtime. My mind's on tomorrow. I know I'm nervous about the tests as I'm not hungry at all and I'm aware I've been snappy at work and not my usual tolerant self. I so want to see Lucy with a baby that I haven't thought about the possibility that it may not be scientifically possible.

My work phone chimes again. It's a text from Sienna:

Any result from the address today? she asks.

Kid in care. Looks like a gun's gone from address. You? She also had a live job running.

Nine-bar of weed seized! A good day all round.

Well done. I'm at the clinic tomorrow, in at lunchtime. We need to see Ben. Set it up with DI. I text.

OK. Hope it all goes well. Give my best to Lucy.

Will do, thanks.

'Who's that?' Lucy asks.

'It's Sienna. Updating me on a result and wishing us luck for tomorrow.'

'That's nice. Do you think we'll be all right, Ed? Do you think it will work out for us?' she asks as she takes my tray away and moves closer to me on the sofa. I try not to provide too much of a pause before I answer but know I'm failing.

'It will be what it will be, love, but whatever happens I adore you and we'll look at every way possible to start a family if it doesn't work. We can look at other clinics or go to America and seek help, but right now we need to start here, tomorrow. Try to relax as I know how stressful it all is.' She gives me a hug.

'Right I'm off. I need to read and switch off. Don't be long, you need all your energy for tomorrow.' With that she gets up and I hear the creak of the stairs as she ascends to the bedroom. I turn up the TV and stretch the full length of the sofa. Louis, our cat, joins me and curls up around my stomach and purrs.

7

BEN

The place is buzzin'. I have the JD Sports bag. The landing the flat's on is alive; full of people just chillin.' I stay below for a bit and look up at the maddening crowd. It's been a while since I've been back here. The last time, I got lifted. I was a runner for Troy. He treated me good; at least I reckon he did. He paid me anyway. We only had one fall out and that was over a Maccy D's. I was young, naïve.

I was on the road and got hungry and bought a large Big Mac meal and a doughnut. I remember it like it was today. I didn't get any receipt to show Troy. When I gave Troy the cash from the deals I'd done, he told me that I was short on the count and I owed him for that meal. He added interest. I had to pay it off by workin' back-to-back shifts for a week, no pay. If I didn't do what he asked then somethin' nasty would happen. He didn't explain. He showed me. He told me to follow him.

We ended up in a bin area at the basement to the block. This kid was there on the floor, he'd pissed himself and he weren't movin'.

Troy told me to help pick the boy up and put him in the large waste bin. I looked around at the two other people who were there and stepped forward and helped. The kid was gagged. Stab wound to the leg and arm. Knife was still in his leg up to the handle. I was told to pull it out. I had no gloves, no nothin', and just did it.

As the bin lid shut, I just stood there with the blade and the youth's blood on me. The youth just stayed still in the closed bin. I ditched the knife. The knife was found, and I was nicked. The police had nothin' on me to say I did it. I just told them I'd found the knife and dumped it and that was why my prints were on it.

The kid survived and refused to make a statement. Case closed. Here I am again same place with a package that could see me doin' serious time if I get caught. I'm wiser now though. I want rid but need to be sure I can do it safely without no one knowing what it is. I know I'm not the only one shooting his mouth off to police. I know this from hearin' what has happened to snitches from people inside. Proper blood baths, man. One guy told me he found out who had grassed on him and he had someone cut the fella's tongue out.

Another guy told me he heard about a fella being shot while he watched telly with his mum. She lived. She wished she hadn't. That won't be me though. I'm too smart to get caught. More people are turnin' up and then I see my man, Troy. He's out on the landing lookin' down. He sees me and I nod. He nods back and moves closer to a girl.

She's got a buggy. I can see the handle of it over the landing wall. She leans into Troy. I see her turn the buggy round and she starts walking towards the lift.

I wait. I know the drill. Troy looks about then goes back inside. His crew exit the flat and form up on the landing. They take up position at each end of the concrete strip. Two more stay on the door. They'll be strapped for sure. The girl with the buggy is comin' through the block door to the outside courtyard where I'm waitin'. I duck back using the cover of the doorway I'm in. She goes over to a bench by the kiddies play area. I walk over to her and sit at the same bench.

'Yo, you got summat for Troy?' she drawls in a north London twang.

'Yeah,' I say.

'He says to leave the bag with me. It's all sorted, and his people are watchin' what's goin on, so no worries.' She scoots up close to me. The JD Sports bag is between us.

She takes it and slips it under the baby's blanket. The baby is asleep. She gets up and starts to leave.

'Troy says come up in ten when it's good. I may be up for you later too if you're game?' She's lookin' me up and down.

'Sweet,' I say. She leaves. Disappears back in the block.

I leave the area for a bit and hang about Archway, then go back. I'm ready for some fun after being away for so long. Never know what might be in it for me, and Troy needs to pay me. As I get to the door the posse, at the front, part and let me in. They're just chillin' to the sounds but alert. None of Troy's firm use gear when they're on point. If they do, then he personally sorts them out. He requires protectin' and don't take kindly to those that aren't up to the job he's payin' them for.

The flat's mobbed and the music's blarin'. I force my way through to the kitchen and grab a beer. I see Troy. He comes over and leans in. Lips near my ear.

'I've heard what I ordered was all there. Come now, get partyin'.' I feel my jacket pocket move. I glance down as a bundle of notes are dropped in.

'Good thing you're back out as I've plenty of work for you.' He moves away and leaves me. I recognise a few faces here but not as many as I thought. I weren't away for long but things can change quickly around Troy. Loyalties have been tested. Some have failed. I grab another bottle and move out towards the music and chill.

The girl with the buggy appears. She comes over to me.

The kid ain't with her no more. She takes my hand and gets in close.

Tonight's gonna be good. I can feel it.

8

ED

Joy Division's 'Disorder' shatters my dream. My ringtone of choice as that's what the phone always brings. I reach out from the sofa where I'd fallen asleep and scramble to answer the phone. I look at the screen. It's Ben. It's three am. The morning of the clinic visit.

I answer. He's speaking straight away, out of breath and sporadic. He's clearly running.

'Yo, I need you now!' he demands.

'What's going on?'

'What's going on? I'm being chased by a knifeman, bruv. He's mental…I've done nothin'…' Ben's breathing is laboured, his speech stilted.

The line sounds fuzzy. I hear a rustle of clothing and Ben's rapid breathing interferes with the signal making communication difficult.

'Where are you?' I ask him.

'Archway…Archway…hang on…'

I can hear his clothing scraping on what sounds like brick, then a thump. In the background there's a voice screaming.

'Yo, come out! You're a dead man, fuckin' dead, messin' with my woman you piece of shit!' I don't say anything.

From the male's voice I have to assume Ben's gone to ground and being sought.

I wait for Ben to get back on. The line's still open. I can hear Ben's laboured breathing. He comes back in a whisper.

'I'm still here. I've done a garden wall; I'm in a bush. I can hear your lot now, there's radio's goin'. What should I do?' He's catching his breath as he speaks.

'Stay there and don't move. What can you hear?' I ask him.

'They're searching the gardens.'

'Have you broken the law?' I don't know that he has, hence the question.

'No, I promise! I've done no more than try to shag a guy's woman. He was the one chasin' me, but I swear I didn't know she was his. I was at a party…'

'Not the party I told you to stay away from?'

'Look, I don't need no lecture right now. I can see torch-lights and shit a couple of houses down. They're gettin' closer.' Ben's voice whispers in a staccato.

'Just stay still. Let's hope they don't find you. If they do, just tell them you were being chased by a guy with a knife and had to hide.' He's gone quiet at the other end.

The line is still live. I hear another voice, it's Fiona, the dog handler I'd spoken to earlier.

'Police. I have a dog. If you're in here, stand up or I'll send in the dog.' There's a brief pause. Silence.

'Sending now. Find him – find him.'

I hold my breath; keep my ear to the phone. Then I hear the inevitable conclusion.

'Get the dog off me! Get it off it's raggin' the fuck out of me!' There's a loud agonising scream. The dog's clearly found flesh and locked on.

'I've done nothin' wrong…get the dog…argh…it's fuckin' biting me…argh.'

The line goes dead. Lucy is now downstairs.

'What time is it?' She isn't happy.

'Go back to bed, love. Sorry if I woke you up.'

'Jesus, Ed. Do they ever sleep? Come up now we've got a big day today.' She's holding out her hand.

'I will soon. I need to make some notes first. They may call back again. I'll be up as soon as I can.'

Lucy shakes her head and leaves. I put the phone down and rub my eyes. I already know today wouldn't be easy, but I never expected the flames to be set on high so early. I grab my notebook and pen and scribe some details in my notebook.

My mind is numb with tiredness and trepidation at the visit to the clinic. I hope Ben's ok.

He's never been one for keeping his head down, but I know he's going to be in all kinds of pain right now. I try to suppress the rising laughter but can't. Maybe he'll think twice before dipping his wick again without establishing some facts first. I lie back, let the endorphins subside, and sleep.

We stop off to eat before going into the clinic. The large Edwardian front door that greets us is as imposing as the process beyond it. The other two on my team had sent messages of support along with updating me on what had happened on their phones overnight. I instructed Sienna to establish what happened with Ben. Covertly, not leaving any digital footprint in the process.

I check my pocket and feel for my phones. They're all there. My phone, work, and source. All charged and all active.

I should have handed my source and work phone to Sienna, but I couldn't. DC Heddon's on leave, so it's just the two of us to manage all the sources.

There's a limit to how many informants one officer should be responsible for. You never know what can break at any time in this world.

I take Lucy's hand and open the door. The receptionist

greets us with a smile and shows us through to a comfortable waiting room. Other couples sit and read magazines. No eye contact here. All engrossed in their own thoughts and crossing whatever they can that this visit will end in success.

The evidence of success is on a pinboard in the way of baby photos and thank you cards. I can feel Lucy's hand has got hotter. I let go and rub her back. She turns and smiles at me, a small comfort in a large and imposing environment but just what I needed. I fill out the obligatory documents attached to the clipboard and hand back the form at reception. We go into the waiting room. Lucy had been organised and brought her own reading material. I'm too nervous to concentrate as I know I'll be required to provide a sample of sperm on this visit to test their vitality and count. They've tried to make the experience relaxing by placing fresh flowers at various places and piping relaxing music through Bang and Olufsen ceiling speakers. Nice to know where some of our money's going. Five minutes pass then a nurse comes in and calls my name. I get up and kiss Lucy on the cheek. Lucy smiles back and mouths 'enjoy'.

The nurse shows me to a side room on the first floor. Thankfully, it's away from the waiting area. She's pleasant but clinical in her bedside manner.

'Here's your sample pot. Try not to let your penis touch the sides and get as much ejaculate as you can. Once you're done, just place the lid tight on the pot and put it in this clear bag. I'll collect it from in here so there's no need to bring it out of the room. Oh, here are some magazines that may help you get the task done.' I take the porn and the pot, smile, and shut and lock the door to the room.

The room's been sprayed with air freshener since the last occupant. Lavender permeates the walls and invades an extractor fan that hums gently in the background. I look at the pot, my name printed on the outside along with a reference number and today's date. Who said romance was dead?

I put down the porn, drop my trousers and boxers and for

some bizarre reason check my watch. I don't know why the time is important. I've no intention of setting a stopwatch or world wanking record. I pick up a magazine and start leafing through.

I start my duty and begin to get in my stride. It's going better than I imagined, which is a blessing as I've never been at my best on any time trial but have been proven to perform well when under pressure according to my last annual appraisal from the previous DI. I'm sure he didn't envisage this scenario when he wrote it. My source phone starts playing, 'Disorder'. I try to ignore it, it's futile.

'Yes!' I'm beyond agitated.

'Yo, it's me, Ben. I'm out. We meetin' up today or what?'

'I said I'd call you.' I'm hostile. Both hands now on my phone.

'Keep your hair on. Who's yankin' your chain you miserable bastard? You sound like you're on the khazi; strainin', breathless an' all that.' He starts laughing at his own observation. My duty is incomplete.

'Look, I'll call you later, I'm in the middle of something right now and need to get back to it.'

'Yeah? Well, sorry to bother you! Thought you'd want to know I was OK after being mauled by a land shark last night. More important than what you're doin' I think? The beast wouldn't let go, bruv. Had me good an' proper. The cop never called it off quick enough. I swear she was messin' with me,' he tells me before he pauses then continues.

'Anyways, I need to see you. I need some advice like. My girl came to the cells, as she was my phone a friend. You always said don't call you from custody. Anyhow, she came and got me, and we had a row then she told me she was seven months gone. You there?'

'Yes.' Still here, ear on the phone an eye on porn.

'Yeah, so I'm kinda shittin' myself now. I'm gonna make sure it's mine but the timin' all fits. I'm gonna need more folding stuff, bruv.'

I say nothing at first. Just raise my eyes and stare at the non-descript walls and breathe.

'Congratulations. We'll talk later, I'll call and arrange where to meet so keep your phone on.'

I hang up and pick up the magazine. There's a light knock at the door.

'How are you getting on? Everything all right?' It's the nurse. My head hangs and stares at my now flaccid cock.

'I'm coming.'

'Well that's always good to hear,' she says.

I sigh, pick up the magazine and start again.

9

ED

'Everything go OK at the wank bank?' Sienna has such a way with words.

'Yes. All present and correct, thank you. How was the beauty salon?'

'Eh? How did you know I went there?'

'Your eyebrows are new.' I sit back in the driver's seat of the covert car and wait for the DI to come out of New Scotland Yard. St James' Park is busy, and parking is tight. I watch for wardens or over-zealous traffic officers. The DI emerges, sees us, and gets in the back.

'Meeting all set?' he enquires.

'Yes. Ben's good. How did you get on with our outstanding parking ticket dockets?' I ask, as Sienna indicates right and joins traffic.

'The Superintendent bounced them all, I'm afraid. Said there's a directive from the Commander that all traffic tickets picked up as a result of covert duty were to be paid by the driver. I did my best.'

'That's a joke, guv!' Sienna is the first to react. I'd heard it was happening from the staff officer to the Commander. I had hoped the new boy could wing it. I was wrong. More meets away from the car now required. The job never makes it easier for covert officers or any officers for that matter.

'Anyway, let's not dwell on it. What happened with Ben last night?' the DI asks.

'He got his arse nipped by Fiona's dog,' I reply.

'Oh. So, he's going away again is he? I hope so. I don't want a criminal on our books.' He's serious. I look at Sienna her eyes squint like she's been caught in headlights or the glare of the sun except it's overcast and daylight.

'With respect, Colin, we want to work with criminals and utilise their knowledge and skill set. That's the whole point,' I tell him.

'Well, he's not on the periphery of crime if he's getting nicked in a back garden,' he replies.

'He was being chased by a male with a knife. He was hiding. Anyway, it's an occupational hazard,' I add.

'Oh...that's OK then...Jesus, what kind of people are you running?'

'The best,' I tell him.

Sienna's face relaxes into a smile. We're heading to Islington. She turns right and heads towards a side street we use. She drives in and parks up but keeps the engine running.

'He'll be here in a minute, Colin. Shove along as he'll need to get in your side.' The DI does as he's told. He's holding some papers. It's noticeable his hands are shaking slightly. It's a common occurrence when you're new in the covert role. You never know what could happen at this crucial point of pick-up and drop-off, or what kind of mood the person who's turning up is in.

I nod to Sienna, get out of the car, and walk around to the front of a building we're parked behind. Bang on time, Ben is outside.

I approach him and ask for a light. He gets his lighter out as I lean in with my Rothmans.

'The DI's here and ready to sign you up so you're officially working for police. He heard about last night so stick to the script and you'll be fine. If you struggle, I'll chip in. It would be good if you had another job for us.' Ben nods and takes a breath of smoke and exhales.

'You better now after your strop?' he says. His face is relaxed, his tone of voice calm.

'I was preoccupied and couldn't concentrate. Congratulations, though. You pleased about becoming a father?'

'Ain't any of my family got to keep their kids. Social took 'em all but I reckon with this baby mother we can do all right, ya know?' There's a silence between us. I can tell by his face he knows I heard him but I've nothing to add. What can you add to that?

'Anyways, thanks for askin' after me so quick after getting a chewing from a mutt! Was all over me, bruv; I swear it were proper goin' for it.' I smile at him. My shoulders start moving and the cigarette wobbles in my mouth as I try to take a drag then we both start breaking into laughter. He balances his roll-up in his mouth while he pulls up his right sleeve and shows me the bandage. The bite just below his bicep. He declined to show me the ones on his arse when the dog let go and re-attached.

'No stitches, they said. Open wound has to heal itself as I could get an infection if they sew it up. I mean! I was the victim!' He pulls down his sleeve.

'Victim my arse! You were lucky you weren't tasered or batoned. What did they nick you for?'

'Can't remember. Nothin' serious. Anyway, the guy chasing me didn't want to make no statement. He got lifted too as he gave a false name and still had the knife stuffed down his trousers. He was wanted too. They just let me out. No evidence. I was in the same nick as the guy though so it weren't pretty. He wanted a piece of me even in the station. Can I get money for him being nicked? I was there…' I ignore him and he stops talking.

I text Sienna and let her know Ben is en route to the car. I turn to Ben.

'The car's round the back. Just get in it. Use the rear near-side door. I'll be watching you. I'll ring you once and hang up if you're to abort, clear?' I look at him to make sure he has listened.

'Sweet.' He drops his roll-up and grinds it out with the heel of his Converse. He pulls his neck scarf back up. All I can see are his eyes and a dark mop of black hair under his baseball cap. He pulls the hood of his jacket up. I say nothing. He walks away and when he's a short distance ahead of me, I follow.

He ducks right at the end of the building. Nothing untoward is noticeable. Our covert car is banked up among other parked vehicles. No one else is about. He saunters along, as is his style. Looking furtive. If uniform see him, he'll get stopped and turned over. It comes with his reputation and the territory. He stops and racks up a gob full of phlegm and spits it out into the road.

He's ten feet from the rear of our vehicle. He looks about and stops. A motorbike's engine is heard. Ben leans up against a random car and gets out another roll-up. He deftly starts making a new smoke as the motorbike cruises down the road. The bike is the type used by a group that do smash-n-grab robberies.

The rider moves in closer to where Ben is. I put my hand in my pocket and feel for the phone. I have it set up ready to go. All I have to do is press the call button.

I carry on walking towards where Ben is. To go in any other direction would look wrong if the rider is hostile to police or an associate of Ben. I notice the engine to the covert car is running. Sienna will be watching the same scene I am. Waiting for my signal to move away or wait. We have an agreed sign for each scenario. I cross the road and head towards a pub.

I could do with a drink. The bike parks up close to Ben. I carry on walking. The rider isn't paying me any attention. The stand goes down then the rider gets off. The crash helmet comes off and a cascade of black locks fall to below her shoulders. She locks the bike and goes. Ben waits then approaches our car and gets in. I carry on my route as the car pulls away. They know where to meet me.

I cross the road and enter the pub. I agreed with Sienna she could do the sign-up with the boss. Ben could do with a fresh pair of eyes over him. I also know the DI has reward money for him for the information about the child at risk. That should keep him motivated for a while. The boozer's full of the usual clientele for the area. I grab a seat with my pint and open a paper that had been left on the table. I figure one drink won't harm and I've done my deposit at the clinic. Lucy gave many blood samples and we were told the results would be back within a day.

I know there'll be a call from the DI in about thirty minutes. I wasn't present for the meet 'n' greet, and he expected I would be. He needs to bed in, and you only achieve that when situations change, and you have to alter the plan of action.

As sure as deer shit in a forest my work phone goes after twenty minutes.

'Hunter,' I answer.

'Where are you? I thought you'd have been here? We've had to carry on without you.' The DI sounds pissed off.

'I can't talk right now I'm in a pub.'

'In a pub?' His voice has gone up a decibel.

'Yes. I'll talk to you in the car. Tell Sienna to pick me up in Chadwell Street. It's a couple of streets away from where you left me.' I hang up. He has to learn the situation we deploy in is different to any other role in the job. It's never straightforward and you must think on your feet. Without this ability, the risk to life for handler and source is high. I down the drink and leave the paper. Sienna is in Chadwell Street. She's out of the car and walking towards me. She gives me a hug for tradecraft purposes only.

'Thank God, you're back. The DI's a nightmare. He was

ranting and raving about where you were. Ben was cool. Got his money and says to tell you thanks. He wasn't expecting anything.'

'He did a good job. He deserves five hundred quid for saving the kid's life. He should've got more, but the DI knocked it down. Thought I'd let him take the shit when Ben saw the value of his worth. Shame he wasn't disappointed.'

'You're a miserable sod today. Even Ben said you were having a strop. What's up?' Sienna asks.

'Personal stuff. Let's get back to the Factory. Is the boss in the car?'

'Nah, he got the Tube.'

'Good.' We set off back towards the vehicle. Sienna puts her arm in mine and leans in.

'You can talk to me you know. I don't bite.' I give her a raised eyebrow and she play-punches me on the arm.

10

BEN

Well that was a hook-up from hell. The new boss man in the fuzz mobile was wound up tighter than a kilo of coke. I like that Sienna though; she's all right and knows what she's about. Ed weren't there, but I saw him lookin' at the bike so I know why he stayed low. I knew it weren't one of my crew. The bike was hot though! We'll have that away one day as the lock she was using was crap. One buzz with the portable angle grinder, break the steerin' lock and *boom*! we're away. Got some money from the new boss man. He said he liked what I did and thanked me, which was cool.

He said it was good the kid was out the house now and safe. I've been in the same position as the boy so I knew it made sense. I just hope he gets a decent forever home. I counted the cash back at my room in the Y. Five hundred notes! I would have thought a grand for that work, ya know? Money's goin' down all the time. Ed says it's the government not giving them as much cash to dish out like before.

My crew's gettin' together tonight for a recce on a jeweller's up west. Last one we did we came away with a load of gold and watches. Our contact is askin' for more of the same and he pays well for what we get. He would though as he's in the diamond and gold business. He pays by weight and market value. I don't do hands-on no more. I'm a driver and an ace one too. Ghost thinks he's the best but I can burn him from a standing start like no other.

It feels good to have got shot of the Spray 'n' Pray. Havin' that kind of firepower about you don't go unnoticed no matter how much you try to hide the fact you got it. As soon as I picked it up calls would be goin' in sayin' it'd been collected. You're a walkin' target for anyone lookin' to make a name or needin' that kind of firepower. I've got some money now which feels good. I grab two twenties and stuff the rest in a sock and put it in an old shoe box up high on my wardrobe. It's temptin' to take more, but I'd get asked too much if I turn up with loads of green. Act discreet to stay on the street. Ed told me that.

The boys drop me at one of our lock-ups where I stored my bike. I don't own the garage, I ain't that stupid. It belongs to a kid's dad. Kid wants to be part of the action, but we told him he had to prove his worth first before he comes on the road. He's away right now servin' the county line. I love this ride. A Piaggio 125cc scooter. I've been lucky and not had a tug from the uniform lot since I nicked it. They're too slow for me despite it only bein' a 125cc engine.

I take my lid off too so they can't chase me. Seriously screwed-up rules they have. Too dangerous they say. For me not them.

I've got a closed-face balaclava on underneath. It can get cold out. I saddle up and go meet Ghost, who is shotgun tonight. I love it when we hit the road. Great buzz and we dominate the street. Ain't anyone stupid enough to do business on our turf. We've got protection from a proper firm. This firm are top tier and run north London. As long as we give them a cut of what we make they leave us alone to get on with what we do best.

I see Ghost at the back of Clerkenwell fire station. He chucks his fag and gets on. He bangs a call in.

'He's here. Let's roll.' We wait while the rest of the crew

join us. Once we're together, we set off mob-handed along Farringdon Road towards the city, our place of work.

Streets are buzzin' tonight, it's warm so loads are out partyin' and they look at us as we pull wheelies and shit. They look freaked out. They know our reputation and stay well clear.

Some will be on phones already to the filth. We ain't got much time when we hit the open road. I don't see what we do as crime. The shops we rob can afford the loss, that's why they have insurance. We ain't robbin' them we're just workin' the system same as they're fleecin' the buyer. They'll scam the insurance and load up the claim sayin' we took more than we did. We've heard it from the others who imitate what we do but get nicked. Property sheets loaded up with gear they never touched. It ain't the police, it's the jewellers. Robbin' bastards.

It goes for our drugs too. It's well known how much the chatterin' classes love a line and they can't get enough of our powder. They still won't shut up though, wantin' us off their streets, ruinin' the country and causing mayhem and murders. They wanna stop arranging dinner parties and needing coke to go with the coffee. It's the likes of them that keeps me doing what I do.

If they stopped, we wouldn't have to travel to them and they could get off their shiny fat arses and come knock on our door for the sniff. They don't try to do you on payment though. They pay up and shut up.

We hit Farringdon and see the planned hit. They're just closin' up but the steel grids ain't down. I mount the pavement. Ghost is straight off the bike and at the window with the hammer. Glass is flyin', people are stoppin' gettin' out phones and filmin' away. We ain't got long. The other lot have their passengers off and they're in the gaff shoutin'. I'm buzzin'! Ghost's back first. I've got the engine running. More people have stopped and started talkin' into their phones.

'Hurry up! We've gotta go!' I shout at the others inside.

The other two come out fully loaded. Then we're off again along the pavements forcing everyone into the road. We're away. Some of the gear drops. I slam on the brake and spin the bike round. Ghost hangs on then leans down as I open up the throttle. He scoops up a Rolex. The watch is still good. I spin it back round, and head towards Clerkenwell. The others have split up now, long gone. I can hear tunes from the plod. They'll be here soon.

I need to park up and lie low. Cameras will be locked on us now trying to work out where we're headin'. The public hate us. Say we're terrorising the streets. We're not fuckin' terrorists, we're armed robbers and drug dealers. It offends me when we get that kinda terrorist label. I'm in Old Street now. The heat's died down and I take the bike to a mate's. I check my watch; we timed it right. Five o'clock. Cops will be eatin' now and not out on the streets.

My mate knows I lay the bike up at his. I pay him, of course. He's good for it and keeps it off the streets until it's not too hot to collect it and get it back to the other garage. I drop it at an alley and text *Yo, check the alley*, then delete my messages. Ghost shows me his haul. Rings, watches and bracelets. The works. I take a bracelet.

'I need this for my woman. She's pregnant,' I say. Ghost is flopping around like he's been shot but his eyes are watering and he's holding his belly while pointing at me, mouth wide open, head back. I'd have done the same if it were him, but right now I can't share his feelings.

'Fuck you. One day you'll dip commando and pay the price. Get this lot to the hot house and bell me later.' He's stopped his dancing, fist bumps me, and leaves. He lives close to here and always has the gear from any venture. He's safe as. He ain't ever had anything away. He gets the stash to the hot house and stores it. It's called the hot house because it's never been raided but is always full of gear fresh from jobs. Once the dust has settled, he takes it to our friendly goldsmith in Hackney who weighs, barters, then pays cash. I don't collect or touch nothin' apart from when I need to.

It was workin' OK when we were just robbin' clothes shops and that. We had a great racket goin' and would nick to order depending on the season. Summer was designer handbags and Ray Bans; winter was North Face coats and gloves. We made a killin' around Christmas on all kinds of robbed stuff. Times have changed though. We've stepped up our game and branched out to better things. We need to be cute around it all. As the risks get greater, our prices go up and our targets get bigger.

Ed ain't got a clue about what I do. I told his boss I were seein' and hearin' this and that when I was out on the road but I'm keepin' clean as I don't wanna go back inside now I've got a baby comin'. He bought it lock, stock an' barrel. I was always told to keep your friends close and your enemies closer. Way I see it is that my work with Ed is doin' just that. He don't tell me nothin' I can't know. I get to find out who's wanted as he shows me photos, plus I get my phone topped up regular. Now and then, like with the kid in the house, I strike lucky.

I don't burn through money. I've done a bit of partyin' but that's cool as I've just got out. I'm at my woman's house now. The walk done me good, let me clear my head before I face her. She'll not be happy I didn't come straight round when I got out of prison but life's full of disappointments. I knock on the door and she answers.

'Well look what the cat's dragged in?' she says.

'Are you gonna let me in then or what? I've had a long walk and I got you summat,' I tell her.

She moves aside. I go in the flat. She's lookin' tired and got a belly on her with the baby. I was hopin' for a good time but I can see that ain't gonna happen. I go to the fridge and open it, desperate for a beer. There's one left. I take it as she can't drink now she's havin' a kid. Ed told me that.

She sits down on a beanbag and lights up. I decline and

roll my own. I have some skunk left and add it in. I give her the chain in my pocket. Her eyes light up.

'Where'd you get this? Is it hot?'

'Leave it a few weeks before you wear it out. You like it?'

'I love it. Where'd you get it then?'

'Never you mind.'

She comes over and pulls me down on the sofa.

'I missed ya when you was banged up. Don't go away again now the little one's coming. He or she will need a daddy, you know.'

'Look, I don't want no hassle but how do you know it's mine?' She lets go of me and leans away.

'I haven't slept with anyone else, that's how I know. We weren't exactly careful! If you think of the timing, it would have been the night before you got nicked when you stayed over here because you heard police were looking for you. Satisfied now?' She's gonna cry.

'Yeah. Sorry. It's all a bit of a shock and I dunno whether I'll be any good at it…being a dad. Look, can I crash here tonight? Don't wanna go back to the Y just in case, ya know?'

'You're on the sofa though. I'm tired.' She kisses me on the head and comes in for a cuddle. I turn on the TV and tune in to the news. Our job's made it to prime time.

She looks up and watches. The CCTV shows us burnin' up the road and Ghost puttin' the window in with the hammer. You can't ID any of us though, which is sweet. Filth ain't got nothing other than shaky phone footage and a few statements from witnesses that will be crap. The bikes we'll ditch or re-plate. I feel good now I've seen how poor the CCTV is and phone camera film ain't worth nothing. She looks up at me and shakes her head.

'Look at that lot, eh? Mugs all of 'em,' she says as she smiles at me.

'Hey, Maria? Make us summat to eat?' She gets up and the long, checked shirt she's wearing hugs her belly curve and hangs just above her knees as she walks to the kitchen. I take a draw and blow out smoke, smilin' to myself. My phone goes. It's Ed. I answer as quiet as I can.

'Yo, what's happening?' I say.

'Free to speak?' Ed replies.

'Yeah, yeah, it's cool.'

'There's been a smash-n-grab in Farringdon. If you hear anything about it bell me.'

'I've just seen it on the telly. Proper job. You lot need to pull your finger out. They're takin' the piss, bruv.' He ain't amused.

'You need to put the spliff out, get off your arse, and find out who's doing it and where the nicked gear is. Call me in the morning or sooner if you hear anything.' He hangs up just as my tea arrives.

'Who was that?' she asks as she gives me a Pot Noodle.

'Just a dude I know seein' if I was comin' out. I told him I'm stayin' in tonight.'

She switches channels and I lie back.

11

ED

Sienna and I finally reach Brent Cross. The Tube journey was terrible, and I insisted we enjoy a morning coffee before soaking up some vitamin D prior to an Operational Team briefing with the Trident Pro-active Squad. Julian Headon House is an odd building set around a courtyard. It was once a stable block and offices but converted to provide more offices when the stables were no longer required. We cross the courtyard and enter the main building. The stairs take us up to the second floor. There are no lifts here. We arrive outside a door marked DI Pro-Active. I knock. DI Nick Nolan opens the door.

'Took your time.' He's one for the banter.

'We're early, get the kettle on, son,' I tell him.

'Oh, don't mind me, I'm just the token bit of skirt,' Sienna interjects as she stares in disbelief at the lack of introduction.

'Nick, this is Sienna Myles. We call her Smiles because of the joy she brings.'

Nick shakes her hand then takes us through the empty main office to his room at the back.

'The team are out on a plot at the moment,' he tells us. 'Milk? Sugar?'

We give our orders and sit down.

'So, what you got then? Tasking meeting spoke about a gun floating around and a guy called Troy? I've got no more than that but I know you're good for work so thought I'd see if it had legs,' Nick enquires.

Nick sits down, takes off his glasses and rubs his eyes. Nick's one of the good guys, an old school detective. You need to have a sound pro-active background to steer this ship. They only take on certain work where guns and gangs are involved. I tell him the little I know about Troy, Fat John, and the police dog indicating where a gun had been laid up under the bath of Fat John's missus.

'It's weak then?' He's quick to grasp this.

'At the moment it is. We've got a source who's close to Troy. They'll be in a position to get some more. I came to you because research has shown Fat John used to convert firearms before he got sent down. I know you've been looking at weapon converters; there could be something in it. Troy is moving up the ranks in his trade of drugs and kidnap,' I tell him.

'Why not the kidnap lot? Get them to have a look?' he replies.

'They won't touch it unless there's a body attached. You know that, you cocky sod.'

Nick sits back and cradles his coffee mug.

'Look, we've got a bit of work going into an arrest phase. I'll speak to the DS on the Pro-Active intelligence cell. His lot can work it up a bit. If you get anything live, call me and we'll react. If I can't respond, then I'll tell you. I'll get the Intel DS to get Troy and Fat John flagged to us. That way we shouldn't get any blue on blue.'

'Our work is done then.' I finish off my coffee. Sienna takes that as a hint we're leaving, along with me standing up.

'How's things with you and Lucy? Still together?' Nick has always been one for direct questions.

'Good thanks and yes we're still together. Trying for children at the moment. What number are you on now?'

'I've thrown in the towel at number three, mate. Costing me too much. I'll have fuck all to my name when I retire at this rate. Single life for me, and the kids at weekends, when I'm not here. I wouldn't be without the kids though, so don't let me put you off parenting,' he says. We let ourselves out.

As we turn left towards Brent Cross, my phone goes. It's our DI.

'Anything from the tasking around the smash-n-grab yet? I've got Westminster Crime Squad's DI on the phone, says he's getting grief again from the business sector.'

'We've contacted who we know and they'll call if they hear anything.'

'Call me as soon as you know. Phone's always on.' He hangs up. Shame his phone wasn't on the other night.

'Have you got any of yours we need to meet?' I ask Sienna.

'Nah, I met them all for this month,' she replies as she pulls the sunglasses down from her head.

'You do know that's the minimum amount of time to meet them? How about upping the face-to-face contact?'

'Oooh…not getting any? Ah…sorry, Ed. Stupid comment.' Her cheeks flush.

'I'm sure it must be difficult for you both right now. You know me, don't think before engaging mouth!' Sienna pats me on the back. It's a comforting feeling.

'Truth is, I want it to happen, but I don't know how I'm going to balance being a father and work. I'll always want to be at home rather than at work and Lucy isn't wanting to return to work until she absolutely has to. When you go through what we are to have a child, then you want to be with them more than not, at least I feel that way now as does Lucy. That could change once he or she is here, but I doubt it. You know who else is having a kid?' I say.

'Well, I know it's not me. Who?'

'Ben, that's who. People like him just seem to churn them

out no problem, despite being off his head on weed half his life. Maybe I should take it up. It might help.'

'Sounds like a plan.' Sienna appears too keen.

I lean against the window of the bus and blend in with everyone else. All occupying their seat and making sure they don't miss their stop. I see Sienna, earphones in and the latest iPhone providing her entertainment. I don't have to worry so much about Smiles. She's a black belt in Jujitsu as well as having a first-class honours degree in psychology. She puts me to shame in the academic achievement department, as well as fitness. I just hope if Lucy and I manage to conceive that the child takes after Lucy in the looks and brains department.

After a long bus journey full of possible fare evasions and drunks we alight and walk towards what we know as The Factory. The Factory is more commonly known as New Scotland Yard. I swipe my warrant card and enter the revolving door that spews us out at the entrance to the lifts for Victoria block. We head for the fifth floor. As we exit and push through the double doors to the main unit's corridor the door to the DI's office is open.

I knock on the DI's office door. I'm now alone in his office.

On his desk is a report from the Commander for Covert Policing. I can't resist and take a look. It's a docket no DS wants to see. I'm on a list for detective rotation.

I take a closer look and see my name is way down the order sheet but, nevertheless, it exists. This means my time is limited on this unit. A unit I love. A unit I had the flexibility with to work from home from time to time and be with the baby. I leave the docket as I find it.

12

BEN

I'm off my head. Pure bliss. Just trippin' with the crew after our blag and countin' out the cash. I dish out everyone's share and they're all cool just wavin' wads of dough about. Ghost goes for his phone and points the camera at it. I ain't that stoned. I know what an idiot is. I bat it out of his hands.

'Why don't you just put a sign on your head sayin' *Filth, I'm loaded*? Don't take me for a mug, bruv. Knock that camera shit off and chill. Ain't no one interested in your Facebook or Insta feed, trust me.' I laugh. Ghost grins as he picks up his phone and dusts it off, blowin' on the screen. Why he loves his phone I do not know. Fool goes around with the latest iPhone. Me? I stick to the old faithful, Nokia 3310. Basic. No contract and unregistered. Ed paid for it too.

Told me to get out and start finding stuff for him. Problem is anythin' I find I roll and burn just for me. He's told me before not to get in the car stinking of weed but like I said to him, it ain't me it's the others I hang with.

I'm just a passive smoker. He just tells me to fuck off and do some work. He's normally happy but I ain't seen him smilin' that much since we've been linkin' up. I'm sure he's got other stuff goin' on in his head but he never shares nothin' personal with me. That's how it goes, I guess.

There's a bangin' on Ghost's front door. It ain't his house exactly as he still lives with his parents'. We all look at each other. We never tell anyone where we're crashin' and dealing out the cash. Never. Ghost gets up and goes to the door. I hear it open. There's loads of shoutin' goin' down in the hallway. I look at the window to the back of his flat. He's ground floor. I slam it open and start climbin' through. Ain't no way I'm waitin' to see who that caller is as they're well pissed off.

I'm unlucky. I can feel hands on my shoulders draggin' me back inside. I get thrown to the floor and roll over. It's one of Troy's goons staring down at me. He's wearing a duster. It ain't a feather one. This one's made of metal and covers all his fingers. He crashes it into my face. I feel the full force. I stick my hands up in self-defence. He drags me up and throws me on the sofa. I can taste blood.

Troy's posse are in the flat makin' sure no one comes to help. There's cash everywhere, all over the floor. My custodian ain't happy.

'Yo, you piece of shit. Rumour has it you've been talkin' to the police.' His face is screwed up like a bulldog. All lower teeth and chin.

'I ain't been talkin' to Five-O, what are you on about, bruv?'

'Don't *bruv* me. What's with all the cash here then? Huh? You all at it?'

Ghost's the first to break. 'Whoa, it's a sideline of ours that don't cross over with Troy's work.'

The thug lets me go and stands up. His shaved head and gold tooth make him look like Goldie. I like Goldie. This guy I want to kill. He looks at me again. Legs in a strong stance, huge arms folded, carryin' major ink work, a dragon's eyes starin' into mine from his forearm.

'Fat John reckons you're talkin' to police. His kid got lifted the other day after you went and picked up that parcel. He reckons you were the last person in her flat. She says so too.'

'Of course, she'd say that, she's a junkie and a whore who

don't want a kickin' when he gets out. Anyhow, why would I care about a kid? I had a job to do and I did it. Tell me summat, if I were talkin' to police then why didn't I give the parcel up to that lot and not drop it where I was told? She's havin' you lot over with her nonsense.'

His eyes squint and he licks his lips. I've made sense. He nods to the other two goons who start collectin' the cash off the floor. No one moves. A show of power. So he thinks. Problem is he doesn't know who he's messin' with. Way I see it, I've got my turf and they have theirs. If I needed a crap, I wouldn't dump in their house.

I don't like bein' shown disrespect. This is gonna cost. If Troy or Fat John has a problem, then front me out. No one can get away with callin' someone a grass then getting their henchmen to rob them in front of their crew and think he can get away with it. I will have my time, just watch.

'Turn out your pockets,' the goon demands.

'Fuck you. You've had your fun and taken enough of what ain't yours. Now do one,' I tell 'im. He ain't movin' and steps in closer, raises his duster hand. I reach behind me and pull out the blade from my waistband. I ram it full down in his thigh. He drops his hand down and falls. I take the knife out and get up. The other two goons just freeze. That's a good sign, means they ain't strappin'.

'Now, fuck off all of youse and go tell Troy I ain't no grass. Leave the money on the table there. If you try anythin' then Ghost here will blow you away. They both look at Ghost as he reaches behind his back to his trouser band.

'Whoa! All right, you've made your point! Troy ain't gonna be happy so watch your back. He said you was mental and for us to watch out. He was right.' He stands up. He's defeated and don't want no more. He came ill-prepared, thinkin' I'd be a push over he could just slap about a bit and get away with it. Prison taught me that death smells weakness. They dump what they'd taken and back out of the room.

Once they're gone, I shut the flat door and bolt it. Ghost comes over. He's got a face on.

'Why'd you bring me in to your games? And what's with making out I was carryin' a piece? You know I don't have one!' He ain't best pleased.

'It's called bluffin' and it worked. You ain't the one with a mashed-up face so go get me a wet towel or somethin'. I need to clean up, make some calls.' I clean up as well as I can. Lookin' out the kitchen window I can see Troy's posse have done one. Man, my face hurts though. I sit down with the others. They're all lightin' up another joint. I join 'em.

13

ED

The engine purrs on idle as we wait in a cul-de-sac for the arrival of Ben. It's early evening and following a call from him I'd agreed to meet up. That and Lucy wanted to talk later. We've had a letter from the clinic. My sample was good. All alive, all swimming but none would be making the Olympic squad and that's a problem. A problem I didn't need tonight or any other night. They hadn't told us that at the clinic. The problem isn't about to disappear or improve unless I make some changes. Even then it's an outside chance. I eat healthily. I know that as I'm sat with an open reseal bag of salad leaves. Lucy's results weren't any better. The amount of chemicals her body would have to endure to stand a chance of the egg taking sounds horrific and none of it without risk.

Sienna is sat with a diminishing packet of chocolate Bourbons and looks to be in Nirvana.

'What did he say he wanted to show us tonight? I'm on a promise so he'd better hurry up.' She picks up another biscuit and begins using it as a prop emphasising her need for speed from our evening's entertainment.

'He said he would point out some of Troy's runners and an address he thinks is a store for the gear. It will help with any lifestyle work. Try to establish links to him. Trident can't house him right now from computer work alone. All the known addresses are historical. Ben was keen and that's something to be encouraged. I'm sure your lover will wait, Smiles.' I grab a biscuit. She slaps my hand causing me to drop it, hitting the floor between her feet.

'What a waste! Stick to your organic shit and get off my Bourbons.'

'Is that what he'd say?' I ask.

'What makes you think it's a he?' she says with a wry smile.

'Random guess.'

'Here's Ben. I can see his weasel grin under that cap and hoody. Has he not heard of washing?' Sienna points down the alley with a biscuit.

We're parked opposite the alley's entrance; nose out ready to go as soon as Ben gets in the car. My eyes are everywhere now. A solitary street lamp illuminates him. He keeps pirouetting as he walks towards us. As he reaches the back door, I release the central locking mechanism and he jumps in. Sienna presses the accelerator and we're away.

He pulls down his hood, takes off his hat and sits back. He has confidence the blacked-out privacy glass will shadow him from view. He leans forward, his face emerging from the cave-like darkness of the back into the low evening light that's infiltrating the main window.

'Lean back, you'll get seen. How's tricks?' I ask him.

Ben does as directed and slumps into the doorframe behind Sienna. I can see him from the rear-view mirror. I don't turn round, just glance up.

'I'm sweet, Ed, sweet.' He appears flustered, wiping his hands on his grey sweatpants.

'Been running into closed doors again?' I ask him as his face has taken a beating.

He laughs it off. 'You should've seen the other guy. This ain't nothin'. Occupational hazard. Go right here, yeah, just here,' he replies as Sienna turns right.

We're heading towards Holloway. 'So, what's with the urgency tonight?' I ask him.

'Have I ever let you down? This is cool. It'll look good for your new man, like. He told me he wants to see some results for his money.' The DI will be pleased his speech would appear to have connected in Ben's brain.

'If it was the DI's money you wouldn't be out of prison,' Sienna chips in.

Ben sits back staring out the window, turning his baseball cap in a twist then letting it unravel. The journey progresses in stilted conversation. We finally get close to the area he said the house was.

'OK…slow down…slow down – we're comin' up on it,' Ben says as he slides lower in the back and away from the window. His hat's back on and his hood's up. Sienna maintains a steady speed. We're now in Carleton Road. I feel the car move as Ben shifts position in the back.

'Pull over here…yeah here.' He's as excited as a puppy near a park.

Sienna pulls over but leaves the engine running. She kills all lights. We're within spitting distance of the Church Estate.

'Let me out and gimme ten minutes.' Ben tries the door handle, but the central locking prevents him opening it.

'You said you were pointing out an address. Where is it?' I ask.

'I am. I need to see if it's live,' comes his reply. His hands attached to the door handle in readiness to de-camp.

'Live?' Sienna enquires as she eyes him in her rear-view mirror.

'It used to be a slaughterhouse before I went away. Ya know, where they cut up drugs or get rid of nicked gear. Troy would keep cash and all kinds of shit there. I can't remember the number so thought I'd take a look, make sure.' He's leaning forward again. I need to set him loose.

'You've got ten minutes then I call you. Don't do anything stupid. We won't be here when you get back out, but we'll meet you round the corner in Anson Road,' I tell him.

'Suits me,' Ben responds.

Sienna releases the internal door lock and with one quick look each way, Ben bails out and merges into the estate. Sienna moves off. She finds a decent spot and parks up. I move the passenger seat back, stretch my legs and rack the back of the chair to recline. I put the window down on the car and get out a smoke. Sienna accepts the offer. We both light up. This is another reason we partner up. We never get asked to swap cars as it stinks. We blame the sources. There are too many rules in this game but when it comes to not smoking in covert vehicles, I believe in a degree of flexibility. Cover must be maintained at all times.

'So, who is it tonight then? Another tap up on Tinder or Plenty of Fish?' I blow out the smoke and ditch the salad bag on the floor.

'Nah. This one's from the gym. One of the instructors. Getting my punishment in a different way.' She turns and gives me her killer smile.

'Did you tell the boss we were deployed?' she asks.

'I tried his phone. It was off,' I lie. She knows it too.

'You lie like a source,' she replies.

I take another drag and tap ash out the top of the passenger window then check my phone. Ben has three minutes. This is all overtime too and that means extra cash that both Lucy and I will need if we're to carry on with the IVF. Ben's good for the money with all the calls out of hours and late meets. Money I desperately need. We've maxed out our credit cards and hanging back from re-mortgaging the house but that's still an option should our treatment costs go up. My idle thoughts are interrupted.

The first crack sounds like a backfire from a car. The second one is more distinct.

Sienna chucks her fag out the window and racks it up via the electric button. I do the same and grab my source phone.

There's no need to call Ben. He's already in full sprint behind us running towards the car. Sienna slams it into reverse, leans one arm on the wheel the other round my chair's backrest and floors it towards Ben. There's no one else behind him. She slams on the brakes as he turns forward from his backwards run and collides with our boot. I get out the passenger side, grab the rear door and fling it open.

All this is at a crouch; my body protecting his. I shove him in the back and dive on top of him. My foot connects with the inside door rest as I pull it forward with my foot closing the door.

Sienna pushes the sports lever on the auto gearbox and the car lurches. A ducktail effect occurs as the rear wheels connect. I keep low, as does Ben. The gunfire has stopped. What sounded like multiple rounds of shot may only have been two or three. Sienna remains focussed as she heads towards Tufnell Park Tube.

'What part of *don't do anything stupid* didn't you understand?' I yell at him.

'It were nothin' to do with me! Get us out of here!'

Sienna tears across the junction at Tufnell Park. I hang onto the internal coat bar as our car hits the speed humps along Dartmouth Park Road. Ben does the same after hitting his head off the roof. She continues until we reach the back of Highgate Cemetery. She finds a spot and pulls over.

'We're good. No contact, no contact,' she says as she flops back in her seat and releases her grip from the steering wheel and kills the engine. Her concentration eases as her breathing regulates. The lights die on the dash and the only sound left is that of the engine pinging as it calms. I sit up, as does Ben. He moves over behind Sienna. I grab him by the throat and push his head back into the rear seat my eyes close to his.

'Never, ever, put us in a position like that again. You *knew* what was going down! Troy was there wasn't he? You knew he was strapped! *Didn't you*!' I demand answers. I let go of his throat and sit slowly back. Ben grabs his neck and massages it.

'Who do you think you are grabbin' me up like that you slack jawed filth fucker?' he yells, but I know he hasn't finished.

'I knew nothin' about what was goin on there. Troy weren't there for your info. The goons that did me over were and this time they were a bit handy. They still use the address though so you should be happy. Here it is…I even writ it down for ya. My neck's sore, man!'

Sienna says nothing. She looks out the window, then offers a fag through the side of the seat and doorframe to Ben. He takes it. She doesn't offer me one. I don't blame her.

'You not gettin' any? I could get you hooked up with a good bird, she'll see you right, no questions,' Ben says as he accepts the light from Sienna.

We all sit in our zones and let the situation wash over us. Nothing's changed where we are. No overt police presence, no walkers, all is quiet. I light up one of my own and Sienna releases the window lock for the rear window for me to put it down slightly.

'So, what happened?' Sienna asks while I remain silent. Ben leans into her headrest.

'I went to where I could remember it was, right. I knocked on the door and next I know I'm hearin' shots flyin' about everywhere. I crapped myself and ran back to youse. I don't know nothin' more than that, I swear. I think it were just someone showin' off, ya know? There were no screams or nothin'. I don't reckon anyone got hit,' Ben explains in his own laid-back street way.

The car is calmer now as nicotine takes effect and the adrenaline of the moment subsides. I've taken the time to reflect. My actions were poor, misguided and misdirected. It's not the first time I've heard gunfire or been subjected to it. Work long enough in London and it comes with the territory. It's not about that though. The business of children is becoming a stress and I know I'm not coping as well as I thought I would. That and the possibility of transfer is becoming too much to deal with. I phone the control room that covers the area. They confirm they've had calls to shots fired but so far the area's been searched with no trace of a suspect, victim or firearm. I tell them if I hear anything from any of our friendlies I'll let them know. The gun could be anywhere now and won't be on the estate, that's for certain.

I end the call and Sienna moves off from our sanctuary.

'Where do you want dropping?' I ask Ben.

Ben turns towards me.

'Holloway Road, near Seven Sisters.'

The journey's quick and this is a welcome relief. Before Ben gets out, I get a twenty pound note out of my pocket and give it to him. He looks at it and signs the handwritten receipt.

We drop Ben in a side street near to where he wants, and he disappears into the night.

'Well that was clever, Sarge,' Sienna says, hacked off.

'Sarge now, huh?'

'What the hell was that all about? If you don't want to talk about it, then leave your baggage at home and don't subject me or anyone else we meet to that again,' she says as she hands me the biscuits. Speech over she crams one halfway in her mouth. I take one.

'It won't happen again, I hope,' I respond, but know I can't promise anything.

She says nothing and we head back to New Scotland Yard to write up notes.

14

BEN

Twenty lousy quid to keep my mouth shut. That's what it felt like tonight after I'd put myself out. Well, I know I didn't entirely do it for Ed. I had my own reasons. See, I banged some calls in and heard that's where Troy would be tonight so I figured I'd go see him and make certain we're still sweet. How was I to know when I got there I'd have a reception party fully loaded and screamin' blue murder? They can't shoot though. Good job it was just some converted piece of shit and not the MAC-10.

I didn't even get over the doorframe. Murder broke loose as soon as they seen me. Mouthin', hollerin' all kinds of shit an' that. Troy was cool. He didn't say nothin' either he just left. That's when the gun came out and I got away quick. Man, they were out that door swift pointin' the piece at me and then I heard a click but no noise. The gun looked old from the quick look I took. I wasn't about to hang around to find out what it was capable of. They must have cleared the jam 'cause they were blastin' into the dark after that.

I was well away. That shooter will be stashed at one of their baby mother's houses now. Tucked up safe and sound to be called on another day. I would have told Ed more, but he weren't in the mood for listenin'.

I'm outside my baby mother's place now. I take a draw on my spliff before I go in. The door ain't locked. I open it and go in slowly. I don't want any chat tonight. I can see her asleep on the sofa. She stirs and her eyes open.

'What time is it? Where you been?' She's yellin' at me.

'Just hangin'. You good?' I sit down next to her but she pulls away.

'I've been waiting up all night for you! Why don't you ring me? Tell me what you're doing?' She's tight. I can't be doin' with no nonsense, not after tonight.

'Look, I'm a free fuckin' spirit. I'll go where I want, when I want, and don't have to tell no one.'

Her eyes flare wide like a seal's.

'You're goin' to be a father soon so you will tell me where you are and what you're doin' as I need to know because of the baby. I need to know you're comin' back, else you can do one and never see him again!' she tells me. From her look I know she's serious.

'What you mean, him? You don't know it's a boy,' I tell her.

'If you'd have come to the scan today, like you promised, you'd have heard for yourself,' she reminds me as she reaches down the back of the sofa and chucks a black and white photo at me.

'Here *he* is!' she yells. She's done and stormin' off. The bedroom door slams and there's a bang on the wall from a neighbour.

I take a look at the picture. I can't make out nothin'. I stare at it and then see the outline clearer. I put it down near the ashtray on the floor.

Over near the window's a crib and some clothes. It's real all of a sudden. I'm gonna be a father and there's no way out of it. She's well up for having it and whatever happens I'll always be his father whether I'm around for him or not. I pick up the photo again and lay back on the sofa. It's warm where she'd been. I lie down and hold it up above me. Truth is, I ain't prepared for this shit. When I was in prison, it was all about what I'd be doin' when I got out and parenting didn't come up. Now there's a kid comin' with my name on it and a woman who ain't gonna let me forget it either. I put the photo back down on the arm of the sofa, find the power button on the PlayStation controller and light up. My phone goes. It's a text from Ed. *Sorry.* Screw 'em all. Time for *Grand Theft Auto* and a smoke.

15

ED

'Thank you for all the work you've been doing. From the reports I've seen it's been fruitful and a good number of seizures of firearms too.' The Commander for Covert Policing looks up from her minutes and addresses the table of operational heads, and me. We're all sat around a conference table on the fifth floor of NSY for a morning meeting.

I represent the Covert Organised and Gang Crime side of the house. The others are after information as the Metropolitan Police are taking a kicking over gun and knife enabled violence. The perceived abuse of it, that is. Carnival is coming as well as the Olympics and that always brings on the pain. The Commander continues.

'There have been a number of shooting incidents across London. Carnival will be upon us in a few months and there's a fear that increased gang tensions will upset the community of Notting Hill and surrounding streets. We need to keep our crime figures down and our seizures up. That will mean an emphasis on intelligence led policing and raids where the information supports a warrant. I've taken the decision to set up the intelligence cell for carnival earlier than previous years. It will be run from Lambeth. Any questions?' she finishes and looks around the table at the blank faces.

There's only a murmur. It happens when all squads have few staff to spare and other pressing operations needing attention. 'Good. In that case, happy hunting,' the Commander finishes, indicating the morning meeting is complete, a scrape of chairs and a rush for coffee the only other sounds heard. For me this is great news as it means more overtime for me to earn. Ben will have to improve his work rate now I've got money to earn and IVF treatment to pay for. Harley Street practices don't come cheap but I'll do anything to make it happen and see Lucy holding our baby, anything.

The fourth floor of NSY is alive with chatter, the low sound of *Sky News* emitting from the TV screen on the wall. I grab two coffees, place a plastic lid on each and head for the office. I kick the bottom of the office door, as my hands are full. Sienna opens it. I hand her a coffee and sit at my desk looking out at pedestrians below coming out from the Tube station like rats exiting a drain.

'Did you get back in time for your promise?' I ask, casually, while I wait for the secure system to boot up.

'Cancelled it. Can't say I was in the mood for company after last night's theatrics. Do you and Lucy get out much?' Sienna asks.

'We try but it doesn't work out that well. Plus right now we're on a tight budget as all spare cash is going on the treatment. Plus the source phone is always going off. It never stops, as you know. Last night I get back and DI Nolan, from Trident, is ringing wanting to see if we've housed Troy yet. I gave him the address. He said he'd get the Intel cell to work it up. He hadn't heard about the shots fired.' The landline goes and I pick up.

'Hunter.'

'All right, mate? How's tricks?' It's another DS from a source unit south of the river.

'Good. What's up?' I ask.

'Need to swap covert cars with someone. We've had ours a while now and could do with a change,' he says.

'So it's nothing to do with your car being compromised three nights ago then getting a dink in the driver's door you can't explain away as fair wear and tear?' There's a brief silence the other end.

'I'll take that as a no then. So, everyone knows?' The DS has taken it well.

'Apart from the Commissioner, I'd say that's a given,' I reply.

The line goes dead.

DC John Heddon has returned from leave. I feel Sienna's relief as she hands his source phone back to him. He gives her a box of chocolates to say thanks for covering. 'Much been happening since I've been away?' he asks. I can see he's already forgotten the password for the work computers.

'All steady,' I respond.

I point to his desk diary where I'd told him to write it before he left. He smiles and gives me a thumb's up. Claire's our office manager. She breezes in and provides a freshness to our stale air.

I never last long behind a desk.

'You done, Smiles?' I ask.

'Too right I am,' she says, as she logs off her computer.

She grabs the car keys and her coffee and we leave the office.

'So where are we going?' I ask.

'I don't know. You gave the shout for let's get out.'

It's lunchtime. We grab a sandwich from a small Italian deli round the corner from the Yard as we head for the car. Everyone is out from the offices enjoying some midday sun.

'I'll call Ben and get the lazy sod up.' The phone continually rings then he answers. His voice a gravelled muffle of incomprehension.

'What time's it?' he drones.

'Time you were out sniffing around.'

'I'm wasted right now. My bird's got the right arse an' all.'

'We need to know more about Troy, what car he's using, phone numbers, associates, everything. You've got to up your game if you want to see some decent money. I want to give you more than twenty quid. You've got a kid on the way and they're not cheap,' I remind him.

'Yeah, yeah, I'm listenin', just it's a bit hot for me right now with everythin.'

I stay silent and await his reply.

'I gave you the address from last night so why can't I have a day off?'

'You've had months off in prison. Get up and get out there,' I tell him.

'Maaan! OK…OK…I'm gettin' up!' I can hear the bed creak. He's like a teenager getting up for school. We're on hands-free and Sienna is trying her best not to break into laughter.

'How about I send the lovely lady you're always with a picture worth rememberin'?' he says. Sienna's mouth widens in an O of surprise.

'Save those for your girl,' I tell him. He laughs at the other end and the line goes dead.

'Where to now?' Sienna sips her coffee and adds two sachets of brown sugar.

'Let's enjoy the coffee. Give the lazy sod time to fall asleep before I call him again,' I tell her. We connect the Styrofoam cups in agreement and watch the world go by.

16

BEN

That dick, Ed, called me again. I'd just got back off to sleep and I can hear him laughin' as he tells me to get up! I hear a knock at the front door. My girl's out already so I'll have to get it. I grab my blade and shove it down the back of my jeans.

I grab my phone and call Ghost.

'Yo, come get me.' The door goes again.

'Who's that?' I say as I hang up on Ghost.

'It's social services, can we come in please?' That's all I need.

'What you want? She ain't here.' I need to get away and the main door is the only way out.

'It would be better if we could discuss this inside rather than on the street.' I need to get rid of these people quick. I open the door. They flash their ID and come in. I shut the door. The place is a state. Beer tins on the floor from last night with cigarette roaches in the ashtray as I haven't emptied it. I can see the bird lookin' about the place in disgust.

'What you want? I'm in a rush,' I tell her.

'Is Maria in?' They just don't listen.

'No. Like I said, she's out. Why? What's you lot got to do

with her anyway now she's an adult.' I'm gettin' right hacked off that I can't get out my own flat.

'We're here to see Maria by appointment we arr—' The door opens and Maria's back carryin' shoppin' and whinging. Time to leave.

'Yo, social's here to see you, I'm out.' I give her a peck on the cheek and hear a car engine cut and die as Ghost pulls up outside. Maria don't say nothin' she just stands there, open-mouthed, like a blow-up doll. I ain't got time for her hormones. I got work to do. I get in the motor and we go.

'Where'd you get this?' I ask Ghost.

The car's a black BMW M135i, auto gearbox, rear wheel drive, three litre, six-cylinder engine. This thing can do 0-60mph in 4.9 seconds. Full spec.

'I've got some skunk to deliver for Troy,' he says.

'Where's it at?' I ask him.

'It's in the door. Car ain't nicked, either. It's legit but modified for deliveries. Troy uses a garage that supplies the motor and does the door work. Quick deal then we're away. I need you to check the money before we do the swap.' I've got nothin' better to do.

We spark up, hood up, and Ghost takes the back roads towards the A406 and the country road out of here.

17

ED

I've heard nothing from the lazy sod. Others are on the phone so we've been kept busy for most of the morning. The late shift still have to wake up, wrapped up in their pits waiting for their body clocks to stir them for their next fix of crime. We drift over to the Bracken Estate for a recruitment recce. There's a girl lives there. She's a street worker but keeps good criminal company. Her fees are high but the product is good quality. To describe it as pure would be a lie. Her old-man-come-pimp has just been sent down for kidnap and blackmail. She knows everything about everyone and what's going on.

My research shows she knows Troy. There's always a risk of running too many snouts along the same trough but that's my job, to make sure the food is given sparingly and the herd not fed at the same time from the same plate.

This potential is particularly tricky. She's always in an entourage when she's at work in the clubs, or back on the phone waiting for an arranged call. When she's out she's quick on her feet. A lifetime spent looking over her shoulder. She knows better than to speak directly to police. It's my job to make a safe line of communication accessible for her.

I do know that she enjoys a smoke. Rolling tobacco only

and she doesn't go cheap. I know this because I've stood behind her when she's bought some. I've followed her and seen her roll up. When she finishes her night shift at the club, she always stops by the twenty-four-hour shop for baccy, milk and bread. I know this because on one of the reports where she did speak to police she said that's why she saw the accident, as she always uses the shop on a Wednesday when she gets the items for the rest of the week.

Today would be exactly the same and a good time to make an approach. It's getting towards the time when she was last using the shop. I open the glove box and retrieve a mobile phone and load up an unregistered pre-paid SIM. A pouch of her favourite tobacco comes with it. The phone's been charged and ready to go.

'You reckon she'll show?' Sienna asks.

'Hopefully. The shop itself is on a main street so we're safer out here than on the estate.' Sienna looks in her rear-view mirror. She can see a dark coloured Range Rover approaching slowly along the road then pulls over a few cars back from us. I'd seen the car in my side mirror.

There are two people in it, a male and a female, and both appear interested in us. They're not plain-clothes police officers.

'Can you see what I'm seeing?' Sienna asks as she glances in her mirror.

'If you're looking at the Range Rover a few cars back, two up and paying us attention then yes. Something's not right; we may have inadvertently drawn out a hostile recce patrol. She'll have to wait.' Sienna moves our vehicle out and the Range Rover does the same. We have a shadow. We don't know who but it isn't good news.

'Drive normally until you think it's time for some fun. If we can't get away, we'll use the agreed tactic.' Sienna nods her understanding and drives towards the junction and turns left without indicating. The Range Rover continues to follow but moves up closer. Sienna accelerates slightly to move away but not to engage a pursuit. We don't want that. She turns into the estate. She knows the estate from other work so keeps our car moving through the side streets heading for the north exit. The Range Rover is still following. I can see the girl in the passenger seat trying to move closer to the windscreen to get a better look at us. It's time to front it out.

'When you reach a decent exit point, pull over. Keep the engine going and let's see who these lot are and what they want. We'll keep our options open for escape,' I tell her.

Sienna finds a spot and pulls over. I get out the A-Z from the side space on my door and open it to the area we are in. The Range Rover draws alongside Sienna's door, close enough to look in but not too close to block us in. We need to act.

'Why do you not listen to the directions I'm giving you? Now we're lost!' I'm animatedly waving the A-Z and shouting at Sienna. Sienna's window is up but they can see in the car.

She's shouting back and pointing at me then at the road. The Range Rover's occupants look confused. Sienna slaps me on the cheek. I get out of the car and slam the door. I wave the A-Z and move towards the passenger of the Range Rover and walk towards the vehicle.

The driver takes the decision he's had enough and drives off leaving me stood at the roadside with the A-Z. Job done.

'Did you get the plate?' I ask Sienna.

'All done. I'll phone John and get some checks done,' Sienna says as she dials our office. They took the rouse. I knew they weren't police and hopefully they'll think we were a crazy couple lost in London. Sienna waits on the phone as checks are being done on the vehicle.

'Go on, John…OK, I'll let him know. We're safe but will get away from here now, cheers,' she says, as she puts her phone down.

'The car has a notice report on it. If seen and stopped all

particulars to your mate on Trident. It's a bad boy's car. We were being scoped for sure.'

'Let's get away from here. We've come to attention and need to do the natural thing and leave the area. I'll have to think of another way to make contact with the female. That slap hurt!'

'It worked though,' she says, as she shrugs her shoulders and laughs.

As we leave the area, I try Ben. His phone rings out unanswered.

18

BEN

I thought Luton was bad, but this place takes the piss. The car we're in stands out a mile with us in it but Ghost doesn't give a toss. He always feels like a gangster when he's doin' a county run, like he's north London's finest when he's nothin' but a gopher. We're in a Maccy D's car park, at the back, outside Dunstable. I'm starvin'.

'What you want? I'm payin' then claimin' off Troy,' I tell 'im. I ain't stupid so made sure I could do it by bangin' in a WhatsApp to the man when we got here. He still wants a fuckin' receipt and it must be regular meal not large the tight-fisted bastard. I'm surprised he ain't asked for us to bring him one back.

'Is that our contact?' I nod at an Audi that's just come near us and lookin' around for somewhere to park. He backs up next to us but leaves room to pop the boot.

'Yeah that's him.' Ghost chucks his fag out the window then drops the glove box. In it is a 9mm handgun, Russian in make.

'What's with the tool, man? You said this was a boot to boot? Standard deal? You can't waste people in a Maccy D's car park. There are people everywhere and CCTV,' I tell him as I try to shut the door to the glove box. Ghost's reacted and has the gun low from the window and leans forward and puts it in the small of his back.

'All's good. I'm goin' on a journey to check the money. If it's all there, then I'll call you on to the exchange point. He doesn't think we have the drugs in this motor. I said I'd call the drugs on if the money's right. He'll check the parcel then do the deal. I'll bell you where to meet me,' Ghost says.

He gets out leaving the keys in the ignition. The Audi's back door opens, he ducks in and it leaves. Screw this. I call Ed.

He answers straight away:

'I've got summat for you but you lot have to be quick.' He's listenin'. I can hear him turning a page in his plod book of bullshit.

'You done?' I ask him. Ed says yes.

'A fella called Ghost is linking up with a guy to do a deal on a kilo of cocaine. He's loaded with a 9mm piece down his waistband. He's way out north though. Apparently he uses the Maccy D's car park to do his deals.' I wait for his weary questions.

'I know this 'cause a mate just told me he'd seen him in Dunstable at the Maccy D's talkin' with a fella in an Audi,' I add.

'How long? Just before I phoned you,' I tell him before more questions:

'No, I ain't seen the gun, but my mate did and said it were the real deal. Says he stuck it down the back of his trousers.' Still more.

'I don't know who else knows this but it won't come back on me. Trust me, I'm good.'

He's writin' all this down and says he'll see what he can do. I know that'll mean sweet fuck all. I know there's nothin' his lot can do when it's another cop shop that deals with the crime and not his London lot. Plus, I didn't tell him the plate of the car or nothin'. It makes me look good though and Ghost needs takin' out the game for a while. He's tryin' too hard to climb Troy's ladder and that's for me to hold, not him. I get another incoming call, so I switch to that. It's Ghost.

'Come now. I'm at the industrial site we passed before the Maccy D's,' he tells me then cuts the line. The stupid idiot has no idea how big the site is and I don't know where he is. I start up and head out towards him. I drive around a bit then see the Audi parked up near a disused warehouse. Ghost comes out from a door to the warehouse and gets in the car quick. He's carryin' a holdall. He throws it in the boot then gets in the front. He's covered in claret.

'What the...?' I ask him but Ghost cuts me off.

'Go man, Go,' Ghost says. I turn our car around and head out. Ghost opens the central console and takes out some wet wipes and starts on his face and hands. There's not much blood splatter but enough that you'd notice.

'Where's the gun?' I ask him.

'I ditched it.'

'You what?'

'I ditched it. Troy wanted a message sent out. That's what he said to do.'

'Let me get this right. You shot them?'

'Don't be stupid! Not them. I shot their dog in the head, noisy bastard. I couldn't hear myself think with it barkin' and snarlin', gobbin' slaver everywhere.' He's trying to wipe a bit of dog spit off his jeans.

'So what's in the bag?' I ask.

'The cash.'

'So you shot their dog and robbed the money?'

'Yeah.'

'You're mental. Troy's gonna do his nut now.'

'He won't. Trust me. He said he'd be cool however I played it with 'em as they were takin' the piss by comin' down south and tryin' to work our patch. He set the deal up so I could deliver his message. A loud an' clear stay away.' Ghost's still cleaning himself up.

'Bruv, you could just have threatened them with the piece! Shot the tyres up!' Ghost's having none of it.

'I ain't wastin' ammo on rubber! The mutt had it comin'. They had no control. Bunch of little league players tryin' to play it big in a man's world. We're London. Not a bunch of carrot crunching wannabes. Shame the cash weren't there though…Piss takers…pull over, I'll drive, as I don't want the motor dinked. Troy said I'm the only driver.' Ghost's grinnin' like the Joker from *Batman*.

I look in the rear-view as Ghost turns round and checks out the sports bag, noddin' in appreciation at its contents. All I can see is wads of green.

'You sly dog, you!' I say, as I know what he's thinking by the grin on his face.

'What Troy don't know…shame they hadn't come with the readies…real shame that,' I say and see Ghost smilin' and noddin' at my way of thinkin'. Cash and drugs all secure with us.

I bang the gear box into drive and whack on Prodigy *Fat of The Land,* lean back into the seat as Ghost lights up a draw and hands me it. Top bit of work, done.

19

ED

It's been a few days since I last heard from Ben. His phone's off which isn't unusual. He's probably been on a bender and hasn't surfaced yet. He could still be pissed off at being woken up the other day by me. As a rule I keep the surmising to a minimum. The people we work with are their own minds. That's one place both worlds don't mix. I'm back in the office to begin another day. I've noticed my hours have dropped as I book on. I have other sources but none as active as Ben, especially out of hours.

I see a file marked confidential and open it. It's reports from the East Midlands Special Operations Unit. I glance through and most of it's not relevant then a log gets my attention.

A shooting of a dog in Dunstable.

The dog was found by a member of the public while working on an industrial estate. Nothing unusual but the finder was an ex-soldier and could see it had been shot with a single bullet and thought this suspicious so called the police.

A forensic vet examined the dog and a 9mm round was found in the animal. Further investigative work shows CCTV of an Audi pulling into the industrial site where the animal was found. Nothing more to go on as there's only one camera working. We've been sent the intelligence as the car is associated to a dealer in London and information suggests revenge is being sought for the dog's execution and robbery of cash.

A drug deal gone wrong. My mind is on Ben's last piece of information RE Ghost, an Audi and a gun. I pull up Google Maps and satellite imagery. Bingo, there's a McDonald's a couple of miles from the site where the dog was found.

I pick up the desk landline, dial and lean back in my chair. It's answered on the third ring with a courteous introduction.

'DS Hunter, I need to speak to Tim Lott, Head of Security. Is he about?' The courteous voice states she'll put me through.

'Hey, Ed, how are you? Long time, no hear.' Tim sounds as bright as he always was. He retired as a Detective Superintendent and joined the security at McDonald's on leaving the job. Security and Logistical Operational lead his new title.

I explain what I need looking at from the cameras at the McDonald's down the road from the site. He agrees to do the work.

'Let's get that drink sometime; I'll ring you when or if I get anything. I'm due a site visit there so I'll handle it personally,' he says.

I thank him and hang up. I wonder what I'll be doing when I finally hand in my warrant card and ditch the phones. Tim was one of the Authorising Officers for Covert Policing; he sounds happy enough in his new domain. My desk phone goes.

'Hunter.'

'Ed? It's Tim. I phoned ahead to see if they had any footage around the time you said they did and they've kept it for me. In the meantime I'm going to send you over a still of two cars, one of which is an Audi. Shows the occupants of both vehicles. It's a start. I'll get the CCTV downloaded and sent over as soon as I get it. This is for intelligence only at the moment?' I confirm it is and give him my job email address.

'That's great. I'm sending it now.' He hangs up. I move the

mouse and unlock the inactive screen. The email's come through and I open the attachment. There's Ben sat in the passenger seat of a black, BMW M135i. Outside the car is one of his associates I know by the street name Ghost. He's talking to an occupant of the Audi parked next to them. Seems like Ben's "mate" was closer to Ben than he wanted me to think he was when he called. I print off the image and arrange a meeting with the DI. Ben will need a different status on our system due to his direct access to firearms and loose Intel providence. He will be designated dangerous for our purposes, which suits me.

It confirms that Ben knows Ghost, who knows Troy, and they're trusted foot soldiers. It also, loosely, indicates Ghost has access to a gun based on Ben's half-truth of a story. Every cloud has a silver lining, even if that silver lining is linked to robbed money, a death threat from a rival drug dealer and a dead dog. Without doubt this will bring the boys out to play and when they come out, so will the firepower. I just need to be in a position to get DI Nolan's team to intercept them with the weaponry before another shot's fired.

20

BEN

I finally call Ed and tell him I've been sick. He wasn't mad and asked if I was better now. The fool. He did tell me we had to meet more though. Some sort of new admin thing or summat as my work was so good but getting closer to Troy meant closer monitorin' or somethin' like that. What do I care? As long as I'm bein' paid.

Ghost's layin' low for a while. Troy ain't havin' it that the lot in Dunstable had no cash with 'em or that they had the nine-bar of weed on tick. He liked the fact he shot their dog though. He thought that were good skills on his part and sent the right message. Don't mess with us. I never got paid for the McDonald's we got on the way back though even when I showed him a receipt. Said I either paid for that or the diesel gettin' there.

He said he would've paid had he seen the money but was pissed it weren't there as he'd been told it would be by another contact higher up the food chain. Truth is the money's at my girl's house with the weed. Troy don't know I stay there so when the heat's off, Ghost will get his thirty per cent cut. I need more money because of the baby. I'm back in the baby mother's good books now. I always know it's best to stay out her way when she's in one with baby hormones and that.

Ain't no one got time for all that screamin' an' cryin' nonsense. She's gotta learn to get on with it. A guy in prison told me that.

I wanna see my kid grow up. No other man can show him how to survive the street like me. I feel it's my prodigal son coming and I can't show him nothin' if I'm banged up. Good job I've got Ed on my side though.

I hadn't called Ed in a while. I didn't like the way he treated me last time over the shootin'. I don't get what his problem is. I need to give him summat good soon though else he'll ditch me. He reckons it ain't worth runnin' me if I don't get them what they need. Truth is I weren't ready when I first got out of prison but I feel like I am now and the way Ed is he won't take no for an answer so I just need to get with the programme.

I needed to test the water, see who was still loyal an' that. From what I've seen of Troy, he's been climbin' high while I've been away. I reckon the time has come for me to step up. Troy ain't gettin' his hands dirty no more and he's rakin' in all the dough. Time's come for him to pay for the way he treats Ghost and me like his bitches.

21

ED

Dusk settles as Sienna and I leave the underground garages of another police site. The rising vehicle trap drops and the echo of the engine dissipates as we hit the surface. The gatekeeper nods and we wait for the security doors to ease aside and release us onto London's streets. We turn left out of the gates and into the one-way system towards Lambeth Bridge. Our task this evening; to make contact with our friendlies and get them motivated enough to keep our company while pointing out target addresses in order for our rapid entry teams to execute warrants, or simply turn them over on the pavement and see what can be found.

Knives, guns, and drugs the order of the evening. These are the nights we love, Smiles and me. John isn't so keen. We contact our sources well in advance of the operation and arrange collection.

Ben was up for this evening's work when I'd contacted him. He was awake, alert and weed-free.

I contemplate the evening ahead as Sienna and I move along the drive-thru lane at the McDonald's near Finsbury Park. Ben will be in Wolsley Rd ready to be scooped up and fed. I know his order now. He's habitual with it.

He's on time as we enter the street. We pull over and dim

our lights. He's seen our car. When he's happy, he stamps out his roll-up and comes over, takes one last look around then gets in the back and we move off. I hand him his large quarter pounder meal, coke and apple pie. You'd think it's his birthday the way his eyes light up.

'You ready to work then?' I ask, as he looks up from bringing the food out from the brown paper bag.

'I'm ready. I hope you are. You'll have results tonight, watch me.' He's already packing away the burger like he hasn't eaten in a week. There's a smell of weed coming from him but he's not out of it. Dutch courage. Nothing more.

The evening starts off slowly. Not many people out and about that Ben knows or cares to point out.

We're completely in his hands. He could be seeing many a villain but we're reliant on what he tells us unless we can identify them ourselves from our policing experience. I like to think of it as working together despite each other. The job sees it as community action.

We hit Islington and as we approach the Tube, Ben leans forward but not so far that he could be seen from the front.

'See the guy there, yeah? Fella with a hoody up and Nike trainers.' I see the guy.

'He's always carryin' weed. He's a runner for Troy. He'd be an easy hit.' He sits back and I get on the phone to the intelligence cell. The arrest team are in the area and agree to take a drive by and check the guy out. We carry on up the road and pull over. After five minutes I see the arrest vehicle cruise down past us towards the Tube.

The guy sees the arrest car then turns towards the Tube. The operator is out the car and chasing him on foot towards the Tube station's entrance.

Thankfully he and his colleagues are fit and take him out in a rugby tackle. As he hits the floor small bags cascade over the pavement and officers surround him and place him in cuffs.

As he's hauled to his feet and led back to the car, he

appears to be limping. The arresting officer leans him against the car and moves the suspect's feet wider as he searches. The officer taps the suspect's legs in a pat down and stops. He's found something solid as he pulls the suspect's elasticated waistband out and retrieves a blade that wouldn't look out of place with a butcher.

A van arrives and the search continues as he's placed in the cage in the back. My phone goes.

'Hunter,' I answer. It's an arrest team officer. She's well away from the van.

'Result. Twenty bags of pills, over a grand in cash and a knife down his trousers,' she tells me. They're more than happy with the result, as am I.

'Good. Call up when you've done the hand over to the prisoner processing team. There could be more.' I hang up.

Ben's phone rings and we go quiet as he answers.

'What's up?' he asks.

'What do you mean where am I? I'm out.' Ben looks at us rolling his eyes.

'I can't get there tonight. What's happenin'?' he tells them.

Ben listens to the conversation. Nodding and grunting at appropriate points.

'Cool. Bell you tomorrow.' He ends the call.

'Good news?' I ask him.

'That address I showed you the other day? There's gonna be a shooter laid down there tonight for a job tomorrow. That's all I know but I should know more when the drop's done.' Ben stops and looks out the blacked-out window, his hood fully up over his face, the peak of his cap protrudes out.

'How will you know?' Sienna asks.

'They want me to lay it down there. How else would I know?' he tells her, as he looks at me as though Sienna has asked an odd question. I address it.

'You can't commit crime, any crime, let alone possessing a firearm,' I emphasise to him.

'It's hardly a gun! You heard it the other night, it were a shock that it fired!' he explains.

'Anyways, I ain't doin' nothing.' But I know who is though. It will deffo move tonight. The guy your lot just lifted was lookin' after it. Word's got out already that he's been nicked. Troy's nervous that the fella's gaff may get turned over.

He was lookin' after the piece. It ain't there no more. It's in transit. That call was from a guy I know who wanted me to look after it tonight. You heard what I said. That's why it's goin' to the safe house on the estate where Troy's bird will take care of it till mornin',' Ben is quick to reassure us. I don't believe him.

'How confident are you that what you've just been told is good?' I ask.

'Hundred per cent! I wouldn't tell you if I thought it weren't. How much do I get if you lot get it back?' he says, too keen to know.

'I don't know. I need to make a call. Keep quiet,' I tell him.

We never tell them any figure. It would always lead to disappointment and a breakdown in trust. I pick up the work phone and call DI Nolan on the Trident team. He answers.

'You lot out to play tonight?' I ask him, hoping the answer is yes.

'What have you got? A bit of weed for personal use?' he jokes.

'Nothing that big.'

'Go on,' he says.

I explain the position as best I can within present company. Thankfully he understands how we work and takes the job on. We drop Ben in a safe area and head back to Lambeth. The main event of the evening is our armed raid on Troy's safe house.

Monitors are on in the main Ops room. A camera feed on the front door of the target premises shows it's not lit up.

Intelligence on the ground has spotted a female enter and not leave the premises, shortly after we'd put the information up. Trident reacted quickly to our call and soon had the address covered and monitored visually. DI Nolan had the place under surveillance already as part of our overall work but hadn't told us. He was keeping the intelligence chain sterile. No gun was seen going in, but the intel fits and there's been recent activity involving firearms in the vicinity that his team have been monitoring. It's only now they've been given the final piece to the jigsaw. Information that confirms they've been watching the right address but never had the right time to strike until tonight.

An out-of-hours search warrant has been obtained. The radio comes alive in the control room as the firearms tactical advisor takes the lead. The officer's body worn video cameras are on for sight and sound. I watch in awe as they creep slowly up to the front door. The door is basic in construction. No fortification here. The signal is given and the enforcer smashes open the door as guns and officers pile through. Shouting is heard and lights in neighbouring flats come on. All thinking it's them getting raided. When they realise it isn't, they go off. A message comes through that the premises are secure and the only occupant, the girl, secured.

The call for a search dog goes out and one is brought up. A lively spaniel shows readiness to work. This is the moment where I sit and wait.

My angst is curtailed when the dog handler radios in that the dog has indicated he's found something. An exhibits officer is with the dog handler. The dog man's video unit clearly shows the dog, rigid other than its tail wind milling, nose on the wash basket in a bathroom that's full of clothes. The handler rewards his dog with a ball as the basket is searched.

In the middle, wrapped in a pillowcase, is a Russian

Baikal pistol. It's been converted to take 9mm ammunition. A photographer documents the find and a firearms officer makes the weapon safe. At the end of the search a small amount of cannabis is found in addition to the gun. DI Nolan was right about enough for personal use after all. The occupant of the flat is arrested. I leave the Ops room and find somewhere quiet and call Ben. He answers straight away.

'We had a result. The gun's been found. Thought you'd want to know sooner rather than later. There will be a steward's enquiry by Troy as to how police came to be there. Be careful. Good work,' I praise him, and rightfully so.

'Cool. I told you it would be there, I told you!' He's laughing and speaking quietly. I can tell he feels good at the fact we'd reacted to what he said and found the gun. It's a good feeling all round. I can hear a female's voice in the background and he whispers he's going then hangs up. Sienna finds me; high fives then gives me a coffee. It is a great result to take a gun off the streets but I also feel nervous for Ben. I know I'm pushing him and I hope he's been telling me the truth about the provenance of the information because if he's closer to it than he's letting on, the consequences for him could be dire at the hands of Troy.

22

BEN

I feel like I've never fallen asleep and there's a bangin' on my Y door. I went back there so as not to lose my room and I don't want Troy to think I'm hiding from him when I've nothin' to hide. The bangs get louder. I throw off the sheet; I'm still dressed from last night.

'Who is it?'

'It's me. Now let me in before I have the door off its hinges.' It's Troy.

'Wait while I get dressed, two minutes.' I sit on the bed and psych myself up. Troy doesn't pay home visits unless it's grief. I have to remember to stay cool like Ed said. I get up and unlock the door.

'About time. The landing was getting busy ya know.' Troy marches in behind his henchmen. The same two I fronted out. I let them in. This is one of them times you gotta face up to what might be comin'. To try to run just makes it worse.

'What's up? Bit early for you to make house calls?' I say to break the ice. Troy stays standing, as do I. There's no room to sit in here and I ain't making myself an easier target by being lower than him. I know I'm sweatin' but hopin' it don't show.

'Had a bit of hassle from Five-O last night. My man got

lifted from Angel and the safe house got turned over badly,' Troy says.

'Fuck me, man! That's madness! They won't have found nothin' there though. You ain't sent me there in a long time to drop off,' I say as he looks around the bare walls, not at me.

'I put the word out for you but the message came back you was busy? Funny really, as I ain't told you to do anythin'?' he says. He's at me now with the kind of look he gives a newbie who wants on-board the action.

'I just told Ghost that. I was out scopin' the streets for a bike. We need to mix them up a bit. It's gettin' too risky out there. I didn't want Ghost along screwin' things up.' He ain't havin' it.

'What could be more important than me, huh? When I call, you dance. If I weren't so generous I'd suspect you dropped a coin to Five-O to get me off your case over the burger and money owed from that firm in Dunstable,' he says, nose-to-nose with me now.

I remain where I am and stare him out. Only a guilty man would look away.

'I may be stupid sometimes but I ain't no grass. I've done time. I see what happens to those that talk. I wouldn't be lookin' at me anyways. I'd be thinkin' on someone else,' I tell him. Troy's eyebrows raise up towards his perfect hairline.

'Oh yeah? Who you got in mind then brains?' I can smell his breath as he breathes out stale smoke.

'It's obvious, ain't it? Your man from Angel Tube. That's your grass, bruv. He happens to be your foot soldier, gets nicked, then your bird's place is turned over that only a few of us know. It ain't me. I know a good thing when I've got one and I like the work here,' I tell him straight.

He stays where he is, looking into my eyes, tryin' to read me like a menu. But this dish ain't for servin'.

'I know it weren't you. I'll always test though,' Troy says. I feel a sharp edge on my cheek.

'Fuck man! What was that for?' My cheek's burnin' and I feel blood movin' down my neck.

'It's a reminder that I own you,' Troy tells me. His minders are close now and I see the blade get given to one of them by Troy. It weren't a Stanley blade, thank fuck, as the wound from that's a bitch to stitch and keep sealed.

I feel my face. Blood is running on a slow trickle. It ain't deep but deep enough to tell me who's in charge. Troy is out the door now along with his goons.

'I'll be in touch. I've a job for you. You won't let me down again will ya?' Troy shouts at me not interested in a reply. I get a T-shirt and put it on my right cheek. I go to my mirror and lift it away. He's left his mark all right. It's as long as my little finger down my cheek line. He must think he's Zorro the way he flashed that knife. I won't go to any hospital as they ask too many questions. There's a guy in the Y who used to be an army medic. He's a good 'un and does a repair for a draw. I go find him to get sorted.

He shouldn't be where I am, but like me, the government don't care about him and he'd rather be here than on the streets. I knock on his door and he answers. He looks both ways down the corridor then back at me.

'You'd better come in.'

23

ED

Last two weeks have been steady. Ben has kept his head down since the gun was found. He's answering his phone but not interested in meeting up, which is strange. Our DI is overjoyed that a gun was recovered and that Ben's quieter as a result. It's lunch. I check my watch and grab my coat. I've arranged a meet up with Lucy in Victoria. Nothing flash but shows me making an effort and with work being so busy I've hardly been about for time to chat. I wonder how long my time will be with the transfer list now being a thing everyone knows.

I've put in a report for retention on the covert command due to my skill set but the job doesn't see that as an issue yet. I'm way down the list so hope this will all blow over. It's been a while since I was in a main CID office on a borough.

Lucy arrives on time and we find a small cafe to eat. The place is lively but not so busy you can't hear yourself in conversation. As I kiss her, I feel her bottom lip's rougher than normal. She has a habit of biting it when she's stressed or anxious. We find a table and get settled in. She reaches across the table for my hand.

'Look, Ed, I've been thinking about the whole baby thing. IVF is already costing us a fortune and we've barely started.

I'm getting close to thirty-five and we know the chances of success for women diminish as we get older. I know you're working really hard to bring in more money but we hardly see each other anymore and you look tired,' she says as she takes a breath and a drink. I take the pause to mirror her behaviour. Despite being at lunch, I'm never off duty even sat with my own wife.

I'm trying to concentrate on the conversation but my mind is on the only entrance and exit, who might come in and sit down, who's loitering or taking notice of us. She's right I'm tired and feel burnt out, constantly alert.

This is the first time I've come to acknowledge the hold the job is having on me. The training and indoctrination now a habit, a trait, I cannot turn off when I want. I was warned about the role before I took it on. Don't give it longer than two years or it will eat you up and possess you like a drug. You will begin to feel weaker when it's not around. I shake the thought off and try to re-engage.

'So what do you think? Should we try adoption? I know it's a lovely thing to do when there are children needing homes and here we are ready to create our own, but at what cost, Ed? Ed?' She's staring at me. I haven't been concentrating. My mind has been on Troy and destroying his empire. I squeeze her hand as she tries to remove it.

'You're right. I have been distant due to work and the stress has been building with the IVF and work. I also don't want to see you pumped full of chemicals with no guarantee of success. We don't know how it will affect you either or what impact it will have on your body. I think adoption may be a positive way forward and I'm more than willing to explore that with you if you like. I think it's a wonderful idea,' I say. She leans over the table and grabs my cheeks in both hands and kisses me, looking into my eyes.

'Oh, that's great, Ed. I wasn't so sure how you'd feel about it. I was afraid you might see it as giving up on IVF too early but it isn't like that for me. You're such a decent man, you know. I'm really excited about this. This could be our life's path,' she tells me as I change seats to be closer to her. The tears in her eyes are ones of happiness and I can feel the same arising in me.

'Let's make it happen, eh?' she says. 'I'll call adoption services and find out what we need to do. A colleague at work went through the process, so I know it isn't quick, but the sooner we get signed up, the better. Can you get the afternoon off? Thought we could do some shopping, get a decent meal later and not rush back home. I'm not due in work until tomorrow.' I'm about to reply when my informant phone goes.

I glance away from her. She's already let go of my hands.

'Answer it. It was only an idea. I'll leave you to it and see you this evening. Maybe we can grab a curry?'

'Sure, I'd love that,' I tell her. She kisses me, gets her coat and goes. I answer the phone.

I don't hang around in the cafe. I pay the bill and head back to the garages and collect a car. Sienna and John are out in the other covert motor on a meet.

I sit in the car in the garages for a while and load up the CCTV footage that had come through from McDonald's on my secure laptop. I don't need to view on fast-forward as the disc has captured the time frame I need. There's Ben. Sat in one of Troy's cars next to an Audi estate. In the back I can see the dog, a Staffordshire bull terrier, as it leans through the gap between the front seats.

I don't think Ben shot the dog. Despite his faults he's never shown me any reason to think he'd be cruel to an animal. I do know he isn't letting on just how close he is to Troy's enforcers. He'd always made out he barely knew Troy but I know different from background work prior to recruitment. It also helps when this is corroborated independently.

Sienna comes through on the speakerphone.

'We're all done here. Do you fancy a beer before calling it a day? Nice afternoon, would be a shame to waste it…?' I take a few breaths.

'Sounds like a plan, I need to be back for seven pm though, I've promised,' I tell her.

'Yay! I'll make sure you're not out all night. See you at The Chapel Bar in an hour,' she replies. That suits me. I can leave the car here and get a Tube to Islington.

'See you in an hour, tell John to get the first round in.'

'John can't make it tonight, he's got to take his boy to football, so it's just me for company I'm afraid.' I think again about needing to be home, as I know once I'm settled in somewhere I need to be dragged away. Sod it though; I could do with a few beers.

'See you in an hour. Guinness for me.' I hang up and lock up the car. The laptop, I deposit in the office safe before getting the Tube north.

24

ED

I grab a black coffee, light up a cigarette and return to my bench. I couldn't sleep last night and the curry we had seemed to sit at the base of my stomach. I hear the first train to London arrive. I take a couple of final drags and stamp out the rest. I find a seat easily at this time of the morning and settle in for a sleep on the route to King's Cross.

'You shit the bed?' John remarks as he enters the office all alert and ready to start the day. I'm on my fourth coffee. Sienna is the next one through the door.

'Oh dear, dear, dear! You sleep here last night?' she asks while eyeing me suspiciously.

'No, I couldn't sleep so came in. Have you got any Codeine?' I ask her as she unlocks her drawer and chucks me a strip. The early start and lack of sleep beginning to bite.

'You can keep them, I've got loads.'

The office calms with the click of keyboards while phones are connected to chargers. We'll know when the DI is in. We'll start getting messages. It's been noticed he rarely comes into the office to see what's happening at the coalface. Something we can all live with. I feed the fish and check the water levels and make a call to Ben.

Best to wake the lazy sod early. There's work that requires

his undivided attention. As the flakes hit the surface of the water, divide then sink, the phone rings out. At least I know it's live. I don't know that he still has it, which is always a concern. As is customary I don't leave a message. He'll see the missed call and realise who it's from. I'm recorded in his phone contacts as *Twenty*. He says that's in light of all I ever pay him.

The phone gets answered just as I'm about to give up hope. It's not him though. It's a woman's voice.

'What time do you call this you arsehole?'

'Tell him Twenty called, get him to bell me back,' I tell her.

'Tell him yourself.' There's a rustle on the line.

'What you doin' bellin' me now? Weren't you ever taught the time, you prick?' For the sake of phone theatre I let his remark go.

'What you doing later?' I ask him.

'I don't know, probably catchin' up on z's that's what,' Ben replies through a yawn.

'Well, don't sleep too long there's a ton of money with your name on it but you need to get out there and get in the mix,' I tell him. His voice has lowered and it sounds like his hand is cupping the mouthpiece to mute it.

'Fuck you. While you was enjoyin' some family time, I was out until about an hour ago graftin'. I'll bell you later,' he says, as the line terminates. I stare out the window at the commuters below.

'I'm on the end of the phone if the DI asks,' I tell John and Sienna as

I grab my coffee and exit the office.

25

BEN

I get in a cab as I ain't waitin' for a bus in this shitty weather. Good job I gotta call from Ed this mornin'. Troy belled me early tellin' me he'd called a meet on with the fam, as he calls us. It's the best family I've ever had so I ain't complainin'. The mini cab scoops me up and I give him an estate to get to.

I never give the proper address, as loads of 'em are grasses. We have a good relationship with the cab firm we use though. They get a decent payout when they pick us up loaded down with nicked gear and take us to the vicinity of the hot house. Our main driver knows we are good for it and waits while we unload the gear through the alleys to the drop. I've come up through the criminal education system to where I am now. I can't say I'm proud of what I've done. I believe it's all down to circumstances that I am where I am, in this cab, headin' for fuck knows what.

The cab stops at the edge of the Anderson Estate, N7. I find the address he's at and knock. A skinny dude comes to the door and just waves me in. I've seen him before at one of Troy's grow houses. There's no one else in but Troy and me. The skinny man's gone.

Troy has rented his flat for the link up. By rent, I mean given him a smoke and told him to make like a ghost for a while. Troy sits down and I do too. The sofa I'm on is crap and my arse hits the floor. Troy kicks things off.

'I had to do what I did. Word was gettin' out that I was weak and we both know that ain't true. You're the only one I really trust, bruv.' He's lookin' at me and nodding his head forward like he's tryin' to convince me he's bein' truthful.

'We're cool. You did what you had to do,' I tell 'im.

'I've got some work and I want you on it. No more messin' around cavin' in shop windows on mopeds and nickin' shit. That ain't ever gonna make you rich, ya know what I'm sayin'?'

I'm the one noddin' now. Cops try that on in interview. Copyin' what you'd be doin' to make you open up and confess, ya know like, trust them.

'I want you and Ghost to take out a guy. This fella, he's called Bling on account that he has his own jewellery and gold place in Hatton Garden. He takes in bent gear and carves it up. Bling gets the gear from a fella in Finchley that has a jewellery business. This Finchley fella takes in high quality nicked bits and breaks it up. Bling collects the diamonds and gold to remake new pieces at his place in the city,' he says. I'm likin' this already.

'So, what's the job?' I'm trying not to sound too keen or greedy.

'Bling's got a pick-up this Saturday from the place in Finchley. I know it's gonna be big. The job's straightforward. Once Bling leaves the shop, he'll be carryin' a briefcase. Take him out on the pavement and have the case away. Job done.' He makes it sound so easy.

'What's the catch? Why me? Anyone could do that,' I ask as politely as I can.

'It ain't that simple. Bling has a security team that shadow him. They wait in the motor and don't come inside the shop. You'll take the MAC-10. If there's any trouble, kill the lot of 'em.'

I say nothin' at first. Just look at Troy. He's sittin' there as if I've just been given his shoppin' list and he's waitin' to see if there's anythin' to add.

'I ain't used one of them toys before man. I wouldn't know how to use it,' I tell 'im.

'Ghost'll handle the shooter. He'll be your pillion; you'll be the rider as you're the best I have. It should be swift and easy. Take Bling out, grab the case and do one before any of his guards realise there's summat up,' Troy finishes.

I can feel myself shakin' slightly. This shit's real. This ain't no Ratners with a pickaxe handle. This Bling dude won't give it up that easy.

'Sounds too heavy, bruv.' I get up and start pacing. Troy lights up a spliff and gives me another small bag of weed and some puff.

'It's been decided you two are doing it and that's final. You've got a little one on the way, so I hear?' I stop pacin' and look at him smilin' at me. How in the hell does he know that? Someone's talkin'.

'You wanted a promotion in the ranks so here's your test. If you wanna be climbin' higher in the firm, you gotta take the work worthy of the status. Now go away and smoke your weed. Here's the address of the jewellers in Finchley Bling will collect from. He should be there around ten as that's his usual pick-up time. Do a recce. Don't try to go in the shop. It will look suss and it's invite only,' Troy explains.

Troy gets up and fist bumps me as he leaves, and skinny man comes back in. I wait a few minutes sayin' nothin'.' When I feel Troy's had enough time to get out the area, I leave too.

I need air and get a cab back to my bike and a trip to Finchley.

26

ED

I'm in the waiting room for the psychiatrist at Empress State Building. My illustrious leader has arranged for us all to have one-off individual sessions to health-check our minds. A box ticked on his form that addresses handlers' welfare. The main doors to the corridor that adjoins the waiting room swing open and the psychiatrist appears.

'DS Hunter?' a demure female asks those in the waiting area.

'That's me,' I acknowledge.

'Come on through, I'm Doctor Curtis. I'm so sorry but I've overrun and only have a few minutes. I'd rather start than leave it, if that's OK with you?' I acknowledge it's fine.

I get up and follow her. She looks like she's just left school. We enter her office. I was expecting a chaise longue, large desk, tall floor lamp and walls surrounded by books.

Instead it's a cubbyhole with two seats and no window. She's picked up I'm disappointed.

'My usual working room is being decorated so we have to use this one. Sorry it's a bit bland and clinical. Please sit down.' I sit and put my paper on the floor. I try to find a comfortable position that looks neutral. I'm realising this must be how a source feels whenever we meet, or at first recruitment.

'So, Edward, do you mind if I call you by your first name?'

'Of course, you can, it's my name. Ed is also good.'

'Very well, Ed. You've been sent by your line manager, DI Colin Ashworth, to assess your state of mind. It sounds extreme but I can assure you it's just a chat so I can see how you are. We have seen more covert officers recently who have found the role a strain, impacting adversely on family life,' she explains.

'OK,' I reply.

'So how are you feeling at the moment?'

'I'm good, thanks.'

'Is that in all aspects of your life?'

'Work is always busy, but that's the same for everyone, I guess?'

'Yes. A sign of the times I feel. You should know that anything we say here is confidential. Anything you share is between us, unless I feel you are a danger to yourself or the organisation. Do you understand? I would encourage you to talk openly. I'm a doctor not a police officer.'

She smiles and sits back, her legs crossed at an angle to me. I've never been good with sharing on any level, let alone emotions, but this could be a long few minutes if I don't say anything.

'I have some concerns about the current policy to rotate detectives,' I tell her.

'Can you explain a bit more what those concerns are?'

'Well, personally, I enjoy this role. It gives me flexibility to work. My wife and I are undergoing fertility treatment at the moment but we'll be looking into adoption too. I'm concerned that I won't be about much for the whole process, or the child, if I'm back on a borough working twelve-hour shifts and having my rest days cancelled.' She nods appropriately and makes a note in a pad she has on her knee.

'Thank you. I'm only making notes for my own purposes

as sometimes it's easy to lose track of a thread when I'm concentrating,' she explains.

'I make notes all day long so carry on,' I offer by way of keeping some conversation going.

'Have you had any fertility treatment yet?' she enquires, tentatively.

'Yes. Three goes. We think it's time to come to terms that it won't be for us, hence the adoption side, not that it's second best or anything.' My brow creases as I realise how that sounds. So often, with Ben, I just rant some instructions, get the job done and move on to the next phone call or meeting.

It's rare I stop and consider the impact of what I'm saying on the other person. She could be going through the same thing herself. You just never know as it feels we are the only couple experiencing these difficulties, which is absurd.

'Adoption is a wonderful thing to consider. I had a friend who went through the process. It is very involved and stressful, so she said. Do you feel you would consider your current role conducive to parenting?' she enquires as she places her pen on her pad.

'I don't know for certain. I don't have kids but one of my DCs does and he raves about how he has time he wouldn't have if he were in a different department.' It's an honest answer.

'I see. The Met does try to look after its staff, where it can, but obviously a service need is a service need and you do have a skill set that's sought after on borough, as so many detectives are leaving and the shortage is noticeable. Of course, the Olympics doesn't help either. It's only a few months away,' she reminds me.

Typical. Claims she's not a copper but clearly has the force's requirements firmly in her mind. My source phone ringtone breaks the silence. I answer it.

'Ed? It's Ben. You about later, I need to see ya?' He sounds coherent and not under the influence of weed. A first.

'I'll get back to you, I'm in a meeting right now. Shouldn't be a problem though. Give me two hours and I'll bell you back.'

'Sweet.'

The call ends.

'Sorry. Occupational hazard,' I tell her as she is making notes and looks up.

'How many times a day do you get called?'

'Difficult to say but a day never goes by without it ringing. Times are all over the place too. My wife is…'

I stop short. I don't want her thinking she's pissed off with the volume of calls and interruptions it causes. I need to stay where I am.

'Your wife feels what?' She's leaning forward slightly like she's hit a therapeutic nerve.

'She feels for them. She says they're lucky to have someone like me on the end of the line. I'm calm in a crisis, apparently,' I lie. She obviously hates the sight of the phone.

'Well, that's very reassuring that she feels she can support you in your role. It must be very difficult for her at times.'

'It can be. She's a vet, so she gets her share of call-outs, but at least she's on a rota.

The doctor looks up at the clock. Therapy time is nearly up. She uses the remaining seconds to bring things to a close. Much like I would with a source. Brush them down and send them happily on their way.

'Well, Ed. That's our time. I apologise again for the short duration. Is there anything else you'd like to say before we finish?'

I think, then work off the same premise all cops do when asked for any questions at a training event. I say nothing.

'Well in that case I'll update your DI that we've spoken and that I have no concern. I'll also be going against protocol and requesting you remain where you are and be removed from the rotation list. You need stability now for you and your wife. You have a brave journey ahead and I wish you the best of luck. I won't need to see you again unless you need to see me. Here's a leaflet with the referral instructions, or you can get them off the intranet.'

I take the leaflet and pick up my paper. She shows me out of the room and as I leave the waiting area and enter the lift I press for the ground floor, where I intend to indulge in a tall latte and a slab of cake to wipe the smile from my overjoyed face. It just goes to show that using the psych services can have its advantages after all. Thank you, DI Ashworth.

I phone Sienna, then Ben.

27

ED

I see Ben as he approaches the entrance to Victoria Station. The early evening crowd of commuters provide plenty of bodies for him to hide among. He knows the drill for this meeting venue. He's to keep walking towards the first escalator on the right. He's to abort only if he hasn't had contact from me or sees anyone he knows. I call Sienna.

'He's on approach to contact point two. Get ready to pick up and follow,' I tell her and she confirms.

I know she has contact as Ben answers his phone and stops going straight. He walks into a newsagent's shop on the first floor concourse. I observe and no one who I feel is a threat follows him in. I wait and observe again at a safe vantage point as he comes out, still on the phone to Sienna. His eyes are scanning around him as he grips the phone to his ear with the palm of his hand. I move away and keep my distance. I watch others around him and keep looking for hostiles to him, or me. I lose him for a second then pick him up again.

He gets onto the second escalator. I allow others on before I join the moving stairs. He's stopped at the top now. I get a text from Sienna saying she's in our final meet point.

At the top Ben doesn't see me but I bump him. By bump I

mean walk up to him. He nearly shits himself then realises it's me. He doesn't do heights either and he's looking down from the upper level.

'We're in here,' I tell him, and he follows me into a restaurant. I move over to the table at the back that's occupied by Sienna and my DI. He has some money for Ben from the last job. I didn't want him coming along, but it was a good opportunity for him to see how we work with so few staff outside, when the car's a no-go due to officers not wanting to pay for traffic tickets.

I hand Ben a menu.

'Order what you like, it's on him,' I tell Ben as I nod in the direction of the DI, who looks none too happy at the prices for what appears to be a standard eatery in the city. Ben appears sober, clean and dressed in the usual hoody, grey sweatpants and Converse. He has a beanie hat on that he doesn't remove.

'How have you been?' the DI asks him.

'Sweet. What you havin' off here?' Ben asks us all.

'I'm not staying for the full meeting. I'm here to pay you then go. Your reward has come through for the last job. How much do you think you should get?' the DI asks.

'Three g's. That gun was top quality. That's my answer. Any less and you're taking the piss man.' The DI swallows and leans forward.

'Times are hard. It's five hundred pounds.' Ben takes off his hat and his forehead is rippled under his black floppy hair. The DI doesn't move.

'Take it or leave it,' he tells him. I don't blame Ashworth. I would have said the same and I had before we met. Ben didn't take it well on the phone but I told him this new boss has his own ideas and wouldn't pay him if he messed him about today. Fact is, he would have been happy with five hundred and wasn't expecting anything more.

'Chill man! I'm messin' with ya. Just give me the green, then you can do one.' The DI slides a receipt over.

'I ain't signin' nothin' till I'm certain it's all there. You lot have just robbed me of two and a half grand,' Ben alludes.

The DI slides over a newspaper and Ben looks in the middle.

'It's all there in the envelope, count it, discreetly,' the DI instructs. Ben does just that and signs his receipt.

'Good to see you again and keep up the valuable work. I expect to be meeting like this regularly and paying you out. Keep to the agreement you signed and don't commit or initiate crime.' The DI nods at myself and Sienna, and leaves.

'Right, looks like this meal's on you then, Ben, we're broke,' I tell him as he looks at both of us strangely.

'What? No way. Now help me with the menu. I struggle with readin' and ain't ever been anywhere other than fast-food places where I can point at a picture.' He laughs but there's a serious note behind his humour.

'I'll order for us,' I say, and Ben nods his appreciation.

The food arrives and Ben looks pleased with his 8oz steak and fries. I added peas to get some vitamins inside him but he ignores them. I can't keep feeling some sense of responsibility for his condition. I need him to stay away from crime to rehabilitate, but if he isn't with people like Troy, then he'll never know what's about to go live.

We have an unwritten agreement. That is, what I don't know, I can't do anything about. It's worked this far, but it's always a fine line to tread with people like Ben. He wants to please despite the way he comes across at times.

'Tell me somethin', yeah?' Ben asks while he pushes away the peas.

'Go on,' I reply.

'Say…hypothetically…there was a guy who was looking for people to come on a job for him…'

'Oh yeah?' I brace myself for where this is going.

'Say this job was about taking out a fella who had loads of money but had been rippin' the organiser off…what could I tell them?'

He sits back and replaces his pointing stick of a fork and steak in his mouth.

Sienna replies, 'Say nothing to the guy. Then speak to us...hypothetically.'

'That. What she said,' I tell him.

'So what's the job then?' Sienna asks.

'I told you it's hypothetical, innit.' He carries on eating.

'I do know somethin' that you lot should know. Remember that guy at Angel who I got nicked when we did that drive around?'

'Go on,' I nudge.

'Word is, Troy thinks he grassed him up while he was in the cells and that's why one of his places got turned over and that gun got found. He says the guy's dead when he comes out. How? I don't know. But he never bullshits around that.'

'How do you know that?' I ask. Ben pauses then looks around the restaurant. It's busy but no one is interested in us.

'He told me. He thought it were me at first but then said he was bullshittin' me, see if I'd break. I tell you, Ed, I was shittin' myself but I never showed it. He grew up with the other guy. He's been workin' for Troy for years and now Troy thinks he's gettin' too big for his boots, like.'

'When did you have this conversation?' Sienna asks.

'I can't remember but it weren't long ago. He don't deserve to die, bruv.' Ben carries on eating.

'How many lives has he ruined, eh? How many lives has he wrecked by pushing gear?' Sienna doesn't hold back.

'Look, right, I ain't sayin' he's a saint or nothin' but the man has to make a livin' and that's how he done it. There's a demand for the stuff and he supplies it. He ain't forcin' it down their throats. He won't deal to kids neither, straight up,' Ben says, as he sits back.

'Who wants a pudding? I'm starving,' Sienna announces. Ben's eyes light up and he looks at me and at the menu.

'Ice cream. Chocolate chip.' There's a childlike glow to his eyes.

'You'll get your pudding once you give us a job. One with legs, and not one that's "hypothetical" or in the *too difficult pile* because it could come back on you,' I interject.

Ben has his arms up and customers look over. He smiles and lowers them in a manner that says he's just messing.

'I've given you a threat to kill and an armed robbery! What more do you want?' he says. He makes a fair point.

'So, the hypothetical case is now an armed robbery?' I ask, with a smile. Ben shakes his head from side to side.

'Look, man, I'm workin' on findin' out more about that one, yeah? It will be soon though. Trust me,' he says, as he taps the side of his nose with his index finger. With the amount of sniff he does, I expect white powder to spill out.

'Take this address down: 16 Waterley Rd. It's Troy's baby mother's house. She holds everythin' for him. It ain't changed since I've been away neither. I've heard she's lookin' after a key of cocaine for Troy. Troy ain't moved it but he's lookin' to move it as soon as he can. It's too hot now with you lot bangin' on doors an' that.' Ben looks at the menu. I look at Sienna.

'I'll have the chocolate ice cream. Double scoops,' I tell Sienna.

'Same here,' Ben chips in before leaning back with his arms across the full length of the bench seat like he's the richest man in the world. We eat in silence. Business is over.

We watch Ben leave the venue and Sienna and I find a Costa and grab a coffee.

'What did you make of that?' she asks.

'I make he's taking us for a couple of fools. Sounds like he's having his loyalty tested on the jeweller.' She agrees with my summing up.

'The things he'll do for food is incredible. Kilo of cocaine my arse,' I mention.

'It was good ice cream though.' She nudges me with her elbow and I spill part of my latte down my shirt. She reaches for a napkin and starts trying to mop it off. I place my hand on top of hers.

'I'll take it from here, Smiles.' She hands me a fresh serviette.

I go back to New Scotland Yard and call the DI to brief him on the threat to life.

The guy is on remand. I phone DI Nolan on the Trident team. He picks up quickly.

'Could be some activity around Troy coming up. Talk of an armed robbery. I know it's not your remit, but it is your target,' I inform him. He needs to know.

'A mate of mine's on the Flying Squad. I'll give him a call, see if we can joint work it for the laugh. If another shooting comes in, it will be good to have a backup plan if this lot go live on it. We'll be out behind Troy tomorrow, to see what he's up to. If we get any images, I'll link up and see if your person can identify them,' DI Nolan confirms.

'Speak tomorrow.' I hang up and turn off the lights as I secure the office door and go and pick up the covert car.

28

BEN

Why Troy chose Ghost for this job, I'll never know. The guy's always asleep. I bang on his door some more and wait. I hear his voice approach. It ain't from inside, it's behind me.

'Bet you thought I were asleep?' He beams the wide-mouthed grin he's known for. We're takin' the bike today and Ghost has my helmet with him. He gives it me and we head away down the landin' towards the lifts. Man the lift stinks today. Someone's either died or pissed themselves, it stinks that bad.

I pull up my bandana over my nose and hold my breath. Ghost's lived here as long as me. I had no choice but to move to the Y. He doesn't wanna leave the manor though. None of us do.

We've taken years to get where we are and our reputations are well known here among the young lot. I started dealin' young. I was nine years old when I got into this game. I'd move anythin' they asked me. They knew that because of my age I wouldn't get charged. Apparently at nine you don't know nothin' so can't know what you're doin' is against the law. Screw that! I knew everythin' I was doin' were wrong. That's why I did it!

The thrill, the buzz, say it how you want, spoke more to

me than any school lesson ever did. I loved bein' part of a growin' empire even if it weren't mine. Troy was just startin' to get his shit together and I liked what I saw. I admired him then, wanted to be just like him.

He got the street name Troy 'cause he'd taken his army in a van and steamed through a street party nickin' everythin'. No one thought anythin' of the van until the back doors flew open and Troy and his crew bomb-burst out with faces covered in his colours by a bandana, armed with bats and metal bars. They robbed the street party of everythin'. Word got out it were him and he was visited by a big firm who run north London.

They told him they liked his style but didn't want it happenin' again. Troy came to an arrangement where he'd pay the family a per centage of each job as a sign of workin' together.

They agreed and he's been rippin' them off ever since. How he's still alive I don't know as this family don't mess about.

I escape my thoughts as Ghost emerges from a ground-floor flat with a garage key. The old dear whose garage he uses doesn't care. She's in her sixties and I swear he's givin' her one as rent. We get to the underground block and he pulls up the door. The door creaks and grinds metal on metal before it gives way and opens up. Inside is a new ride to us, all plated up. It's one I recognise. It's the bird's from behind Saddlers Wells theatre, that time I met Ed. Turns out it were worth goin' back at the same time the followin' day. She's an actress appearin' on stage there. She was parkin' up and going to rehearsals. I don't care though. We got the ride through initiative and attention to detail. She should've invested in a better lock and not parked it in the same place at the same time each day.

Complete lack of respect for the way we work makes our lives a piece of piss. The bike's powerful though, a Yamaha YBR125. It's a new model and could be our ride of choice in the future. It doesn't take us long to get from Wood Green to Finchley. We take the A406. Our hit will be comin' up soon. I feel good behind the throttle and the way the bike handles gives me confidence.

A line of white before we left has helped too. I see where we will be. The place looks like a fortress. Big letters spell out The Gem Shed. It all looks legit despite not havin' windows, but there are cameras on the front.

I roll slowly and check out the two black doors. Bling can go left or right out the shop. The road's busy too so we can't mess about. The pavement's wide though so I can easy ramp it. I park up further down the road against the opposite footway to the shop. Ghost raises his visor like me. I stop the engine.

'What you thinkin'?' Ghost asks.

'I'm thinkin' it will have to be quick, no messin'. You get me? Up on the pavement, bosh and away. There are cameras so I'll switch plates again. If we can nick another ride, that would be cool. This one's powerful but we need a 250cc to be sure. I hope he gives it up without a fight as there's gonna be people about that could get caught in the gunfire,' I remind him.

'When's that ever bothered you?' Ghost whacks the back of my helmet.

'Look bruv. It's one thing slotting a rich rip off jewellery merchant but I ain't in this to take out an innocent. What if a kid got caught up? I'm gonna be a father soon, ya know?' Not even I can believe the words comin' out of my mouth. Ghost's just laughin'.

'Good job you're the driver then. It's all on me, man, so take a chill pill and let's move away from here. We need a route for gettin' away,' Ghost reminds me. He's right. I won't be on the trigger, but I'm bringin' it onto the job. I shake that thought off and turn the bike around. We head towards some shops and figure out a quick route away using the back roads. The A406 will be too busy and crawlin' with Old Bill when we do it. We need to be off main roads and hidin' in the background.

I think about whether I should let Ed know about this job just in case it all comes on top. I need some insurance if it goes wrong and I get lifted. I'll see closer to the time. I've dropped hints but not given anythin' concrete. Technically, in my mind, I've told him. I just ain't put the filling in the pie. I could make a load out of this hit. Troy can't know one hundred per cent what's in the briefcase.

Some of it could go on the missin' like the money and drugs from the other day. Troy needs to pay well or lose out. That's the way of the world. My world. My way.

29

ED

'So how do I look?' Sienna asks as she turns around.

'Like a million dollars,' I tell her.

'Why thank you kind sir. Exactly the compliment I needed,' she replies.

She's dressed to draw attention. We're in the covert car away from the club the potential frequents. It's a late start for us. The potential's just surfaced from Farringdon Tube station. Sienna is relaxed in her tight white top and leather trousers, mid heel shoes, hair down in a loose curl below the shoulder, make-up now being applied in the vanity mirror. She also carries a suitable black handbag.

In it is a small can of hair spray. She has no intention of using that on her hair. She'll use it if the situation arises to fend off an unwanted attention-seeker.

There's no police protective equipment going into this club. The only protection she'll have is her wit and skill. The backup is John and me.

We have the plans of the club from the licensing officer and Sienna's attended the club off duty so knows the inside too. The importance of visiting the club before deployment is vital and she knows it. When she's in there she doesn't want to appear out of place.

The risk tonight is greater from criminal and any off-duty police who may be inside. That risk is now necessary to manage.

'You know I'm here for a good time, boys, so you two will have to wait it out until I see fit to engage her outside. It may be quick, or I may be having such a laugh I won't want to leave.' She starts applying lipstick and I can see John taking a glance up from his phone in the back. She catches him and winks, causing him to react immediately by looking away.

'I want you taking a fag break on the hour. I need to see you regularly so I know you're ok. There's no phone signal in there and it will be too noisy to speak. Minders block all the exits, but we have an Observation Point organised close to the designated smoke area out the back. We'll see you. If nothing's happening then re-apply your lippy outside. Ten minutes after that, leave.' Sienna nods and I continue.

'We'll know if it's going good, as we'll see you with her in the smoking area or outside the main entrance. We won't lose contact. I've organised some backup if it all goes wrong. Either way, we'll all meet up at The Smithfield Tavern and debrief after that.' I need to know she understands the situation.

'I hope to be de-briefed in there,' she replies. I look at her, my eyes unsure at what I've heard.

'I'll be on my best behaviour,' she says as she raises her eyebrows.

'That's what bothers me. Here's some Commissioner's money to make an impression, don't blow it all. We'll need a kebab once this is done,' I tell her as she takes the money and starts putting it down her top. I stare at her.

'Only kidding! What's up with you tonight you're not always this highly strung.' She puts the notes in her bag, writes a number on a twenty and puts it in her shoe.

'If it doesn't work out this time, we'll attempt it later in the week. What I'm saying is, do your best,' I reassure her. At least that's my hope. Sienna leans over and pinches my cheek.

'I'm a big girl now and can look after myself,' she says, as she exits the car and puts her bag on her shoulder as she walks in the direction of the club.

'Just me and you now, John.'

He leans forward from the back seat.

'So…are you and Smiles…you know…?' I turn and face him.

'Is your mind anywhere else other than your dick? No, I'm not,' I tell him as he shrugs his head and raises his eyes.

'Cool. I might try it myself then.'

He sits back and manspreads across the back seat.

'Mess her about, John, and you'll be history.'

'See! I knew you had something going on with her,' he retorts. I say no more. We get out of the car. I lock and alarm it and pray it will be there when we need it later.

'You're looking smart yourself there.' John says, as he looks me up and down.

'Let's hope we can get through the door, without showing out, if she needs us. We are her backup,' I remind myself as much as John. He lights up and takes a drag.

'She'll be in and out, job done. You just watch,' he says as he offers me a light. I hope he's right.

30

BEN

I'm freaked after today. I've no idea why but doing that recce made the shit more real. Bling ain't gonna just hand over the case. He's got minders for a reason. They won't mess about either. Deffo they'll be tooled up an' all. Bats, poles, car wheel braces. The kind of hardware we carry when we're out.

I feel wired, but without the toot in my system. I'm gettin' grief from Maria as she's gettin' bigger and wantin' to know where I am an' that. I ain't no dog. I'm a free man. I've done my time. I need to get some stuff for the kid but I ain't got no clue where to go or what to get. My whole family ain't ever kept a kid beyond hospital. No matter if they've tried to do a runner to another hospital to have it.

The social have always found out. As soon as the kid's out and screamin' it's taken away.

Was one time we could see the kid as family but now we're considered too high risk like we'd nick it! Man knows there ain't no value worth nickin' there so why would we have it off? World's messed up, I'm tellin' youse.

It's late now and I need out. I need the streets. I need the freedom of the road with no one tellin' me where I should be or what I should be doin'. I bell Ghost.

'Yo, what's up?' I ask.

'Just chillin', what about you?'

'I need out of these four walls, bruv. My heads bangin' after today, I don't know why, like,' I tell 'im.

'Sweet. Let's do a club or somethin'. Farringdon has a no ticket night on, we could try there?' He sounds confident despite the fact we'd never get in there by how we dress and our attitude to waitin' in a line.

'Let's take a look. Worse case we could do a bit of work down there when they're all spillin' out pissed on their phones.' I can hear laughin'. He's high and up for it.

'Twenty minutes I'll be outside. Let's have us some fun tonight.' Ghost kills the line and I don't bother gettin' changed. I know what fun he's talkin' about and I'm good to go.

31

ED

Sienna's been out having a cigarette but not with the potential. She's not given the lipstick signal so the recruit must be somewhere in the club and hasn't taken a fag break. I just hope she won't be lured away before Sienna can get to her. The club itself is heaving. My senses are alert to potential trouble.

Bouncers are controlling the entrance outside. They have their fingers in their ears like they have tinnitus. It's busy. They often switch the larger front of house to go inside and deal with an ejection from the dance area. Sienna isn't stupid. She knows when the risk is too great and will get out. The robbery squad got us this OP on the understanding we were using it to combat drug dealing.

It's a vacant upper level flat that has a good view of the welfare tent and outside smoking area. Both well used. John is covering the front on foot. By covering, I mean he's being discreet in various bars using the warmth of the evening to drink outside. He won't drink alcohol. He's assured me of that...I can remember a time I would have been in a club just enjoying life and not having a care in the world. Now I wouldn't take one step inside unless it was work. That and the realisation I've matured and have responsibility above and beyond myself. Lucy's desire for children enters my mind. I feel an increase in heart rate at the same time. It isn't out of the same desire.

My desire is what I'm doing right now, binoculars at my eyes, glassing the outside behind a net curtain and hoping for a successful evening's work. I don't bother looking for John. He's a tough cookie and will be on point if the shout goes up to get Sienna out. We've always worked well in these situations. Sienna is the newest recruit to a small unit. I'm glad she's arrived. She's brought fresh perspective and outlook to how we work and a younger mind that's unaffected by years in the police, getting steadily worn down through politics.

My phone vibrates in my pocket. I turn away from the window so the screen doesn't illuminate me. It's our DI.

'How's it going?' he enquires in a genuine, wants to know, tone.

'Sienna's inside so our subject must be in there. John is covering the outside.' I keep it brief.

'Good. Look, I'm calling to let you know there's been a message sent out that concerns the club you're at. Rumours are circulating that Troy's mob's turning up at the venue as a show of force. If they turn up, I want DC Myles out of there and all of you away from the area,' he says then pauses and awaits my response. I continue observing through my binoculars and consider what he's relayed.

As much as I enjoy disagreeing with him, on this occasion he's right. I have respect for the fact he's made the link between our deployment and this separate request. Any message from our tasking group means another intelligence feed has mentioned the club. There's a need to assess and feedback any information as to the truth behind the rumour. Knife crime is on the up as well as shootings so it's a serious risk to manage.

'I'll make sure she's out at the first sign of Troy or his crew arriving. We have great knowledge around this lot and I have good cover. I won't put DC Myles at any further risk,' I reassure him.

'I know you won't. Keep me informed as things develop and let me know when you're all safe and stood down.' I confirm I will and he hangs up. My phone goes again. It's a text message from John: *motorbike arriving. Two up.* I take a look through the binoculars and can see a 125cc Yamaha bike arrive with two people astride it. They cruise past the entrance slowly, looking at the line of clubbers. Both doormen see them straight away and are on their radios; they know why they're there.

Like a lifeguard knows when a school of sharks has arrived. The two on the bike have gained the attention they desire. In my mind they're scanning the crowd for opportunity to rob or rival gang members to carve up.

I text John back, *Got them. Aw8 further instructions.* He acknowledges with an emoji thumbs up. I call Ben. The phone rings and I keep the bike and riders under observation. They've both stopped and the pillion is looking around as the main rider goes into his pocket and picks out a phone. I see him kill the call at the same time my ringing ends. It's Ben.

The little shit's out and about and must know something's going down at the club tonight and hasn't told me. On top of that, Sienna's inside and he'll know her on sight. Now another two bikes have arrived; all two up and milling around as though they're corralling cattle. I check the back and Sienna's out with the potential, talking, having a cigarette. Right place, wrong time. I pray this is the final contact before the club kicks off. Two are off the bike and one's Ben.

Both keep crash helmets on and the pillion has a rucksack over his shoulder that appears to have contents by the way it hangs at the bottom.

I text John: *Move to position B. Observe and control.*

I see him look at the phone, place it in his pocket and move away from the bar he was outside. He makes his excuses to those he'd decided to chat with to maintain his cover and not stand out.

The pillion has the bag open and he's checking the contents. While he's doing this, the others ride around outside. All this tells me they aren't looking to go in. They're trying to draw the rival gang out or biding their time at the watering hole for the stray to break from the crowd and become their prey.

That's the way they work. The pillion with the bag is moving away from the pack towards the entrance. His eyes are everywhere as the others move around on their steeds in anticipation of the main event. At the same time Sienna exits the club and starts applying lipstick. It's the final sign she's finished and moving out to our next meet point for de-brief. I look for Ben. He's still about, looking towards where Sienna is. I grab my bag and get out of the OP taking two steps at a time down the stairs.

I finally get to the ground floor and start running around the block towards the vicinity of the club's front door. I see John, he's intercepted Sienna and asking for a light as they walk away. The pillion approaches them. My instinct is to move towards them but it would serve no purpose. I know what I've seen and I don't like the look of the guy with that bag.

He isn't delivering pizza. I'm twenty feet from him now. His hand goes into the backpack.

He's found his prey and started the stalk. His eyes are locked on John and Sienna. His preparation for the final pounce is nearly complete. He's beginning to retrieve the object he's located in the backpack. As his arm retracts, the contents of the bag still remain hidden. John sees me and doesn't acknowledge. I don't know who the pillion is as he still has his helmet on.

I'm suddenly dazzled as the area floods with light and the sound of a helicopter causes everyone to look up. People either disperse or make the mistake of looking up, drawn in by the illumination. The helicopter hovers over backpack man who starts moving away as the light tracks him. He's running now and at the same time uniform are turning up.

Cops bail out of their vehicles and start chasing. I recognise Fi and she doesn't hesitate as she lets her dog off and it brings the guy down. His screams are drowned out by the sound of the helicopter as the dog rags his arm around like a tug-toy. The backpack is still on the floor, left as he fled. As quick as I see it, a bike appears; it's Ben. He accelerates towards the backpack. Police and public part as he leans down, grabs it and makes off.

There's panic as the bike pushes through people at speed causing them to dive out the way.

He passes me with millimetres to spare and is gone. Officers run back to their cars as the light from the helicopter remains on the suspect while he's being secured. The other bikes have gone. They were away the moment the helicopter arrived, and uniform followed. Backpack guy is left to face his demise alone. No one will catch Ben. He's well away.

John and Sienna have used the cover of the crowd and commotion. They see me and John nods and mouths, 'OK?' I nod back and we split towards the agreed meet point. My heartrate is up and I'm desperate to get clear of the conflict area.

I take a steady walk towards the street and our covert car. I stop, look in windows, cross the road and back again further up. I'm not being followed but I don't relax. I can't relax.

I have control but remain alert. Ben has screwed up. Why he took the backpack will need to be established as well as why he was there. Question is, will he acknowledge it to me? I doubt it very much. All I have is the fact that he answered his phone and killed the line at the same time I rang. That and wearing the same sweats and Converse he wears every day.

32

BEN

The place is buzzin' with people. I take a slow ride along the line, nodding at everyone, makin' sure they know we're about. Ghost had a call from Troy who said another firm were over on our turf. Fools. We'd done a drive by at Ghost's bird's house and picked up a piece, just in case it got tasty. I don't like guns myself. Prefer a blade to do the talkin' with. Thing is with Troy, he don't care as he ain't out here doin' it. He just sends out the riders to deliver messages and sort his shit out. I seriously thought we'd just be out for a cruise and the random take down if the phone looked right. Ghost and I go back a long way. He's like a brother from another mother to me. We always roll together.

Just like cops have their favourite players, well that's Ghost and me. He's got the gift of moving gear in and out of stash houses unseen by police. He can make nicked gear and drugs disappear quicker than any dude I know. By disappear I mean he don't just ditch it he sells it on quick for good money. He's the only person I'd lay down my life for, I'm tellin' you the guy's a legend with me. Word's gone out and more of the crew turn up for the laugh and to see what's goin' down. There are no rivals here yet, unless they're inside. They'd be mad to be in there without askin' permission before visitin'. We all wanna' good time but this is where we work. This is our house, our plot, our livin'. They've got their own honey pot and ain't takin' a scoop out of ours. The other lot are just fuckin' about outside now, poppin' wheelies and riding round in circles and figure-of-eights. They're itchin' for some action.

I can see the thick and suited out front have seen us already and are talking into their radios. They'll be doubling up security around the place and makin' sure all exits are locked down. They hate us but that comes with lettin' us deal there. They get a good cut from Troy and they know it. Sure they play the game with Five-O, too. Grabbin' drugs that's being smuggled in from outsiders, but they don't touch any of Troy's soldiers. Plod are happy and the club gets a good rep for co-operatin' with the war on drugs.

Thing is, there ain't no war on drugs. That ended a long time ago, when the streets won. I'm tellin' you. Even politicians are sniffin' powder. Where do you think they get their gear? Damn right, from people like Troy and me. The minister's foot soldiers, who they can't even pay decent benefit to for being out here peddling this stuff so they can stay smacked up running the country. Man they got problems, I tell you. They want someone like Troy in charge. He'd show 'em how to make money and get people listenin' to what's goin' down. No messin', just doin' it. Put up and shut up.

Ghost taps me on the shoulder and I lower the throttle so the bike's ticking over. You never, ever, kill the engine. Ever. You do that you're a sittin' duck. He leans in.

'Right, I'm gonna send a message. First one I see out through the door gets slotted, bruv. I don't care who they are. If anyone's there tonight that I see as an outsider they're gonna get a lesson in respect. Everyone who goes regular knows the score, and who runs things in there, so it's fair game in my head.' I nod at him and he taps my crash helmet.

'Wait about for me. You'll know when I'm done then come

get me and we're away, yeah?' I nod and he gets off. He puts the backpack on one shoulder. I know what's inside it.

Thing is, I didn't think we was doin' anythin' tonight other than movin' it away and layin' it down. It's too late for me to call Ed. My phone goes. I mess about tryin' to find it. When I do, I see it's come up with Twenty, Ed's fake name. Ghost is still here. I can't talk right now so I kill the line. I'll call him back tomorrow. He'd go ape shit if he knew I was out here with Ghost and a gun waitin' to kill someone. It's too late for all that. I'm here and that ain't changin'.

Ghost's headed toward the main entrance. There's loads goin' in but ain't anyone come out yet. I hope no one does or the gun jams or summat. Ghost's a hot head and he doesn't give a shit. All he'll see is people comin' out from a party that weren't invited. He doesn't care who they are. Bang! They're dead. I see him drop the backpack off his shoulder, crash helmet still on. Bouncers are lettin' people in and friskin' them. They ain't concentrating on us anymore. Our wheelie show was all designed to get Ghost closer by distracting them, letting them get on with their jobs so we can do ours.

It's then I see her, or at least I think it's her as she's got a load of slap on. It's the cop bird that works with Ed. I'm sure it's her. She's out front now puttin' on lipstick. I rev the bike some more and keep lookin' at her then back at Ghost. He's seen her too. I know he won't know her. It's game on. Fuck! Fuck! I can't think of what to do. I hate the filth but she's different, she ain't like the others. She cares even though she can be a stroppy bitch. Ghost's hand is in the bag now, he's squarin' up to take a pop, I know it.

I thrash the throttle. The rear wheel skids like mad. The wheels then grip and release me towards Ghost. I can't let him shoot her. I'm gettin' close now. His hand's in the bag. All I can do is grab him and say it's hot. Then I see 'em. They're arrivin' quick.

The copter's lit the place up. Ghost's been caught in the light trap. He's left the bag and he's off. Five-O are everywhere. I just keep my head down and keep goin'. I bank the bike and lean down, grabbing the backpack handle on the way through. I straighten up then carry on. I don't give a shit if I hit anyone, but I don't. I've got out. Ghost? I don't know where he is or what's happened. All I do know is that Five-O ain't got nothin' on him as I've got the bike and the bag. They'll keep him overnight and sling him out next day, as there's nothin' at all to keep him on. I'm cool.

33

ED

We're back in the sanctuary of the covert car. I'm in the back and John's driving. We're alone in our thoughts, each concentrating on the outside world, making sure we're clear of trouble. John pulls over, lets two cars go past, then pulls out again. A few yards further he does the same thing, then U-turns. I go with the stop, start, pirouetting of the car. None of us are taking further risk tonight. Anti-surveillance is providing a necessary comfort for us all. Once I'm satisfied we're safe, I tap John on the shoulder.

'We'll go to the Turkish place in Green Lanes. We could all do with food.' John nods, checks his mirror then U-turns again and heads in that direction.

Sienna's in the front passenger seat and turns in my direction.

'It went well. I've told her I'm a recruiter. She wasn't put off at all; in fact she needs the money, she says. We've exchanged numbers. She'll call in a couple of days. I told her my number was on the twenty. She appreciated the note. It was a scary place in there I can tell you, gang-bangers from another turf, that's for certain. It just felt like it would kick-off so I took the initiative to engage early and get out of there. She felt the same which was handy.'

She turns back around and racks the seat back to recline.

'What about you, John? You have a good night chatting up the ladies with your droll pick-up lines and bedside manner?' She's smiling at John as he turns her way.

'I'll have you know I was very professional and had your back all the time,' he replies as she laughs and closes her eyes.

I text our DI and tell him we're all safe and sound. He replies he'll *see us tomorrow*. 'So, what happened back there, Ed?' John knows my silence means something. I'm usually vocal after a job. This time I feel differently. I need to establish from Ben why he was there and what was in that bag before I can commit to any thoughts out loud. He was a fool to ride in and grab the bag. There must have been a gun, drugs or both in it to take that level of risk. Why was the passenger interested in Sienna and John coming out the club?

Until I can firm up the facts I shrug it off. It's not that I value Ben's resourcefulness over these two; it's how things can be unclear until fully investigated.

'Call it instinct. I didn't like the rider on the bike.' John looks in the rear-view mirror and our eyes connect. He knows I'm talking shit but leaves it. I look away first.

We arrive at our destination. John parks the car up. 'Usual?' They both nod and I do the honours and get the tab and food to take away. Tonight needs to end for all of us, but only on a full stomach. I check my personal phone, there's nothing from Lucy.

34

BEN

I turn the piece from side to side checkin' it out and wonderin' if the rusted piece of metal would ever have fired. I have the ammo that was in it. There were only three rounds. I have my sleeves pulled down so my skin doesn't touch any of it. This is what I need for protection, I'm thinkin'. Not this piece of shit but summat heavier with more firepower. A Glock. Well impressive and looks the part when you pull it out and hold it side on like in the films.

'What's that doin' in here?' It's Maria.

'Just lookin' after it for a mate. Be gone tomorrow. Promise. You wanna hold it?'

'Don't be a tool. I ain't getting my dabs on that. Why'd you bring it back here, anyway? You know I could do time if this place got raided? Do you want your kid being born in prison? You never think about anyone but yourself.' She says her bit then flops down beside me on the sofa.

Ain't no way I can keep it here and the Y ain't good either. I have a plan though. I stick it back in the backpack.

'Ain't that Ghost's bag?' she says. The girl's got eyes everywhere and a memory like a camera.

'Yeah, what of it?'

'What of it? If it's his gun he can keep it at his house can't he?' She's lookin' at me like I'm thick or summat'. I can't tell her he's banged up as she'll wanna know more about where I've been.

'This is business right. Business that you do all right out of so keep your trap shut or your mouth will end up wrapped round the end of it and a bullet through your skull! Is that enough questions now?' She's looked away with the right hump. Conversation done.

Next mornin' she still ain't speakin' to me. She'd stayed downstairs all night, so I had her bed all to me-self. I slept like a baby. I try Ghost's number but his phone's off. He's either out and not turned it on or he's lost it to Five-O.

I don't wake her as I creep down, just go past and look at her lying there drooling like a bulldog. I can't believe she's havin' my kid.

Until it's all DNA'd an' that I ain't believin' her. She could have been screwin' loads of blokes when I was away despite all she's said to link me into it. It was a one-night stand that was all. I was stoned and could barely get it up. It's all bullshit, gotta be.

It ain't that I don't care about her, because I do. She stuck by me through some bad times. When I was banged up, she visited me twice then stopped. She wrote, but I needed someone to read them to me and I didn't want that. I just don't wanna be tied down at this time in my life. I've gotta feelin' big things are gonna happen for me now and I can't have no ankle biter wantin' me all the time. I'll see her right though. I always do even when I sound off at her and make threats an' that. She knows I ain't gonna do nothin' to her. Anyways I need her gaff when it's good to lie low. I know Troy says he knows where I live but he ain't who I'm bothered about, it's the filth. I don't need them on my doorstep.

I grab my pushbike from her kitchen and get out the back.

I know where I'm headin' and take side streets and alleys to stay away from the main roads. Police always stop me, always, and this is heavy shit I'm carryin'. I get into the park. I cycle over to the main bushes and look around. It's quiet as it's early. I tip the piece out under the hedge and kick some leaves and dirt over it so it can't be seen. The bag I ditch in a roadside skip.

Now it's breakfast. Man's gotta eat while he works. I find a local cafe where we sometimes hang out and order a full breakfast. I'm flush and fuckin' starvin'. The Turk owner knows me. He knows I pay when I turn up and don't do a runner once I've finished. I check my phone. No calls yet. It's before twelve so ain't anyone up. I text Ed though: *Bell me.*

35

ED

'Where did you get to last night? You were out for ages, I didn't bother calling you.' Lucy's not happy. The milk has barely touched the cereal before she's off on an interrogation. I understand that it's difficult for her to come to terms with my work, long hours, never knowing where I am, who I'm with and why. But there's a reason for all that. It's covert police work. It would shatter her world of animals, kindness and compassion and just become one hell-hole with no rope to get out of.

'We had some work on and the signal wasn't good where I was so you wouldn't have got hold of me. How was your night?'

She's joined me at the small breakfast bar.

'I looked up some stuff on adoption and arranged for us to go on an open evening tonight. I've taken the day off. Why don't you do the same and we can hang out, you know…try to relax and be a couple for a bit.' I use the moment to stuff my mouth full of cornflakes so I can delay the reply. There's no way I can take leave today. We all need to sit down after last night and run through the next approach. Plus I need to see Ben.

'I can't take today off. I'll try to make sure I'm away at a reasonable time so we can go.' I lean towards her to give her a kiss, but she turns away and takes her tea into the conservatory. It's an occupational hazard in the police, you never know what time you will be away from duty, ever. It was bad enough in my early days in uniform but even worse now I'm covert. The people I work with rarely keep regular hours unless they're so far up the pecking order they can turn their phone off at five. I've met a few but not many.

I can see the leaflets she's been sent from the adoption services, surreptitiously scattered on the breakfast counter. The smiling faces of a sibling group beam off the page. I turn the page over and start reading but then shut it. My mind is full of work; guns, drugs and where they may be and for how long. As if on cue, my source phone vibrates, and I read a text from Ben. *Bell me.* He never uses the money I give him to top his phone up. I hear the door go as Lucy leaves, saying nothing. I dial Ben's number and it's answered immediately.

'Yo, Ed, what's up? Ben's voice sounds edgy.

'I'm calling you back.' I'm clipped in my reply.

'Who rattled your cage this mornin'?' He makes a fair assessment of my mood.

'Where were you last night?' I ask.

'I was out and about workin' for you, why?' His voice becomes hesitant.

'Really? I heard you were outside a club that nearly kicked off.' Fuck it. He can have some of my wrath.

He pauses before replying.

'What if I was? Is there a law against seein' your mates now? Anyways I heard somethin' about that you'll be interested in.' His voice eager to switch subjects. I let him have his moment.

'Go on,' I say.

'There was another gang at the club lookin' to cause bother, right. They wanted to buy a gun off Troy, I know where that gun is if you're interested?' I'd make a good guess as to where too but decline. I let him know enough though.

'The one you scooped up in the backpack off the road? The one belonging to your mate?' He's gone silent at the other end.

'I saw you take the bag. What was in it, Ben? Don't fuck me about.' I know what was in it now. I also know he's lying about it being for sale.

No one brings a gun to a club to sell and certainly not to a rival gang.

'Look right, I know what you're thinkin'...that the gun was in the bag, yeah? Well you'd be wrong. It was my mate's clothes. He was comin' to stay at mine after we'd been out that night. Anyway, I now know you were with that bird from your office. I knew you was doin' her!' Arrogant little prick thinks he can sway my mind by bogus blackmail.

He's pissing himself laughing. I'm not. I hadn't realised that he'd seen Sienna. It's unfortunate but easily explained away. Just not to him unless he digs further, and she needs a cover story.

'You're way off track. So where's this gun?'

'In a bush in Caxton Square Park near the kids' play area. I ain't touched it before you ask; I heard it had been laid down there. A few people know about it, so it won't come back on me if you find it. You'll have to be quick though. These things don't hang about long. I only heard this morning,' he says.

'What if a kid finds it? The world you're in is fucked, Ben.'

He's saying nothing. Lies and more lies. I have to take him on face value. He gives me the location again so I can confirm what I've recorded, and I hang up.

I ring DI Nolan. 'I've got a gun for you. An easy recovery if you're interested?' Thankfully he is. He says he'll get a team out to look. I give him the details and hang up. The adoption leaflet catches my eye again. I pick it up along with the covert car keys and head into the office.

36

ED

I have a new message. It's a picture sent by DI Nolan. The image is of a Russian Star pistol in situ under a bush. I reply – *anything else?* A short time later the response comes back – *Nothing.* Although I'm happy the gun has been recovered, my gut tells me that it should have been with ammo. If this was in the backpack Ben's mate had, then it was taken for a purpose and not just to pose.

I can't help but think Ben has the ammo, or it was on a separate bike that made off and never linked up with Ben to hand it over. There's no way his mate was reaching inside the bag for a change of top. I ring Sienna and tell her the news and then the boss. The DI is in a good mood.

'Great work, Ed. We need more results like that. I'll await your reward report for Ben and we'll see what we can get him for putting another gun up. Money's tight but I'll do my best. The informant budget has been cut but there's always room for manoeuvre where guns are concerned. I'll see you later.' He hangs up as he sounds in a rush to get to yet another meeting.

The other two haven't arrived yet. I sit at my desk and open my bag. The adoption leaflet greets me first. I start reading it as I sip the takeaway mocha. The bitter taste of coffee clashing with the sweetness of the innocent faces staring up from the pages. I realise I do care. I care that each and every one of them finds that forever home and has a fantastic life. I just don't know if I'm capable of delivering it for any of them when I struggle to do that for Lucy and myself.

I log-in and check the overnight crimes for London. The usual stabbings, shootings and assaults stare out at me including the nightclub incident. It's a mention only and nothing more. Mainly because we prevented it from escalating any further. The public won't hear about it. If the crime didn't happen, that's what counts.

I hear the door swipe being activated and Sienna strides in all smiles and glee. She's carrying two takeout cups and my spent one is replaced with a fresh fill and a ham roll.

'Thought you wouldn't have eaten.' she remarks, as she spies the adoption leaflet on the desk.

'So, that's why you've not been your cheery self then? Pressure or choice?' she asks, as she sits at her desk adjacent to mine.

'Choice. Just not enough space to have them all.'

'The amount you two are on you could buy a mansion and give them all a home.'

Sienna hands me the leaflet back and gently squeezes my shoulder.

'No contact from the potential but I wasn't expecting a call this early. She'll work out if I can keep her on-board. I'll try to jack up another meeting as soon as she makes contact. Any news from Ben?' I shake my head to the negative.

'He's bang at it, you know. One of these days he's going to bring us all down the way he's carrying on, he's off the chart. If you ask me, we should ditch him.' She turns to her computer as it warms up and spreads her written contact sheets on the desk ready to input on the secure system.

'I've no intention of ditching him. Unless he comes back on DNA or gets caught red-handed on a job, then he stays on. Besides, he's got a child on the way, he can use the money.'

'You're too soft you. You should've been a social worker.' She's staring into the screen as she types.

'Trust me, I've met many social workers and some of them are anything but soft,' I reply. I get through the security checks and the secure system comes to life on the screen. The DI has been in and authorised the reward report I'd typed for Ben. I'd calculated the reward on our matrix and made it fifteen hundred. He's knocked a thousand off and authorised five hundred. I lean back, hands in my hair looking at the amount.

Five hundred pounds for something he could have sold to the right buyer and doubled his money. The price of a gun is what someone is willing to pay. How am I meant to encourage him to talk to us when we pay paltry money?

'We'll go out when you're done and pay Ben. DI's happy for me to pay him,' I tell Sienna who nods in agreement. I leave the office for the short trip to covert finance.

37

ED

London bridge station buzzes like a hive. Londoners moving to avoid each other and get to their final destination. Our destination is pre-determined by fate, luck and some planning to make sure we're not being followed. That means by the police service or Ben's contact and associates. Sienna is in the station awaiting the arrival of Ben. John is tucked up with his own work back at NSY and I'm on a concourse opposite the station entrance, waiting for the shout from Sienna that she's seen Ben arrive.

These meets all need planning and preparation. I have routes and meet points all over London but you always have to make adjustments on the day as the places never stay as they were when we walked them through months ago. I check my watch; it's thirteen hundred hours. I know he'll be on time today. He always is when the Commissioner's wallet is open. My work phone goes. It's Sienna.

'He's out, wearing a black hoody, baseball cap and ridiculous shades, he'll be in sight in 5, 4,3,2…now,' she says, and hangs up the phone. I take over and observe. I'm looking for a police surveillance team to outwit or any other dodgy character that appears to be following him. Our meetings are private matters and not for voyeurs. I stay where I am and ring his phone. He answers immediately.

'Yo, where you at? I ain't got time for all this messin' about today.' Eloquent as he always is. The line remains open as I walk him through our route to the meeting point.

'Cross the bridge first, then wait on the other side.' He does as he's told and leans against the wall, Borough Market side. I watch to see who might be paying interest to him. All's good.

A male then catches my eye. He's six-one in height and wearing a North Face coat, jeans and Timberland boots. He was behind Ben when he came out of the station. He's crossed the road at a distance and has slowed his pace down. I carry on using the open line.

'Ignore the steps on your right that lead down to Southwark Cathedral. Keep going straight ahead.' He nods and walks as directed. Phone at his ear.

'Under the railway bridge you'll see an alley into Borough Market. Go slow.' He saunters along taking in the people and traffic as he approaches the entrance to the alleyway.

'Take that alley and continue walking unless I direct you otherwise.' I wait to make sure he's heard me. I watch him turn in then he speaks.

'Cool, see you on the other side.' He hangs up his phone. I'm already off the concourse and crossing the bridge further down. The male has hung back but is now six people behind Ben and going in his direction. I mirror his behaviour six back from him but take the steps down to a cafe area and pass them to the opening that leads to the market.

As I arrive, I see Ben exit the cut through. He can't see me. Ben gets on his phone and starts looking around.

'Where are you? What the fuck's goin' on?' he demands. I can see Sienna at a stall in the market on the edge of the open space. She too has a discreet watch of Ben.

I ring her.

'White male. Six-one – dark puffa and boots. If he comes

through that alley then we'll have some fun shaking him off,' she agrees, then hangs up. She knows the drill.

I'm back on Ben now. 'Keep walking past all the stores through the market. Stop at the stall that sells cheese on your right. Go in and have a nose around.'

He's not happy but agrees to do it and stays on the phone.

'I hate markets. Nowhere to get a bike through.' He starts laughing.

'Good job you've given all that up then,' I tell him as he carries on meandering around and enters the market area I'd asked him to. The owner already has her eye on him. I would too.

There he is again the same guy doing the same thing. He looks like a footy from a surveillance team on his first deployment. He's hesitant and unsure of his environment. Another male suddenly approaches him. He looks around and then a wide grin spreads across his face and he embraces the stranger and kisses him on the lips.

I relax.

'OK, dude, keep walking until you exit the market. You'll be in Stoney Street. Walk to the end and turn right into Pickfords Lane. Call if you see someone you know and need to abort.'

'About time, big man.' He hangs up. I text Sienna and see her move away and filter past me. She turns left away from Ben. Our final destination is welcomed by all of us.

Ben is never comfortable hanging around with us. He prefers to keep it simple and meet in the covert car. I get a round of drinks in and we all blend in looking at the replica of The Golden Hind.

Ben takes off his cap and shades. His eyes have large bags under them. He's lost some of the bulk he had when he left prison. His face shows signs of healing but the tissue is still red and raised from his cheek wound. In truth we're all exhausted. Each of us in our own way tired of the habitual patterns to earn money and try to right wrong. Some things can be overcome; other things need to be accepted to move on. My home life is dead; my work life is where I feel alive. Alive among those people society seeks to incarcerate and reject as useless, not worthy of good fortune or happiness. I see Ben in me. My path could have gone his way were it not for a chance in my early years. I had love and direction. Two things he's never truly known.

'Can I smoke?' Ben asks.

'Sure. That's why we picked outside to chat,' I confirm with him. Part truth but more so we could get Ben out quickly if we were compromised and couldn't leave him. We have our agreed compromise strategy in the event of someone who knows us, or him.

Ben leans back and smokes. Sienna and I give him time to chill out and get used to where he is his before we start talking shop.

'So when's the baby due?' Sienna asks.

'To be honest, I ain't got a clue. She don't tell me nothin' no more as she's got the right hump with me cos I'm never there.'

Sienna nods giving the impression she gives a shit. I'm sure she does, but she isn't on the phone to him each day listening to his tales of woe like I am.

'You got any baby stuff together yet then?' Ben is enjoying Sienna's attention.

'I will once you lot give me this bit of wedge. I plan to get a cot and buggy. The money's all good yeah?' he asks. I look at Sienna. Ben clocks this glance.

'Yo, I know that look. We use it all the time on the street, when summat's not right. If this money ain't all there then I'm callin' it a day and you can get some other mug to do your dirty work.' He's getting agitated. He leans forward and puts out his cigarette in the ashtray and gets out another. I offer him a light and he takes it and sits back, pulling his hood back up.

'It's all here but not as much as we'd hoped to get you. It

isn't us. It's the boss who decides on the pay. Cuts have just started and they've looked at the pot we use to pay everyone like you.' He's not impressed.

'I ain't a puppet. You lot are having a laugh pullin' my strings thinkin' I'll dance to your tune for nothin'. Why'd you lot not go and rob a different budget? You lot are mad I tell you, mad. If it weren't for me, you wouldn't have got that gun,' Ben exclaims, his voice rising in pitch.

'Keep it down. It isn't the likes of me that make the decisions. It's my equivalent of Troy that does. If it's any help, we're as pissed off as you that it's only five hundred notes.' I decided to pull the pin early and let him know the amount. I never tell them before we meet.

The chances of being set up and robbed are always present. Five hundred could be five thousand, could be fifty thousand.

'Five hundred? Five hundred, for a gun. Fuck me, Ed. I could have gotten a thousand for that on the street and more. There's a big demand for this type of thing, ya know? I guess I can live with it though,' he says.

I pass over a newspaper. He knows what to do. He signs the sheet inside and takes half the paper with the envelope and cash. He pushes the other half back to me. He won't count it. He never does. I always do though and get an independent check done on the amount.

He's the type who would easily allege I'd taken a fifty off the top for myself. He then does something I've never seen him do before. He takes a twenty-pound-note from the envelope he now has in his hoody pocket and hands it to me.

'Here, get a drink out of it. You did me good. I shouldn't have disrespected you like I just did.' I look around. I don't know why, as I've done nothing wrong, but it feels wrong.

'That's kind of you but I can't accept that. Get something for the baby with it. I'm certain,' I tell him. He puts the money back shaking his head smirking. He sits forward.

'Troy's plannin' something big. A robbery. He says the

people on the job will be tooled up.' Ben looks about before continuing.

'Some fella is collecting gold and he'll have minders with him. That's gotta be worth more than five hundred notes if you get that job, right?' He looks to Sienna and me. We remain non-committal and wait for him to carry on talking. He doesn't though. Why would he when he clearly knows more than he's letting on but doesn't know if it's worth giving up? I've no doubt he'll be on the "job", but he'll keep his cards close unless we discuss money. We never discuss reward. It isn't in our gift to give.

'You know we won't discuss money. What we will discuss is the finer detail of this job. Where, when, who's on it, vehicles, weapons, you know the score, Ben. Thing is, you're not the only one who talks to us. What if someone else gets wind of this and tells us first? You'd get nothing.' I dangle the bait and wait for him to seize it. I sit back and light up my own cigarette. Ben looks out to the Thames. He's thinking the message through. He knows I'm not lying, well at least he thinks I'm not.

Fact is, there is no one else talking about it and he is one of the best in terms of Troy and his gang-bangers. He turns back as Sienna comes over with more drinks and some food.

'Here, eat this,' she says. Ben looks at the house burger and fries. His pupils widen. He's unsure at first.

I know he's thinking this is all some psychological ploy to make him talk. In a way it is but it was genuinely presented and both of us hope he'll eat rather than give up the information. He will tell me. He knows I'm interested. It all sounds good. Not for the potential victim but with any luck the whole thing can be nipped in the bud before the victim gets whacked. We hope.

'OK...OK...here's the deal,' Ben says as he leans across and grabs the plate.

38

BEN

Five hundred notes! They're havin' a laugh, I tell you. They always want me to go where they want, do what they want, when they want. I ain't got any choice. If I don't then my phone never stops ringin' 'til I answer it. Last time I never answered it for days. Next thing is a knock at my girl's door and she says there's a parcel for you. Who was it? Ed, that's who it was, dressed like a postie. He handed me some clipboard with the message ring me on it. I signed it and he left. In the parcel is a new phone all loaded ready to go. The cheeky bastard had his number in it under our agreed name!

I swear it's harassment but I can't report nothin' to police. I'd be a mug and no one would give a shit or believe I was tellin' the truth. I'm well away from them now and can feel the wedge of cash still in the envelope in my pocket. I need to get shot of it quick.

If I get stopped by the filth with this amount of money, then questions will be asked that I ain't prepared to answer honestly even though I honestly got the money for doin' a decent thing. Well, kind of. The gun is safe with that lot now and ain't with Troy playin' the biggun' and shootin' the place up.

I see the shop I need. I'm back in north London now. The shop's empty. A bell beeps as I open the door and a geezer comes from out back wipin' his hands.

'What can I do for you?' I can tell he ain't keen on seein' me again. Tough shit, I say. He runs a motorbike shop and he ain't legit. He moves nicked bikes all over. He ships them all over the world in containers. How do I know? I nick 'em for him.

'That's no way to treat a customer,' I say.

He looks out the window making sure I'm alone.

'I need a new lid. Mine's too hot now.' He nods and disappears out back. He returns with a new lookin' Arai. It looks the bollocks.

'How much for cash?' I ask. He turns the lid over in his greasy hands.

'Hey, watch the oil on the paintwork,' I tell him. He looks at me, and stops twirlin' the helmet.

'These are worth seven hundred. I'll do you it for four fifty.' He doesn't give me the lid. He thinks I'll do a runner with it, and he's right.

I get the wad of cash out and count out four fifty and push it towards him. He puts the helmet down, his side, and scans a few random twenties in his light box. He's happy the cash is good.

'There's no box with it but it's never been used,' he says.

I just take it and leave. He's beaming away like he's had me over. Thing is, he's a stationary target. Whenever the moment comes for me to show him who is boss round here, I know where he'll be. My bet is he's owin' Troy protection money. I'll make sure I'm the one doin' the collectin' come payday. The lid's a beauty. Matt black, mean looking.

There's no fancy sticker on it or anything that would pick me out.

On CCTV it will just appear a dark mass, it's perfect for

what I need. I'd already spent fifty before I got here. It's amazin' what you can buy if you say the right things. I bought a machete from a little hardware store. No camera's blinkin' at me. I told the owner I'm a trainee gardener for the council.

It feels weird walkin' with it stuffed down my leg and the handle in the band of my trousers. I weren't gonna risk carryin' it in no bag. I could've bought stuff for the kid with it, like I told Ed, but there ya go. Needs must.

It's a fact that so many like me are just out to survive. I ain't the type of guy who goes lookin' for trouble, it just finds me. It always has. I'm not sayin' that's because I had a rough upbringin' or it's all society's fault. I don't care what anyone thinks. I organised my own education. Home schooled on the street. Only lesson I needed was weight and measures with a bit of accountin'. School was never an option as I got expelled over nonsense.

The kid I stabbed in the school canteen made it to be a man and he's all the better for it, trust me. Ask Ghost, because he's still got the scar in his side to prove it. I'm back on my manor now, hood up, shades back on and prepped ready for anythin'.

I see Little Z in the play park. He nods at me out of respect.

His bro, Big Z, is doin' time for murder so Little Z has taken on his role as Park Keeper. He don't do lawns an' shit, but he does take care of the weed.

'Yo, was up?' he says. Eyes about now. I know he's loaded, waitin' for the buyer to turn up.

'How's your bro doin'?' I ask him.

'Ain't been to see him in a while.'

I nod, but I know the good a visit does. It keeps you connected, like you know you ain't been forgotten. Ghost kept me alive with his visits. I had to calm him down at one point as rumours were gettin' out that I was some kind of faggot.

I sit next to him on the roundabout and start to turn it. He holds on.

'You gotta get that VO and go see him. Get your social worker to sort it out. He won't see you grow up unless you get your arse there. I'll get someone to cover your shifts here while you go. Be good for you an' 'im. See where you don't wanna end up. You've had a good run out here. You ain't been nicked. You're ten now though, so game on. Courts think you old enough to know right from wrong, see? You'll get a slap for a first offence. As soon as you hit eighteen though, then you're game on for the big house an' that ain't any fun. You might think you can handle yourself but there's always some fool bigger than you.' He's noddin' but he ain't truly listenin'.

'Anyways, enough of this shit, I'm your order so hit me and I'll be off.'

'It ain't you man.' He's stopped the roundabout.

I grab him up.

'It's me and if I don't get my two baggies, then I'm gonna introduce you to hell, boy.' I let him see the handle to the machete. I see him swallow. He knows I ain't messin'. He looks about then we bump fists and shake, and I feel the product in my sweatin' grateful palm. The boy needs a lesson and he'll get that from Troy. I'll pay Troy. But this boy needs to know it ain't all swings and roundabouts in this world.

I pick up my new helmet and head for my girl's house and an earful, then a chill out with smoke and fun.

39

BEN

Ghost's late. Filth let him out. Nothin' to hold him on. I'm at the meet point, bike revved and ready and he's not answerin' his phone or nothin'. The professional side's gone. He's become shoddy. Then I see him in the distance just daudlin' without a care in the world. I ride up to him and pull up the visor.

'Where the fuck have you been?' I ask him. He climbs on the back.

'It weren't my fault. Troy's laid the Spray 'n' Pray down with a baby mother of his and she was kinda busy if you get me? I couldn't get it while she was doin' some guy. I just watched the TV with her kid and waited. The dude must have taken a pill because he took forever! Anyways, I'm here now so let's rip up the road and get this shit done.' I playfully head-butt his helmet and we have a laugh.

We both feel the tension. It's the same before we go to work, a risin' feelin' that this could be the last one if it gets tasty or the filth turn up. I shake my head to get rid of the thoughts and Ghost batters my helmet with both hands. He knows me so well. This is one of the worse bits for me, the ride out to the snatch zone.

There ain't two ways about it, we're targets for the filth. Hotter than a Maccy D's apple pie. Just 'cause I ain't carryin' the shooter, I'm still game on for being sent down if we get caught with it. If we lose it, then it's Troy who'll be dishing out justice.

These toys ain't easy to come by with a decent amount of ammo. We know word is out that he has one around him and the amount of doors Five-O are puttin' in to find it is noticeable. All the wrong ones, mind you. That's 'cause I ain't told them where to go.

Truth is, after gettin' a lousy five hundred for the handgun I ain't gonna give this baby up. The North Circular Road is crawlin', which is great for us. If any Old Bill sees us, they'd never catch us in this traffic. Windows go up as we ride by. We stand out. We know we do. It's the way we dress. No leathers and boots. We ain't heavy on health and safety. We're fuckin' invincible.

We both feel this as we weave in and out of cars. Every now an' then one don't move over so they lose a wing mirror. They don't own the road. We do. More flash the car the greater the feelin' of power over the rich who all think people like us are worthless pieces of pond life who ain't any good to society. Thing is, we are the great society. We are the ones who take out their trash, clean their houses, wash their cars, and pick up their litter. Well, not people like me because I don't work and they do. They also don't rob people, like me, but you get the point?

My mind's ramblin' as we get closer to the junction with Regents Park Road. We wait and turn right towards Finchley. The weather's not lookin' good. We need this done before it pisses down. Wet and wheels ain't a great mix when you're in a hurry to get away. I take a left at Cyprus Road and a right at the end. We get close to the shop and ride by slow. Ghost bashes my shoulder, then nods at a dark windowed Volvo XC90.

Two goons sat up front readin'. Bling must be inside. We were lucky. I waste no time and leave the area. I double back and park up in a side street. Ghost looks in the bag and without takin' out the gun he checks it's still there.

I do the same with my machete that's down my trousers like a sword. I've taped up the handle for better grip and it feels good. I push up the visor.

'You good?' I ask.

'I'm good, bruv. Let's mash him up.' Ghost takes out a small wrap of white and does it.

He don't offer me none. I never do the white when I'm on the bike. I need a clear head. We move out and park up on the opposite side of the street to the Volvo and back up. The driver won't be able to see us in any mirrors and it don't matter none as they've both switched off, heads not in the game. It's a good sign they're expectin' no bother. Just the usual pick up and take. Their delusion is about to haunt them. My ringtone goes. I take a quick look. It's Ed, why would he want me right now? Does he never know I'm busy unless I call him?

'Who's that?' Ghost asks.

'The Mrs.' Ghost accepts it without further comment. Then he does somethin' he's never done. He grabs my phone.

'What the fuck are you doin?' I can't turn fully to get it back and he's holdin' it above his head as he looks at the call list, laughin'.

'Since when has your Mrs been called, *Twenty*? You got some other dealer? Some other bird?' I manage to get the phone back.

'Mind your own and stop askin' shit. He's cool. I should introduce you sometime. He was in the Ville with me.'

'That don't sound right? All the time I visited you, you never mentioned this guy,' Ghost says.

'I did. You weren't listenin' just bangin' on about how good it was outside gettin' laid an'...hey, we're on, we're on!'

I lock down my visor and Ghost does the same. The lower half of our faces remain covered in a bandana. The bike goes from tickin' over to redline. I floor it towards the man carryin' a briefcase cuffed to his wrist while talkin' into a mobile phone. We've got no time to waste. The footway is clear, no people just him and us as I ramp up the pavement. Bling turns and looks at us, fear in his eyes. The same stare every robbery victim gives off. Pure panic and disbelief it's happenin'. We're stopped now and the fella is smashing Ghost's hand with the phone and screamin' as Ghost grabs at the briefcase and tugs it.

'Do him, do him!' Ghost's shoutin' at me as he's gettin' battered by the guy. He can't reach the shooter. I can hear sounds of shoutin'. Bling's back up's out an' runnin'. I have no choice. Ghost steadies the bike as I jump off. I draw the machete out of my trousers and yell at Ghost to lean back. He does, still hangin' onto the case. The blade lands on Bling's wrist. The fella ain't noticed! He's still hittin' Ghost. They say this can happen when the adrenaline kicks in. You don't feel it until you look down. I give it another wild swing through and down and then the tension releases and Bling collapses.

I get back on the bike. Ghost grabs the machete now shoutin' for me to go as the first of the minders is near. I slam the engine again and the back wheel spins and the smell of scorched tyre rubber fires off. Ghost hangs on to the bag as a minder reaches out to grab it. He misses and we're away.

I look in the side mirror and see Bling is on the ground, claret everywhere. One minder's on the ground with Bling while the other looks on at us, phone at his ear. I don't think about it. I just keep gunnin' the engine and get us away from the area. We're in Barnet now having done side streets, duckin' and divin'.

I can hear sirens comin' from all over. The shout's gone up. The filth will be arrivin' in force.

Ghost hasn't let go of me and is leanin' against my back

with the briefcase and his bag. I can feel his quick breathin' in pattern with mine. We're in Avondale Rd and I see a little estate. There's a small garage block and I pull into it. It's clear of people, just closed units in a square. One has a door that's been forced open. I get off the bike and push it up enough. It's full of junk but we can get the bike in, and us.

Once we're inside, I shut the door as far as it will go. A small chink of light is comin' through the bottom. I take off my helmet. Ghost's already done that. He's put his phone light on. I follow the beam down to where he's lookin'. I can see why the tension had slacked off. The gold weddin' band glints in the beam then my eyes see the rest. I turn and chuck up.

'Fuck! What we gonna do with the hand now?' Ghost asks, still lookin' at the shattered bone, blood, gristle and fingers.

'Man, you proper took him out. He could die,' he says. Like I don't know.

'You don't say! Fat lot of good you were,' I tell him. Ghost turns the torch in my eyes.

'Knock that off, you're blindin' me.' He lowers the light.

'I should be bashin' you up for what you just said. I COULDNT GET THE GUN, MAN! The guy was all over me and he weren't givin' in.' Ghost's pacin' around, then he stills himself.

He's calmed right down and so have I. The post-robbery tension subsides. We look at each other and start laughin'.

'Let's lie low here for a while. What's in the case?' I nod at the case at Ghost's feet.

'I ain't touchin' that! His hand's still attached. Try cuttin' the chain with the machete,' Ghost remonstrates.

'No way! That could break the blade. It cost me fifteen quid! Troy ain't gonna cover that now. Give it here.' I motion with my hands for Ghost to pass me the case.

Ghost kicks the case closer to me. I get out the blade.

'Yo, spark up your light again.' Ghost does as he's told. He shines it on the steel and my clothes. I'm covered in blood. Ghost is too. This ain't good. I slash open the side of the briefcase. The knife hits something solid, a box.

I cut away at the leather and take the box out.

'Go on, man. Open it up!' Ghost's overexcited mood is catchin'. I slip off the lid.

'What's inside?' Ghost demands, leanin' over to see.

'Two bagels, that's what.' I lean back on the bike.

'There must be summat else in there, man?'

Now Ghost's keen to get his hands dirty. He shines his torch inside. He brings out a small velvet pouch. I hold the phone light while he pulls open the drawstring. As the cloth unfolds the beam picks up a huge rock. It's the largest diamond I've ever seen. Trust me, from all the jewellery shops I've raided, I've seen a lot. Even in this poor light it sparkles.

'Is that it?' Ghost asks.

'Is that it? Have you lost your mind or are you just comin' down off the toot you plugged your snout with earlier? This is worth a fortune, I'm tellin' you,' I say.

Now, seein' the hand just danglin' from the bracelet it's attached to, don't seem that bad. He'll live, I reckon. Barnet hospital ain't that far away. Plus we all know this deal ain't legit either so in a way he had it comin'. The filthy robbin' git. At least now the sale of this will see the cash get put to good use and keep the estate well fed in brown and white. That's my food of choice off any menu.

'I'm carryin' that,' I tell him. He hands over the diamond. There's nothin' else in the case. Why Bling didn't just stick it in his pocket, I'll never know.

'We need to split up now. I'll go on foot. You take the bike an' the shooter and lay it up. Burn your clothes too,' I tell 'im. Ghost nods his head rhythmically.

'You'll need to ditch the fella's hand as well,' I add.

'I ain't takin' that anywhere. Let's just leave it here. No one will find it.'

'Are you kiddin'? Have you not watched *CSI*? He were grabbin' you up, proper, man. There'll be all kinds of shit under his nails that could link back to you. You need to ditch the hand in a river or summat, but it can't stay here,' I say.

He's keen to get away as I am, but we need to make sure we're covered before we go anywhere. He sees an old carrier bag on the floor and takes it. He puts the hand on the ground and puts his shoe on it while he eases off the metal cuff that's dug into the flesh. It comes away and he kicks the hand in the bag. He ties off the ends with the handles and puts it in the bag that carries the gun. The rain's started. I move among the streets using the weather as cover. No one comes out when it's pissing it down. Even the filth don't like gettin' wet. The scene of the crime will be gettin' a drenchin' too. It's all good in the hood.

I try some alleys first, lookin' over fences until I see what I need. Today that need is clothin'. Being skinny means at times like this I can just grab clothes off a line and know they'll fit. They'll be baggy but not too small or tight so I won't look like a prick. I see my prey. The patio door scoots over and the owner disappears out of view. I do the fence and grab a T-shirt off the line. It'll do. It's damp but don't have blood on it. She should've brought it in rather than leave it.

I see a bin, ditch my own top and put on the T-shirt. I wouldn't be seen dead in a Spurs top but needs must. My helmet I left with Ghost. It's a risk but the police would have to prove I was at the scene. Ghost won't grass. I check my pocket and feel the weddin' band I removed from the hand. Seemed a waste to leave it. I feel better now.

The machete is history dumped in a wheelie bin. We passed the dust lorry on the way out of hell, it's bin day round here. Everything's going my way. I removed the tape from the machete handle too.

I wore gloves. What self respectin' rider wouldn't? They're in another bin. I get my phone and dial call return.

'Yo, it's me, what's up?' I ask.

'I need to meet. Where are you?' Ed sounds cool for once.

'Golders. Can you get me from there?' Cheeky I know but sometimes he's cool for rides.

'Meet me outside the flower stand Temple Fortune Lane. Twenty minutes,' he says.

That's my ride home courtesy of the Metropolitan Police.

40

ED

'Shouldn't you be getting Lucy a bunch of those flowers while we're waiting for Ben?' Sienna nods in the direction of the flower stall as she picks her nails and perches her feet on the dash of the covert car, her flip-flops discarded in the foot well. She's decided on the relaxed approach to waiting this time, her seat partly reclined, shades on, hair tied back and up.

'At least I can claim it on expenses as a prop bought for tradecraft.' She looks at me then lowers her glasses down her nose to reveal her disappointment.

'Last of the romantics alive and well in London, I see.' She pushes them back up and stares out the window.

'What do you reckon Ben does all day? Every time we meet he always claims to be busy and yet he does nothing. Where does he get his cash?' she enquires. All questions I have no intention of answering or asking him.

'He's clearly an entrepreneur,' I reply. It doesn't wash.

'You're kidding me? He wouldn't know a day's work if it hit him in the face. Unless it's a wedge of notes we hand over, he doesn't care. He's got a kid on the way and he's barely at home from what I can see. I was doing some checks on him the other day as his authority for use and conduct renewal is coming up. He's been stopped twenty times this month! His baby mother has called police twice to prevent a breach of the peace; he's a close associate of a guy renowned for gang violence, firearms, possession and supplying class A drugs. He's a time bomb, Ed. Dangerous. He's a liability.' She says her piece and nonchalantly watches for his approach.

'Out of those twenty times stopped he's never been nicked. The times she called police she was under the influence of drugs or alcohol and had the arse because he hadn't bought any more back. As for his associations, that's why we use him and classify him at the highest level. I don't see your problem,' I tell her. She gives off a short burst of laughter.

'That's where you and I differ. I don't mind Co-Handling him with you as you deal with it all. He's never called me, because he always calls you. I reckon he thinks you're a soft touch,' she says. Now it's my turn to laugh.

'I don't know what gives you that impression, it's not like I've bought him some second-hand baby clothes, new bottle steriliser…'

'Don't tell me that's what's in that bag?' she says as she looks into the back seat where a Mothercare carrier bag resides.

'I didn't buy them. A mate was having a clear out and told Lucy she could have them for when we had a baby. She finds it too upsetting to have this stuff in the house, so I said I'd get rid of them to charity. Technically that's what I'm doing.'

I know what she's saying. Ben no doubt thinks he has me wrapped around his little finger, but the fact is I have to work with the guy and he brings in results like guns, drugs and near-dead children. He will have his methods of working, as do I. He knows the boundaries and what will happen if it comes back on him. He will fall, not me. The point is, he's still a human being, struggling in his own warped world of violence and crime.

He forgets others have lives and issues as I've forgotten Lucy in all the chaos that's been going on.

I too get wrapped up in work; bury my head in the sand when it comes to her feelings.

Point is, I can't manage my own and have no space for others close to me. Ben? He's my work. That's why I can donate these things that will: help his girlfriend, help the baby, bring some peace to his home life and prevent uniform turning up at his door. I need him out on the streets, not banged up in Pentonville prison.

'So what's in the fancy gift bag by your flip-flops?' I ask as she picks it up and opens it.

'Just a new baby beanie I knitted with a Stone Roses lemon motif …' she tells me beaming with pride, cuddling the beanie against her cheek. I see Ben approach and unlock the doors. The back door opens and the skinny frame of Ben flops into the back seat. Sweat is running down his face. He's wearing a ridiculously large Spurs T-shirt.

'Never had you down as a Spurs fan. What did you make of the result last night?' He sits back and tucks in behind Sienna so he can see me. I'm duty driver for today.

'Yeah, it were good, we deserved all the points we got.' He wipes his forehead with his arm.

'Hey? You lost and never put a ball beyond the keeper other than over the crossbar,' I say. He doesn't reply. He's on edge more than he normally is. Once we move off he relaxes.

He once told me his greatest anxiety is getting found out he talks to police. Every time he gets in or out of the car, he fears he's been seen and needs a couple of days clear of no one asking him whose car he got in or out of before he can relax.

'My mind's not on it, Ed. I've been charity shoppin' for stuff for the baby. My other T-shirt was too old and stinkin' so I bought this one. None of them had nothin' for the kid though. She'll be fumin' when I get back.'

I couldn't have asked for better timing.

'Check the bag next to you,' I tell him, while looking into the rear-view mirror.

'I ain't touchin' nothin' that ain't mine. I know what you lot do, fittin' people up an' that,' he says, just staring at it.

'Just open the bag up will ya and stop complaining,' Sienna says. Her attention has worked on him. He opens the top and reaches in and brings out the babygros. I look at his face in the rear-view. He looks shocked yet surprisingly happy at seeing the size of the clothes and the feel and smell of them. Freshly laundered. Something he doesn't experience. Sienna hands him her bag and he pulls out the hat. His eye catches mine and he quickly shoves it back in the bag.

'All this is for me? Whoa, I wasn't expectin' that. I thought youse would just start up with, *what's goin' on*? *Why ain't you callin*? *Where are the guns*? You know, the usual shit you ask me,' he says.

'We'll get to that, don't you worry. We're heading back Camden way, is that any good to you?' Ben leans forward and pats my shoulder.

'Yeah, yeah, that's sweet man. I'll show you a garage on the way. He deals in bikes an' shit like that but his main business is sellin' blow out the workshop. He's over Dalston but it ain't that far off.' I check my external mirrors; U-turn and head back towards the city.

It hasn't escaped my mind that he could have charity-shopped much closer to home, he isn't wearing his habitual coat despite the rain and that he couldn't get comfortable for the whole journey as something that appeared to be in his back pocket prevented him from sitting properly. I file it in my mind and continue driving.

I have no reason to search him or suspect him of doing anything different to what he has explained. It doesn't stop me feeling uneasy. Questions arise in my mind, regardless. Not forgetting the traces of blood I could see on his nails, from the rear-view mirror, when he patted my shoulder.

41

ED

'I'm so glad you could be here tonight, Ed. It shows me just how important children are to you and it's not just me driving the bus.' Lucy takes my hand as we enter the room at the Social Services building where the adoption evening's taking place. Most of the couples are in our age range. Thirty something's seeking solace in the "right" child.

I don't believe in the right child. I simply wish for a connection, even if that's just from the photo. They're laid out on many tables with a brief information sheet and the child's social worker's contact details. Lucy leads me over towards a lady at the far side of the room. She greets her like a long-lost friend.

'Hi, I'm Janet from the Family Finding Team, and you must be Ed? Lucy has told me so much about you, and I'm so glad you could get here tonight.' Before I can drum up an appropriate response Lucy cuts me off.

'So am I, Janet. He's a tough one to pin down sometimes!' Janet gives an understanding upturn of her lips.

'Well, help yourselves to tea or coffee and have a wander around and see the children who are currently seeking a forever home. I'm aware you're wanting a child under two but as I explained on the phone, the children here are ones who have been in foster care a while and need placement. Please don't discount them as they have so much to offer the right family.'

With that Janet makes her excuses and moves towards another couple seeking her attention. 'Who was that and why don't I know you've been making arrangements and discussing our life without me?' I'm calm but it needs addressing. Lucy puts her arms around my shoulders and whispers in my ear.

'Because you're never at home. If I didn't do something, then we wouldn't move forward.' She kisses my cheek.

Conversation over. The pictures on the tables show faces of hope. Hope that one of us will connect and seek further details and a follow-up visit or contact from the children's social worker. To me it's a room of utter sadness and despair.

From confused children having an unwanted photo taken, to couples like us. Couples who seek completion through other's inability to care or nurture their own offspring. I can't say that love would be absent as so many parents faced with the removal of their children put up some resistance. I can only hope it's out of love rather than a wish to battle the system.

That's where Sienna is right about me, but she mistakes a soft touch for compassion. I was lucky enough to be shown it by my own parents. If only they were still alive to support me now. They would have been here with us and been by our side all the way through the process. Not interfering; just being there. To this day I will never forgive the drink driver who ended their life. Ever. That single act led me to join the police. My sense of justice increased tenfold. I was eighteen when it happened.

Lucy hands me a coffee.

'You were miles away. Were you thinking our future child might be here in one of these photos?' She looks into my eyes over the rim of her cup.

'No. I was thinking of my parents and how they would've been here.' She never met my parents.

'Here, have a biscuit,' she says as she takes my hand.

There's a tap on a mug. The gathered throng are introduced to some house rules re confidentiality and fire exits. I can hear music that gradually gets louder and realise it's my source phone. All eyes are on me except for Lucy's who gives the appearance she isn't with me. I press answer and weave through the people to the exit at the back. It's Ben.

'Yo. That gaff I showed you today? It's live right now. A key of white's just been dropped off. It's gettin' cut and bagged there. You lot will have to be quick mind. They don't mess about.' I can hear he's outside from the sound of traffic noise.

'How do you know this? How long has it been there? Who else knows? Have you seen it?' I ask the questions rapidly as I'm not in the best of places to speak openly.

'Look man. You ask me the same shit every time. If I give you somethin' then I'm cool around it, ya know what I'm sayin'? Ain't nothin' can come back on me. I ain't stupid.' They're questions I have to ask. He knows that but he doesn't know I'm being short and not approaching them in natural conversation because I'm corralled in a social work building looking at my potential future family.

'Leave it with me. You're not to go back there, is that clear?' I hear him laughing down the phone.

'You don't trust me do ya? I ain't been there and I'm not there now. It's bang on the money though. Anyways, I owe you for gettin' me the baby stuff an' that. She was well pleased. All down to you.'

'That's good to hear. Leave it with me.' I hang up and switch phones. I put a call in to a DS on the Westminster Crime Squad. They have a pro-active duty around the smash and grabs. I figure they'd fancy getting some kind of result around a motorbike for the figures and as a bonus a good quantity of drugs. He bites my hand off.

He has a team out looking for work. He'll get the warrant and search the garage. I check my watch. It's eight PM. I take a deep breath and re-enter the room. The introductions are over. I look for Lucy. She's already chatting to another social worker. I look for the coffee and another biscuit.

42

BEN

I'm back at the Y now. The key of cocaine safely deposited at the garage. I didn't take it in. I was a shadow to make sure it got to the right place. I'd met Troy earlier and gave him the pouch and the diamond. I kept the ring though. It's gold and heavy so must be worth something. I'll take it to a Cash for Gold shop I know. They take anythin', no questions asked. I hear *Fire Starter* by The Prodigy. It's my Troy ringtone.

He's well pleased with me after loppin' off Bling's hand to get the prize. That's why he's had me on the shadow for the drugs run. Sometimes it ain't about the cash, it's enough to get the respect from an elder.

I answer it.

'Yo, what's happenin'?' Troy doesn't sound too good.

'I'll tell you what's happening, the last drop's just been raided by Five-O, that's what's happenin'. My spies on the scene tell me a mutt's just been sent in that looks for drugs and that. Now why would that be I wonder?'

'I dunno? I tailed the parcel along with Dwayne and Ghost. Dwayne took it in. Do you think someone seen it? Is that what you're sayin'?' 'He's fumin' now.

'Of course, I'm not sayin' someone's seen it! How could they when it's in an old petrol tank that was goin' in for repair? We've got big problems. Way I see it, someone's talkin'.'

Troy goes silent. I feel like I can hear my heartbeat gettin' quicker. There's no way he can know it's me. He's just guessin'.

'What you want me to do?' I ask him.

'Nothin'. I'm handlin' this end of business. I'm givin' the same message to all of youse close to me. Don't screw with me. When I find out who's grassin' then they're dead. You can put that message out.' He kills the line. My breathin' slows down. I lie back and stare at the ceilin'.

Another result for me means more money comin' from Ed. Screw Troy. Screw the garage man for rippin' me off for my helmet. Greedy arsehole deserves some time away for fleecin' me. I know he'll have been nicked. I seen him take the tank and cut it open. The package removed and the prep start. He prefers to work alone. He says too many eyes make too many spies. They'll both have to get out of bed early to catch me.

43

ED

I'm in early today. Sunlight is seeping through the window blind and leaking across my desk. I fire up the computer and open an email from the Westminster Crime Squad DS. Attached is a list of property seized, with photos. He's overjoyed with the result as is his borough Commander. A number of stolen scooters were also recovered along with the cocaine.

I click and zoom in on a picture of a crash helmet. I already know 'whose it is, or was, before the picture enlarges. It's Ben's. The one he was wearing on the night I saw him outside the club. I can't ask the DS what he intends doing with it or its significance, as it will alert him to my source being the possible owner.

I do know that he's seized it as evidence and can link it back to a recent smash-and-grab.

If he gets authority to swab for DNA and prints, then Ben will have some explaining to do. It's all down to money; he could get lucky and they may discount its importance. It's still circumstantial. It puts the helmet with his DNA at the scene. It's weak in that respect but it's something we can both do without.

My DI is already all over his record on the secure system.

Each risk assessment I submit comes back with more questions from him to justify continuing Ben's use and conduct. I'm beginning to feel that every aspect of my life is becoming a battle of justification. My landline goes.

'Hunter.' It's the Westminster DS.

'I see you've opened the email I sent you. Fantastic result last night, thanks for giving the work to us.' The DS sounds upbeat. He's in early. Must be so the team can start interviews of the garage owner they've nicked with the gear. I decide to take a chance. If I have some answers, then it may assuage my DI.

'What's your plan?'

'We've been given the go ahead for forensic on all the property that could link someone into one of our robberies. If we get any positive hits, then I'll get back to you to see where the owners are so we can nick them.' That answers that.

'Great work. Get back anytime and thanks for doing the job.' I hang up. I have a strong feeling Ben is on borrowed time. Not just from this but also from the blood on his nails I saw in the car. I take a walk over to the coffee pot and refill an already warm mug. When I get back to my desk, the pan London Overnight Serious Crime Bulletin has arrived. I open it and scan down the list looking for anything relating to guns, gangs and drugs. My eyes rest on a GBH and Robbery in Finchley.

Two males involved, motorbike used and the victim's hand hacked off with a machete. Only witnesses are two people who were with the victim. Victim is now stable in ICU at Barnet General. I look at the venue; it's not a million miles from where I picked Ben up. He was in the area, I'm certain of it.

He must have ditched his coat that would have been covered in blood and somehow got hold of the T-shirt. It's all supposition on my part, of course. It's not like he had a crash helmet with him as his was found at the garage raid. Maybe he'd left it there for the garage to dispose of? If so, why? I think I know why, but that would be in relation to the smash and grabs not this robbery. Yet again, I have nothing substantive. It's all circumstantial.

A large part of me doesn't want to believe it's him. The part of me that believes our working relationship would deter him from the crime business he was used to. I put it down to the stress of the baby stuff, for me, not him. He's not been nicked. If he is, then I'll deal with that when it happens. The priority now is to get into Troy and destroy his empire once and for all. For that I'll need Ben. The other potential recruit of Sienna's has failed to call back but there's still time, there's always time. My DI enters the office, he looks in a good mood.

'Just got back from the tasking meeting with all the Pro-Active Superintendents…'

'Superintendents and Pro-Active don't actually correlate, you know?'

'Very funny. There's going to be a huge drive around gun and knife enabled crime. This includes bike gangs doing these smash and grabs. I see you've viewed the overnight bulletin.'

He's nodding in the direction of my screen as he fills his mug from the coffee pot.

'That robbery in Finchley has tipped the balance. The community are quite rightly upset and fearful of repeat attacks of the same brutality. I thought Ben could help?' I spit my coffee out. Not the best of reactions.

'Sorry…went down the wrong hole. I'll speak with him, see if he knows anything, although it's out of his normal working area and that level of violence is a first. These gangs normally target premises for diamonds and gold not people. It sounds like a one-off targeted attack to me. I understand why the community would see it otherwise.'

The DI isn't interested. He's latched on to the community aspect.

'On the matter of Ben, I've submitted another reward report for last night's raid on the garage. Would be good if it could be greater than the last one? You know, show a bit of faith in his information and risk getting it?' I take a glug and sit back in my chair, pressing the space bar to refresh the screen.

'He'll get what he gets, Ed. I have the feeling he's closer than he's letting on to many of the crimes he's reporting. His volume of stop and search by uniform concerns me.'

'I'd say it goes heavily in his favour. Shows we, as the police, are all over him and others that hang with him would never suspect him of being a grass. Great cover for him.'

'It's CHIS or source, please. Grass is such a negative word.' He verbally raps my knuckles.

'I'll have the reward processed today. Get it to him as quick as you can and make sure he's worked hard around Troy and the rest of the smash-an- grab lot. If we can contribute to catching who did this robbery, then that will be great for the unit.'

With his speech complete, he collects his mug and starts to leave for his office.

'Where are you going?' I ask him.

'To my office, why?'

'Not without the coffee pot, sir…last one to drain it refills it…' He takes the pot and smiles as he leaves.

44

BEN

Back in my manor now and it feels like home. Troy is up country doin' business. He loves a trip to Birmingham does our Troy. I wasn't on the escort crew for that Jolly. The firm he's linkin' with don't mess about or nothin.' BMW or Birmingham's Most Wanted. Keepin' it mean in green. Green cos it's their colour. Troy reckons they have the contacts to sell the diamond. I say they're lookin' to rob him. Thing is he don't have the rock on him. I've got that. He's given it me back for safe keepin' while he talks money with them.

He also sees his drug line as good for them too. All sounds great as they called him on to the link up. Word travels quickly in our world when someone's doin' good in the game.

Right now I'm round at hers. Her being Maria. She's chilled out now she's got the stuff for the baby. She says she feels good about it and us. She sees me makin' an effort.

I feel rough though as I'd partied hard last night and just need a break to die quietly on her sofa.

'You can't stay down here. Social could come round any minute and they ain't impressed with you not being about for me and the baby.' She tries movin' the pillow from under my head but I just grab it and turn away from her.

'If they see you here, in this state, they'll know there's drugs bein' done here. They won't let me keep the baby. Are you listenin'?' I roll over and look at her.

'Jesus Christ! Your eyes look like piss holes in the snow and you stink of weed. You've gotta leave.' She's stood over me now, fag in her fingers held high against her right cheek. Her little finger's at the edge of her mouth. A mouth I'm sick of seein'. I ain't got the time to deal with this shit right now. My phone goes; it's Ed. Thank God.

'Yo, it's me.' I sit up and she gives me her fag and goes to the kitchen. Ed answers.

'I've got something for you from last night. Meet me today outside the ambulance station in Smithfield. You've got an hour and bring your game on. It's time for work.' I register what he's sayin', just.

'Yeah, sweet, see you in a bit.' I end the call and ruffle my hair. Ash drops from where I'm sat forward. It's too late to stop it markin' her carpet. I go to her bathroom, lock the door and undo the side panel to the bath. I check the JD Sports bag. Ghost had to move the shooter on so now it's here. What she don't know won't hurt her.

There's no way she'll remove the panel and go lookin'. Even if she did, she'd be on the phone to me like a bullet out a gun tellin' me how useless and selfish I am and to get the stuff out of her house. Thing is, in my mind, this is kinda my place now too. She's havin' my kid so by rights what she has is mine.

I replace the panel and leave the bathroom. I see her purse on her bed. She won't miss a score. I'll get it her back once Troy pays me out for work owed. He said he'd sort me out once he's back from Birmingham. Ed's paying me today too so all's sweet in my world. As I leave, I see Maria on the balcony to the block talkin' to one of her neighbours.

She doesn't say nothin', just turns her back as I go.

It'll not take me long to get to Smithfield on foot. That's why Ed chose it to meet up. He knows I never get my arse out of bed for when he wants so today he'll be well pleased with me. I'm hopin' it's good money he's givin' me 'cause I'm well broke and need to get some new trainers. I can tell him she wants a cot an' all so if he sees one of them, he might bring that one day. He'll have to pay for my cab back to hers though as I ain't bein' seen carryin' no kiddie crap. Won't do my rep any good.

I'm on the circle now and can see the side of the ambulance hut. I don't wait outside. I go to the wall where all the cars are parked and sit up and wait. I can be open here as it ain't hot for me. I can see the top of the big house from where I am. One place I don't wanna end up and that's number one court at the Old Bailey. I've had a good run of it lately and no one on the street's sayin' police are lookin' for me.

I see Ed's car come round and drive by me. I know where he'll be parkin' up for me to get in. That drive by means all's good for me to link up with him. No messin' about today with 'go here and there'. I hate all that carry on.

45

ED

I see Ben and he's seen me. From my brief glance he looks like he's slept rough. His hood's down, his mop of hair's clinging to his head. An achievement when there's a curl to it. I park up in a small side street, get out and sit in the back and wait for him to approach. He skulks over and tries to get in the side I'm in. He part opens the door then shuts it and goes round the other side. I can see him through the tinted glass looking around before he gets in. Finally the door opens and he flops down beside me.

'Yo, where's the good lookin' one? Why's it just you?' he says, as he looks about.

I press the key fob and centrally lock all the doors. My first lunge at his throat is good. My grip is strong around his scrawny neck. I force him into the rear seat as I lean over him my face near his. His eyes as wide as a crack addict having an orgasm.

He's trying to decipher what's happening while putting up some resistance.

'I'll tell you what's happening you lying piece of shit. You're not sticking to the rules and coming to attention where you shouldn't.' His eyes are confused and I lightly release my grip so he can speak.

'What the fuck are you doin'? Have you lost the plot? I could get you nicked for this, you're a cop for fuck's sake!'

'What were you doing in Finchley the other day? Why did you have blood on your hands and your crash helmet turn up at the garage raid? A man had his hand chopped off while being robbed not a million miles from where I picked you up so start talking.' I release my grip. He sinks back in the seat and rubs at his throat.

'You're lucky I don't mash you up good an' proper, man. That stunt you just pulled ain't cool. I don't know about no man gettin' his hand cut off other than what was in the Metro. Plus as a rule I don't do Finchley. As for my helmet, that was bad luck. I left it with him that's all and there ain't no crime in that.'

'There's a crime in it when it could be linked back to smash and grabs *you* were on where CCTV caught you wearing it!' I tell him as I sit back myself, mirroring Ben. I haven't got long before Sienna turns up. I'd purposely dropped her at a shop to get some cigarettes and said I'd meet her at the car. I shouldn't be alone with Ben; it's not protocol. Screw protocol though. He's making a fool out of me.

'Where's my money? I want my money! I'm done with this shit!' Ben's sat upright now.

'Move closer to me and I swear I'll beat the living crap out of you and dump you in Tottenham for another gang to finish you off. You've been playing me despite me looking after you. If you get nicked, then it's game over. Back to jail you will go and the letter to the judge won't be worth the paper it's written on. It will show you've been messing us around and committing crime, serious crime like chopping a man's hand off!' It was always going to be a long shot, but I needed to see his eyes when he was confronted with it. Instead he flops back and stares out the window.

'I can't believe you thought it were me just because, what, I had some blood on my hands? It's a liberty. I was out that way with a mate. He got in a fight with some guy an' came off worse. I treated him like any mate would. It were a busted lip, bled like a bitch on her period. I ain't been anywhere near Finchley or no guy in Finchley. I got a lift from my mate to where we met, and he went off with my helmet and dumped it at the garage for me to collect. I didn't have time to pick it up 'cause I heard what was there and phoned you. *You* told me not to go back there and I didn't. It were more important to me that you got the coke.' He takes a breath. I say nothing.

'How was I to know your lot that raided it would be interested in a crap helmet? They ain't got nothin' on me with that. People are always using my lid. I don't ask them what they're gonna do? Far as I'm concerned they need it to comply with the law, end of.'

He finishes his summing up. I feel ashamed at my behaviour. I feel under pressure from all fronts in my life. The thing is, I know he's lying. Everything he says is a lie with a dash of truth but not the whole truth. Sienna's back at the car and gets in the driver's side.

'Ben? Can't believe you're early. What's up with you two? You look like you've had a lover's tiff?' She unwraps a Magnum and hands one to Ben and myself.

'We're done. He was just leaving,' I say as Ben looks to her and then me.

'Leavin'? I ain't goin' nowhere without my money. You said you had money for me? Where is it?'

'I said I had something for you. You're eating it. As you can see, language is all about interpretation, now get out. I'll be in touch once the reward for yesterday's job is ready.'

Before I've finished, he's out the car and he slams and kicks the door. Sienna has the engine on and with part of the Magnum gripped in her teeth she engages the auto box to drive and floors it out the side street leaving Ben ranting about killing me. A half-eaten ice cream lies on the road. Two fine examples of spent opportunity.

'Are you going to tell me what's just happened? I've got his cash here, all seven hundred and fifty pounds of it.'

Sienna has turned into St John's Street. She carries on eating, using the stick and remaining ice cream to emphasise her questions.

'Look, it's best you don't know. He got the arse at something I challenged him on. It wasn't safe to give him that amount of money.'

'Wasn't safe? He looked fine to me. If you're not going to tell me, then fair enough but don't expect my contact sheet to reflect anything other than what happened.' She places the spent stick in the side door pocket.

'I wouldn't expect anything less. You might want to remove the chocolate moustache though.' We're at lights now and she flicks down the internal visor and drops the vanity mirror. She produces a small pack of wipes. Before she's had chance to do a once over our vision is obscured by cracked glass fragments and a loud smash of glass.

I never saw the bike rider draw up alongside and neither did she. The brick shatters the front screen rendering visibility nil. The retreating sound of a motorcycle engine the last thing we hear. By the time I look up from the crouched position I've assumed, the lights have changed, bike's long gone along with the assailant or assailants. Traffic's now moving around us, making no attempt to stop and help out.

'Are you OK?' I check Sienna's hair and scalp as she sits back in shock.

'Yeah, yeah, I think so. Thankfully the windscreen didn't implode. How about you?'

'Shaken up, but same as you. I think we both know who was responsible for that.'

We're both out of the vehicle now. Sienna looks beyond me from the driver's door she's leaning on.

'I think you could be wrong,' she nods to look behind me. I turn round and see Ben on the opposite footway. He stops, looks over and carries on walking away. He's seen what's happened but doesn't approach. I wouldn't expect him to come over. If it wasn't him directly, then he could have called it on with one of his cronies. If he hasn't, then we may have a problem. A covert car isn't any use if it no longer protects the occupants from unwanted attention.

'One thing's for sure. It's time to ditch this motor.' I put a call in to the office. John picks up. I explain the situation and after he's enquired how we are he bursts out laughing.

'I'll get the car recovered, Ed. You'll have to wait with it though.' I give him our location and Sienna and I push the beast off the road and out of the traffic.

46

BEN

Man that boy done good. Brick went straight through the windscreen. Yeah, I put the call in, damn right I did. The man's a fool takin' me on like that. He felt all pumped up behind his badge and his Five-O mobile. My gang ain't bigger than his but when it comes to it, they always respond when a shout goes out. They listen to anythin' I tell 'em.

I told them his car had cut me up at lights and I couldn't get close. One call is all it took then POW! In goes the mortar and the fool's down a windscreen and stuck on the road. There's been no call from either of them. I know they both seen me. I made a point of lookin' over and leavin' them to it. Never return to the scene of the crime, Ed says. Well, big man, that's the kinda advice I'll always take. It ain't long before I'm back at my room in the Y. I'll be stayin' here most nights now. It's too risky to be with her when the shooter and the gem are there.

Plus social are wantin' to talk with me about what part I intend to play in the baby's life. How do I know that now? I don't even know what I'm doin' later let alone that far ahead. She's been givin' them all the bullshit about what her plans are. Truth is she's no better than me.

She tells them she don't do weed no more but I can tell

you she smokes like a good 'un whenever I bring the fun over. She just ain't botherin' to pay for it, is what she means. Still, I can't do a day without it neither so I get where she's comin' from, pregnant or not. If I were her, I'd do exactly the same. Both my parents did and worse. It ain't had any bad effect on me.

Unless you're livin' a life on the road, then no one can tell you what it's like for real. Every middle and high-class roller thinks they know how they'd survive because they're always tellin' us what we should be doin' with our lives and how we should be leadin' em. I know my life ain't all sweet but it ain't artificial neither. It's down-to-earth survival of the fittest out here. By rights I should be London's strongest man by my record of livin'. I done Feltham, I done Pentonville and survived both systems juvenile and adult.

I've lived with hard bastards that would cut you up just for lookin' at 'em wrong or standin' too close in the slops queue.

I'm doin' all right now. Troy has my back and I have his. He wouldn't be trustin' me with those items if he didn't. I swear, if anyone gets caught with those then they're doin' serious time. That ain't gonna be me though. Nothin' can come back on me from the gem and the Spray 'n' Pray, nothin'. I see Troy talkin' to the boy in the park. The kid looks battered to hell.

Man, I didn't think he'd give him that hard a lesson. His face looks like one of them balloon toys inflated then twisted in different places. He don't look good but here he is out doin' it like the good foot soldier he is, keepin' the street and the community in food.

'All right, bruv? What's up with him?' I talk to Troy but don't ask the kid.

'You know what's up with him. I've docked your wage fifty notes for the weed and the trouble you two gave me. Good job you're here, as it's payday,' Troy says.

Troy brings out a wad of notes the likes of it I ain't ever

seen in a long while. There's gotta be four or five grand there. The man's crazy carryin' that amount of cash in the open. He could get robbed. Not by one of us but by the filth. Man gets stopped with that amount of money and they take it and you along with it. If you can't account for where it came from, then the dough's history. He knocks some notes off the roll then hands me them. From what I saw him rake out, it's only three hundred. Three hundred for all I've been doin? He's havin' a laugh.

'Whoa! This can't be it, Troy? Not for what I done for you.' He takes me away from the kid and grabs my neck and pins me up against the slide ladder. It ain't my day for gettin' choked.

'You're right. I've got it wrong. I've forgotten you owe me fifty. For the disrespect it's gone up to a hundred.'

He takes the notes from my hand and he drops the two hundred in twenties on the floor.

'From the marks on your neck it looks like I ain't the first to grab you up today. Who else you been upsettin'?'

He doesn't have hold of me now. The money's blowin' away but he ain't lettin' me pick it up. If I had a blade, I'd do him. I need to get another now the machete is out of action.

'Come now. Let's take a walk while you pick up your pay.' I get off the slide steps and start pickin' up what's left. Other kids are about. I know a few have had twenties away from the ground where it's blown from me. I'm left with forty quid out of the three hundred. Troy doesn't care.

'The BMW boys ain't happy with me. They're sayin' they heard about the robbery and claim the diamond came from their turf. They're giving me a week to bring it back to them or they'll be sendin' a crew here. It'll be a bloodbath. Them lot are tooled up for battle and don't mess about. I'm down a couple of guns but we still got the automatic and a clip of ammo left, is that right?' I nod at him.

'They still at your bird's place?'

'Yeah, both bits are still there behind the bath panel.' He

ain't in a mood for games. He's hit on some serious shit now and word's out. Birmingham's Most Wanted could soon be London's Most Wanted.

'Here's what I want you to do ...'

After he's finished his preachin' he gets back in a waiting motor and leaves. I just flop down on the grass and hold my head in my hands.

47

ED

'You're certain you never got any index or description of the rider?' The traffic officer is doing her job, treating us like any other victim of a fail to stop accident. She looks at the windscreen again while rattling the pen in her mouth.

'And it was a brick you say that hit it? Where is that now?' I don't know as we haven't looked for it. I lie, as I don't want it seized as evidence and checked for DNA. It's in our boot.

'Look it all happened so quickly. Neither of us stood a chance at seeing what was thrown. I assumed it was a brick but I could be wrong.' She still isn't convinced I'm telling the truth. She must have had a bad experience of covert officers and their cars in the past.

'I need to see a brick if that's what you said hit the window. Are there any witnesses?' I've had enough now.

'Witnesses in London. You're having a laugh. Best bet is the traffic cameras. See if anything has been picked up on that. In the meantime we need to sort out another car, so can we crack on?' The traffic officer isn't amused.

'Look. You lot may think you're God's gift to policing but I've got a job to do too. Who was driving?' Sienna says nothing.

'It was me,' I reply. I know what's coming next.

'You're suspended from driving until I can establish what's happened. You're being un-cooperative as far as I'm concerned and hostile at the very least. Was anyone else in the car before, during, or after the 'accident' that I need to speak to?'

'No.' Another lie.

'Right, I won't offer you a lift back anywhere. Wouldn't want to "blow your cover" and I don't suppose you'd both be seen dead in a marked traffic car, anyway. I'll wait until the recovery truck arrives. I'll check the cameras. Once I'm satisfied it was a random event with no provocation from yourselves, then you'll be re-instated to your original driving classification.' With that she shuts her book and goes to sit back in her car.

'What are you on today, Ed? You weren't driving, I was. I was happy to have said so. You've put me in a right position now. I just don't understand you lately.' She's right.

I have changed.

'Look I'm the higher driver classification so if you said it was you she would have added that to my charge sheet. I just hope the camera's broken or not showing anything clearly.'

Sienna shakes her head in disbelief. We grab what we need out of the car and head for St Paul's Tube station. The sun provides a much-needed respite from the coolness of the traffic officer as we meander the streets towards the Tube. There's been little conversation between us but Sienna's source phone has been active while we walk, providing me with a welcome break from having to explain myself.

I remember the words of an old DS when I was a DC. He told me the more we screw up the better we become. Don't break the law and don't repeat the same mistake twice.

Only Sienna can make me feel like I've failed. Me? I was just using different methodology to extract the truth, and it didn't work. My source phone beeps indicating I have a text. I'm guessing it's from another source we're due to meet up with later. I pull the phone from my pocket and am surprised to see a message from Ben. I open it: *It weren't me earlier but I know who it was – bell me.* It would appear our hostile has turned friendly again. I speed-dial his number. He answers immediately.

'You calmed down now? Picked all your teddies up from the corner?' he asks.

'I think I'm missing one,' I say.

'Look I've been doin' some thinkin' since you strangled me in the car. I ain't ever seen you so angry before and it must be 'cause you actually give a shit.' Finally the penny's dropped.

'Truth is though, you've got a bad way of showin' it. Just like my old man in that way, but less aggro. I'm ready to stop dickin' about now. I need another meet as there's some heavy, heavy, shit gonna be happenin' soon that I don't want no part of. Bottom line is I need your help as much as you need mine. So, you up for it?' Inwardly I'm beaming, and it must be showing on my face as Sienna is pointing at the phone miming, 'Who is it?'

'Yeah, I'm good if you are. Meet me at 2 p.m. bottom of St Paul's Cathedral.' He agrees and hangs up. I'm about to put my phone away and tell Sienna when another text comes through from Ben: *Bring the money*. Some things never change.

'Right, Smiles, you've got the cash Ben doesn't want so we may as well do lunch on him.' She stops walking and holds her hands up across her eyes and looks up to the sky seeking divine help.

I wait until she looks through the cracks in her fingers at me smiling as she hits me lightly over the head with her bag.

'Don't worry, we'll need the money again this afternoon when I get another chance at redemption. Lunch is on me; not literally, obviously.'

'Thankfully. You're the last plate I want to eat off.' Surprisingly she links my arm. It feels reassuring. I accept the gesture as tradecraft and nothing more. Truthfully, I welcome the physical contact after this morning, and the calming effect it's produced.

Lunch was peaceful. Our private, work and source phones remained quiet for the hour we had. I opened up to her about what was happening at home, how I felt ill-prepared to be a father. She listened without judgement, didn't offer advice or solutions. It's exactly what I needed. Once we'd finished eating, we left to meet Ben. The steps to St Paul's are crowded, perfect for us. Everyone is out enjoying the sun and some respite from the world of work. Everyone except us, that is. We've worked out a route for Ben to take once he arrives here. On this occasion it won't be far.

'I hope he's here soon as his ice cream could end up on the asphalt again,' Sienna states. I see him on the other footway and phone him. He picks up.

'Go to the end of this street and turn right opposite the lights. Cross the bridge across the Thames then stop. Get a shift on though. Your ice cream is about to hit the deck,' I explain as he hangs up and does as directed. Sienna's ahead of him as we cross the millennium bridge. I'm following up behind. The sun dances on the Thames surface like a glitter ball in a 70s nightclub.

Days like these make every working moment in London worthwhile. The sights, sounds and smells of the city attack the palate, making me glad to be alive and doing what I do. We reach the other side with no problems at all. We find a pub and sit in a bay at the back of the bar. Ben grabs the ice cream and starts cramming it in.

'OK, Ben, what do you have for us?' I ask.

'How's about a fuckin' *sorry dude,* eh?' he says, and I acquiesce.

'I'm sorry for the incident earlier, now what's happening?'

He's still eating scoops but pauses in between.

'It's Troy. He's in the shit and wants me to bail him out. He went up country to see the BMW boys the other day, you know who I'm talkin' about?' Sienna and I both nod that we do.

'Cool. Well that robbery you were grillin' me on earlier in the car, the one I had nothin' to do with, yeah?'

I don't reply. 'Anyways, the thing that got robbed off the guy was a diamond. The jeweller he came out of takes in nicked gear from all over the country not just London. He'd had a delivery of this diamond a week ago from a punter in Birmingham. It was from an Asian family who got turned over and loads of gold was taken with it. It was all worth half a million. The BMW boys heard it had gone south and tried to get the rock back, but missed it as it got robbed before they could get down to the jewellers and rob him. Are you still with me?'

'We're with you. So where does Troy come in?' I ask.

Ben is furtive now. He stops leaning forward, runs his hands through his hair and vigorously scratches his scalp like he has nits. This feels like the first time he has ever given us anything decent. It feels great; to us, not him.

'Look, Ben. You're doing the right thing. You need the likes of Troy out of your life so you can get on with being a decent father and not getting killed. I'm certain we – the police – pay better than him – on time and a decent amount of cash. Cash you've legally obtained.' I pause while he digests the ice cream and information. Ben looks up at that point, a small smirk on his face.

'As far as I'm concerned it's been legally earnt. I can only go on what you tell me and what turns up as a result. It's your risk if you mess up or lie about the provenance. You know the truth of where it's come from. I have to ask the questions you hate.'

He's looking more relaxed now.

'Let's eat something proper while we're here. You look wasted.' We all grab the menu. Both Sienna and I having to choose something on top of the lunch we just had. Needs must though when you're in a hearts and minds campaign. Sienna has us in sight as she goes to the bar and orders. Ben leans in.

'Look, Ed. I'm in deep shit man. He's comin' down heavy on me now. He had a meetin' with the BMW boys and they know he has the diamond. He's been lookin' for the right buyer in the city. He's got some decent contacts there. All look legit but some do deals under the counter for the right price. He can't sell the rock as the diamond's too hot. The Birmingham mob had the feelers out down here. They heard a rock was being offered up. They did the maths and came up with Troy. Troy's small fry compared to them boys. He's got a week else they're payin' a visit down here and they won't care whose door they knock on. It'll be a war the likes of which you lot ain't ever seen,' he tells me.

Sienna puts drinks down on the table and sits back. I summarise what he's just said, to her.

'So where do you come in?' I ask.

'He's wantin' to set them up. He's gonna call them on to a neutral place that ain't been decided yet. Troy says he'll bring the diamond in exchange for four keys of cocaine. The rock's worth jack to Troy but way more to the BMW boys. Thing is, he ain't gonna hand over the diamond. He's gonna rob them of the cocaine and mash 'em all up. Well, I say him…he wants my mate, Ghost and me, to do it. He wants us in a shadow car, come on the plot at the signal and waste the lot of them with a Spray 'n' Pray he's got. This is way above my pay grade, Ed. If I don't do what he says then he'll shoot up my bird and the baby with her, then kill me after I've watched her die. That's the level of shit I'm in right now and I can't see no way out for me. This ain't about money no more.'

His head hangs down. His shoulders are slumped. He's worn out from telling the truth for once and he knows there's no way back now he's told me. Too many lives are at stake to go back on this. Sienna reaches out and places her hand on top of his. His hands are outstretched on the table as if in prayer. He flinches then sees it's her and his face relaxes.

'You've done well telling us that. We'll sort it out but we're going to need your help more than ever now. Where's the gun and the diamond laid down?' She releases his hand and he sits back up.

'I dunno. I'll soon find out like as Troy will want Ghost and me to go get it. He won't keep the shooter and the diamond together though. If the place were robbed or raided by you lot he'd never live with himself on a double loss.'

He takes a large swallow. His Adam's apple sinks and rises like a fishing float. He knows where they are. He still doesn't trust us after all this time. I guess being grabbed by the throat by me didn't help. He's stepped way over the line now and he'll feel like he owes us. He doesn't though. He'll have to toe the line, if he doesn't he's dead. He takes the cash inside a carrier bag. He looks in and sees the envelope among a couple of tops.

'The clothes are neutral. He or she will need something to grow into.' Sienna flashes her great smile. She chose the clothes on the way to the meet. We both used our own money. We both care enough to see the job through and the newborn clothed. There's no guilt on my part. I did what I had to with Ben. You'll do anything when life is at risk.

'Keep that phone on and stay in contact. We'll be in touch after we've worked out a plan to see you right and the gun recovered. Don't spank all that cash. If you appear flash now, it'll stink with them. This is serious, don't screw it up,' I tell him as he nods, pulls up his hood, grabs the bag and leaves. Sienna covers him as he exits and I pay the bill, keeping the receipt for a claim on expenses.

48

ED

Our tiny meeting room contains an excited DI Nolan and our buzzing DI Ashworth. That level of excitement will soon disappear as the job gets underway. I've never managed a job that went to plan or ran as the source said it would. This isn't Crime School for Dummies. These people mean business. Business based on lies and deception.

Both Troy and the BMW boys know it and will come prepared for a war. The deciding factor will boil down to guile, firepower, bottle, and luck. Nolan knows this too well. This is bread and butter to him and his team. Ashworth is an unknown factor.

'So, Nick, what's the plan now you've heard things from us?' DI Ashworth poses the question that Nolan already knows the answer to.

'Way I see it is getting the MAC-10 back's a priority. If we can get evidence of the jewellery robbery from any addresses all well and good. If they've got nothing to turn up with then there's no bloodshed. I haven't spoken to our equivalent team in Birmingham. They may have a team wrapped around this lot, anyway. We'll have to disclose our interest. It could save a lot of time and work, prevent blue on blue wherever the meet point will be. That's something we need to be in control of,

Ed. Your friendly will have to engineer that. We need to know as early as possible.' Ashworth nods in agreement, which is a good sign. I respond to Nolan.

'I'll put pressure on the friendly to house the gun and hopefully the rock too. There's no corroboration that either exist. The jeweller and buyer weren't forthcoming. Your team must be prepared to react if I get a call and it's on.' Ashworth hears this and cuts in.

'I'll need to know immediately that call happens, Ed. This isn't a decision a DS can take alone I'm afraid.' I nod in agreement. Ashworth wraps things up. Nolan and I agree to call each other later to discuss updates.

49

BEN

This is where I need to be after today's shit. The place is full with decent fanny, weed and white. Troy is gettin' us all stoked and ready for the off with the BMW boys. His idea of gettin' us prepped is to throw a party before things hot up. Show his troops he's the boss but respects us. This one's in a boozer. He's taken it over as a private function. He ain't paid for it. The licensee is behind in his protection money. Tonight he'll pay the price for that in booze and fags.

The job won't be on straight away. Troy ain't no fool. He knows someone else on this team is talkin' and it ain't me. Yeah, I talk to Ed but someone else is talkin' to the BMW boys. Whoever that is will feedback to 'em that he don't give a shit. So much so he's thrown a party. That's how much he cares about that lot. Ya see them boys up north know this ain't all gonna be legit. How? No one rocks up like Troy did and offers to take on four keys of white like that. No one.

They don't know him, never done business before. All they want is a chance at gettin' the diamond and they know that he ain't gonna turn up with it neither. They'll see it as a chance to show Troy they can operate outside Birmingham if they so choose and take over his line. Why deal with Troy when they can control it all?

This is my problem with it. Troy ain't gonna be there and he's leavin' it to Ghost and me to deliver the message. Ain't no way it's gonna go well. No way those boys will show up and go, 'Yeah sweet, here's your gear, now where's the diamond?' They're gonna stick a gun in our face and go, 'Where's the diamond?' They ain't gonna be satisfied with no picture of it and I ain't got anyone else to bring it on and take it away while we test the coke. The whole job stinks and they know it. I'm a dead man walkin' and so's Ghost. He don't know I'm tryin' to bail us out of it. How can I tell him?

'Hey, Ghost, I'm talkin' to the Feds and they reckon the job sucks.' He'd kill me himself there an' then. I grab a drink and weave my way through the bar area down to the basement where the music's at. The whole floor doesn't need dry ice.

The smell of weed is pure bliss and I inhale me some as I get on the floor and bust my moves. Ghost's here. He's coppin' a feel of some bird's tits. She's tryin' to get him outside. She knows he's got food but there's no way she has any cash. Ghost seen what happened to the kid from the park and he ain't takin' no risks with this sort.

He sees me and gets rid of her. I take over her seat.

I shout down his ear, 'Come up top we need to talk, bruv.' I point up and he nods. We move out across the floor and back up to the bar and outside. When we get out a police wagon's here. The filth are kittin' up ready to raid the place.

'Yo, Ghost, it's time to go. Look at that flash mob, man. Bunch of Storm Troopers gettin' ready to dish out some bad vibes down there.'

I take a picture of them. For no reason other than to wind them up. They ain't interested in me though, which is a first.

As we move off, I see Troy and his minders. Looks like they got word early and did one. Nice of 'em to give us the heads-up. The blacked-out rear window to Troy's Audi Q7 shifts down and he waves us over.

'Get in.' Ghost and I do as he says and the motor drives off. It's the first time I've been in his car. Plush, cream leather seats that look untouched. The rest of the inside looks like it's been recently valeted. If the filth were to stop it and turn it over there'd be nothin' to find.

He always keeps his cars clean like that. This one he bought cash and's all legit with the law. He told them he'd come into some money through gamblin' in the casinos. They didn't believe him but there's nothin' they could do to take it off him.

'Take a right,' Troy instructs his driver. He says nothin' to us until we're back on the estate and down in the garages. The goon drivin' brings the car to a stop in Troy's space and kills the engine. I look at Ghost and he ain't lookin anywhere but out the blacked-out window where he sees nothin'. Troy turns back from the passenger seat. Let's take a walk. He never talks in his car. He's always sayin' the filth could have it bugged. We move away and he starts.

'Yo, pussies. The work I got lined up for youse is bein' brought forward. You'll go tonight in the motor parked next to mine. You'll meet them at the Toys R Us in B19. The exchange will take place. By exchange I mean you'll fill their sorry asses full of 9mm. Once the job's done get the coke out their car along with any guns and bring them back here.' I can't think straight.

'Yo, Troy man, why the rush, bruv? I thought they weren't gettin' the gear till next week?' Troy turns on me. 'What's your problem? You got summat better on tonight that can make this wait?'

'No, course not,' I reply.

Now he's laughin' summat horrible like it's his first time on the weed. His driver's shoulders are givin' it some too.

'What's so funny?' I ask.

'You took the bait straight away! You should have seen your face! Fuckin' picture, bruv. A fuckin' picture.'

Some joke. Ghost and me now join the laughter out of sheer relief more than anythin'. I know that soon he's gonna mean it though.

'The car you'll use is that one though. Ghost you take the keys and pick up Danger Mouse here when I give you the nod. It could be anytime soon. I took a call from my man from the Ham. He says they'll be in touch. Part of me is thinkin' they'll be bringin' us some good gear we can knock out. Fool boys them BMW lot, I tell you they've picked the wrong firm to mess with. Now get out of here. Keep your phones charged and on all the time. You're good guys, I won't forget you with this one. You'll be seen good, no worries,' he finishes, and his minder opens the rear door and he gets in.

Ghost moves towards the car Troy has given us then stops as Troy looks out his window. 'Leave the car until I call you, then come an' get it. I don't wanna have that out of action before the job. You're on your feet from here.' The window goes up and the Audi reverses as the garages descend into darkness, the headlights fading to a point.

'Now we're deep in the shit with this, ya know?' Ghost states. I'm surprised Ghost feels the same way. I think he shit himself in the garage when he saw Bling's hand on that handcuff bracelet. Ghost's had the same message from Troy. Put up and shut up or his family dies in front of him and then he follows.

Troy would do it too. It wouldn't be the first time. He's out on the street 'cause he's good at what he does.

Ed has made me look at myself though. My current situation and lifestyle, as well as responsibilities. Thing is I earn good money off him for using my skill set and gettin' back the guns and drugs he wants. It's like child's play to me. At least it was until now. Now it's pure grief an' I hate the way Troy still sees Ghost and me as his patsies. It's OK for him gettin' driven around in his flash Q7 like one of the untouchables. He deserves all he's got comin' and when he's away, it will be my world then.

I'll be the one gettin' the driver an' doin' the deals, makin' others go do my runnin' and laundry. Screw him. Screw Ed. Screw the Police!

All I need to do now is move the gear on that's in Maria's house. If she finds it there, she'll go spare. Ghost's gone now. I'm back on the street, on my own, doin' my thing the only way I know how. Movin' one piece of gear to another place, to another. Right now, though, I ain't got another place lined up. Then I remember the kid in the park. He'll do just nice.

I get back to her pad and she's out. The bath panel ain't been removed since I put it back. I'd left a telltale there and it's still in one piece. A simple bit of wood that looked like it should be there but would be on the floor if someone else had moved it. She doesn't believe in cleanin' that often neither.

She's gotten better now the kid is comin' though. She really wants to keep it. I've seen the way she's been, not takin' anythin' other than a puff of smoke. She was never much for the drink and she's down to two fags a day. Social reckons she stands a good chance of bein' able to work with 'em in a mother-and-baby unit or summat like that so they can see how she is when the kid's here. It's her first but it ain't my first. I don't see 'em though. I'm a 'risk' accordin' to the social. But with this one they reckon they can work with me 'cause I'm a bit older now.

I was sixteen when I first became a father and didn't know no better. I've grown up now, seen a bit more of life an' that. I ain't ready to settle down but I don't think I'll mind bein' about for the baby when it comes, ya know? Weekends an' that for an hour or so. I grab the bag the MAC-10's in and open it. It's all there, still with the clip.

I sit down a minute an' think.

I may need this on the hurry up for my own use. If I take it to the kid, then who knows what he'll do with it or say about it with his mates. Fuck it though. I grab the bag and head out the room over to the estate.

I hate movin' bits out in the open. It doesn't matter whether you're inside with whatever is being laid down or outside shiftin' it. The feelin' you're being watched is always there. You're waitin' for the jump that could come from anyone, anytime, anywhere.

I reach the kid's block. The lift is fucked so I take the stairs to the fifth floor landin'. I know which door is his. I got him into this game, you see. I rap on the door and wait. I can see no one through the kitchen net that looks out onto the landin'. I can hear a telly inside though, and the kid's mum shoutin' at him to eat his tea. The voice gets louder, then the door opens up. She ain't pleased to see me.

'Can't you hang around with blokes your own age? He's not in and not coming out to play.' She goes to close the door but my foot prevents it.

'He should've told you I'd be comin' over. Now where is he? This won't take long.' She says nothin'. She don't need to as the kid has appeared behind her.

'Mum, leave it, yeah? He's my mate, he's helpin' me out loads.' She turns away and leaves us to it, shakin' her 'ead. When she's gone, we go into the kid's room.

I ain't been in here before. All my work with him was done on the street. Take this, take that. The kid was a natural and loved the money he was gettin' for shiftin' pills an' that. He always got the money and never short-changed anyone. Ever.

'How you been?' I ask him.

'Better, I guess. My face still hurts. What you want anyway? We've not got long, she'll be in here soon.' I take a look around his bedroom. He's well looked after that's for sure. He has clean clothes hangin' up, models, toys and shit like that.

The kid can read too. He has a bookcase. It's a perfect drop zone for the piece in the bag. All aside from one thing. Me. I can't do it to the youth. It was one thing teachin' him a lesson outside but another seein' how he's livin' and cared for. He could be one of the ones from this shit-hole sink estate that could be different. Problem is I don't wanna go back out again now I'm here. I can just dump it safe and go. His mum's back at the door again.

'What's going on? Jake, go get your tea, now.' The kid shrugs and leaves. She ain't happy.

'It's time you left. You can take the bag with you. Whatever is in it isn't wanted here. Take my advice and do one from his life. He's a good kid who doesn't need any more visits from you. You must be the one he told me about who got him the hiding. He won't be out there anymore doing your running, now leave or I will call the police.' She's feisty, I'll give her that. Her nose is close to mine now and she's just starin' me out.

She's a fit bird, works out an' that. Looks like she could hold her own, but she's still nothin' to me.

'He'll be where he's meant to be or you'll be kissin' little Jakey goodnight for the last time.'

I should've realised when she smiled what was comin' next. My bollocks scream in pain as the bitch knees me good an' proper. I double over an' stagger for the front door to get away.

I'm not runnin' you understand, I just don't need no filth comin' with what I have in the bag. Anyways, little Jake ain't my problem. I wait in the stairwell while I get my breath back. I need somewhere else to lay this gun down and soon.

Ed will need to know it ain't with me and where they can get it if they need it quick. I don't have to tell him straight away though. I can wait until I think the time's good for me and the money. Ed findin' the weapon ain't gonna pay that much. Look at the last one. It'll be better pay for me if it's on the street about to get used, then the price will rocket.

It won't be me carryin' it. It'll be Ghost. He'll only get a five stretch though and he can do that standin' on his head. I'd see him right when he got out; give him a decent position with the new blood in my gang. Times are about to change for the better round here, you watch.

I get back to Maria's place. Put the panel back on the bath and re-set the telltale. It's time for some weed.

50

ED

'Penny for them?' Sienna asks. I look at her then back across the Thames, sipping the fresh nectar of the first morning's coffee. The small coffee hut near Lambeth Bridge provides a welcome stop after the meeting with Westminster Crime Squad. They'd had prints and DNA from the crash helmet and it all came back to Ben. His true ID anyway

They've asked me to ask my friendly if they know where he is. I told him I'd ask, which of course I won't. I've arranged a meeting with the CPS to discuss the situation and if there are grounds to delay arrest in the circumstances. I doubt there will be. They'll see it as a criminal playing the system despite his involvement on a more serious operation. That's why the meeting's been scheduled for two weeks' time. If Westminster catches him before then, well, that will be unfortunate.

The case is weak, as Ben has already pointed out. I finally answer Sienna.

'Lucy wants to try fostering with a view to adopt. The whole kiddie thing's been on my mind recently, hence my predictable self has become unpredictable,' I tell her. Sienna raises her Styrofoam cup in recognition of the truth in the reply. We get back to the covert car and place the drinks on the dash. The windscreen steams up. The standard cup holder section's full of phones and cheap notebooks.

'You'll make a great dad. I can see you with a baby or toddler; I think you'll be surprised how much it would suit you. Stop you being such a miserable selfish bastard, anyway,' she jokes.

'Have you ever thought about having kids?' I ask her. Sienna reaches for her cup and tentatively lifts the lid and sips before replying.

'No. Kids aren't my bag. I'm a single and a career woman at heart and proud of it. I don't do baggage of any kind, unless it contains limited clothing for a tropical holiday. I have dreams about where I want to go, where I want to be and children aren't a part of that. I'm too selfish for parenting and proud to know it.'

I contemplate her reply. I admire her ability to be brutally honest yet totally sincere. It's why she's a great handler and detective. She reads people so well and can communicate with all walks of life. John is the opposite. A good detective but would rather be at home with family than putting in the hours we do.

'Any calls from the woman you bumped last week?' I ask.

'I had a text saying she'd be in touch soon. Could be she wants to bring something to the table rather than turn up empty handed.'

'Good. Let me know when she's ready to meet. Would be good to get her on-board. Start up our new wheels and let's get across town and meet some of yours before lunch.'

Sienna starts the engine to our Mercedes GL350 BlueTEC. The black paintwork, low profile tyres and alloys coupled with blacked-out rear and side windows give it a street appearance. My source phone starts ringing. It's Ben letting me know he's up and about. Whatever that means I hope it's good for us both. Time is running out. Results are required and quick.

51

BEN

I can't remember gettin' up at this time. I'd be gettin' in but never up. I check my phone again for the time, nine-thirty in the mornin'. Truth is, I've been up all night on a bender of weed and booze. I feel like death but I can't shake the shit off Troy has brought to my door. My head's spinnin' with noise and chat.

I find myself sayin' 'shut up' at random times to no one but the air. My mind's completely messed up right now and if it don't get respite, then I don't know how it will all turn out. Today I've gotta make plans and start decidin' how I'm gonna play this with Ed. He won't let up on me now he knows there's a sniff of a gun about. He'll want it off the street, but this time he wants someone with it. Cops are always lookin' to pin summat on a dude. They're never happy with gettin' the gun. Have to have someone to rag about with it.

I need to make sure all's cool with my man at the garage. I'm near there now and the front grill to the work bay is halfway up. I duck under and see him out back makin' a brew. He turns and sees me and carries on doin' his own tea. He don't offer me nothin'.

'What do you want? I'm busy and not up to chatting after getting raided and a night in a cell. Some arsehole's talking and for all I know it could be you.'

'You finished, Mr Preacher Man? Do I look like the kind of guy who goes talkin' to the filth? I've come for my crash helmet.' He tosses three spoons of sugar in his mug, stirs and lobs the spoon on the workbench.

'You're out of luck. They took it along with a load of bikes, parts, clothing, the lot. Cleaned me out. I've got no choice but to shut up shop and take to the mattress. I'm not doing time, so they can come find me. I was lucky to get bail. Troy arranged a good brief for me. Know anyone that does passports, ID, that kind of stuff?' he asks.

He doesn't suspect me at all. 'I can ask about, like. I used to know a fella, but he's retired now.' All lies but makes me look good.

'Forget it. What else do you want?' he looks like a bag of rottin' meat that's oozing a leak. His face is alcohol red and he's sweatin' like an Arab. The guys been knockin' back some shit since he got lifted.

'I wanna use this place for a bit. I've got some goods I need layin' down, short term. Now your place has been turned over it ain't likely to get done again. It would be ideal, put you back in Troy's good books,' I tell him as he drinks his tea.

'What is it you need storing?'

'You don't need to know that. I just need the space for a couple of weeks. I'll see you right.'

'Get me a passport and you can use whatever you like,' he clearly doesn't believe me.

'I told you, I can't get you that right now. Besides those things don't come cheap. Tell you what I can do though, I'll open this place up and keep it lookin' like it's business as usual while you make for Spain or wherever else you got in mind. How does that sound?' he's thinkin' about it. I can tell he's tempted as all he was gonna do was have his tea, lock up and run. This way no suspicion will come about until he's well away.

'Done. Here's the key. There's nothing left worth taking, anyway. Customers have collected their own legit stuff and plod got what they wanted too. Good luck.' He throws me the key. I can't believe my genius sometimes. Now I have a place to lay the gun down where I can get it easy and an account for my crash helmet if I ever get nicked and they start askin' questions. There's no law against workin' at a place and lettin' your crash hat be used by anyone who needed to test ride their bike after repair, is there?

I don't think so and there were so many I lost count of who, what, where or when. Sweet as. There's not just my DNA in that lid alone. Loads have used it but the filth will focus on me. He didn't ask me what was in the bag as he left for the last time. He knows he's goin' down for a long stretch. I don't blame him for doin' a runner and givin' it a go. A supply charge comes at a price in terms of jail and that's a place he thought he'd never see. Add the nicked bikes into the mix and a conspiracy to steal 'cause of the helmets an' that, and he's goin' down.

Shame really. He used to be straight as a level until I came along. Troy was lookin' for a decent mechanic to work the bikes and conceal class A in fake tanks and hollow frames. Troy didn't give him a choice see. He spread a rumour the fella was into kiddies. He'd told him he'd spread the story far and wide if he didn't cooperate. All bullshit and lies but you try tellin' that to us lot when we're at your door all tooled up.

The rest, as they say, is history. Every good lock-up has its day though and I like bein' part of this one especially when I was responsible for crucifyin' it.

I wait until I'm certain he's away. The place is all locked up from the inside. I get a set of ladders that are leanin' against the main garage wall and go into a little office room out back. It's cleared now apart from a desk and chair. I ditch the steps and look about for any old carrier bags. I check under the tiny kitchen sink and I strike gold.

The guy weren't much of a hoarder but he didn't like to get rid of his plastic bags. I grab four and go back into the office. I put one each on my hands and then cover my feet securing them off at the top. I climb on to the desk and remove the polystyrene ceiling panel.

I find a couple of good metal ceilin' supports and hoy the bag up and place it across them. I replace the tile and climb back down. I look up. You'd never know it's been moved. I take off the bags and stick them back under the sink, hidin' them in plain sight.

The filth are done and dusted with this place now. They'll have moved on to the next mug. I take a seat at the desk. I've realised I'll be OK bein' here. I didn't need the bag routine but my mind's kinda paranoid right now. Technically I own this place according to the law of the street. I could see myself workin' on bikes an' that. I'm good on engines, especially gettin' bikes started without keys. Now that, I'm shit hot at. Nah, this seems strange.

One minute he was here and the next he's gone. I can't escape the fact that it was all down to me. I have a temper and when someone disrespects me it just triggers it. I guess he weren't that bad. He'd talk to me when I came by with a bike that needed a new identity.

He'd been in the community longer than Troy and me but he couldn't accept the rules had changed since he first opened up.

I guess some people have no respect for youth and innovation when it comes to business and work.

I feel good now. I've decided this place is where I'll be crashin' for a while. I feel safe here with a shooter in the roof and a fuck off steel door that locks good and tight. You can't tell if someone is in or out from the outside when all the grills are down. It ain't a huge place but it has a toilet, microwave and runnin' water. I can shower at her place or just not bother. Fact is, I'm in control of my destiny here. I still got phone signal and this is proved by Ed droppin' a text: *Where u at?* I gotta laugh when he does these.

He's tryin' to sound like my mates would 'cept they wouldn't leave no question mark at the end. I called him on it before in the car and he laughed too sayin' he just slips into the lingo.

I can't be arsed to see Ed today. He won't have any money. It'll just be the same old nonsense about what *he* wants, what *he* needs, what *he* expects to see, like I'm some kinda magician pullin' coke and guns outta a hat for him and his cronies.

I check my tracksuit trouser pocket and the pouch is still there, the rock diggin' into my thigh remindin' me to take care of it. The ring is in there too. I rolled it in bog paper so it doesn't mark the stone. I know I gotta get shot of it. The price of gold is good right now. I just ain't had chance with everythin' bangin' on around me.

I look at the state of my clothes and think of what Troy wears. Different clothes each day. I can't remember a time I had new anythin' – that I'd bought, anyway. I'm gonna need to go shoppin' soon and look for summat else to wear. My threads have seen betta days and need seriously upgradin' before they fall off me.

I go back into the main garage pit area and in a corner is the previous owner's bike. He must have had it elsewhere and brought it over when he got out. A Kawasaki Ninja 250r in green. I can't see him comin' back for that now. I know that the bike's legit. It's quick too. He only just got it. His pride and joy he called it. He must have it on tick and that's why he's left it. He won't be needin' it like I need it now. I just blank Ed. I bang in a call to my bird though. She answers after four rings:

'Yeah? What you want?'

'Well that's a fine way to speak to the love of your life, babe?' I laugh.

'He's right next to me, so it can't be you.' A small chuckle and a yawn tells me she's been sleepin'. The baby is good. She says the doctor told her it may come early so we have to be prepared an' that.

'I was thinkin' of comin' by your place this evenin' and chillin' out with you? You up for that? I can bring summat for the occasion?' I hope she says yes. She yawns again.

'Sure, come over and while you're at it bring a takeaway, that would be great. Indian. I can't stand Chinese right now. Neither can your baby, he kicks like a horse when I eat it.'

'Sweet. See you later tonight, around eight. I'll bring you what you want, trust me.'

'Last time I trusted you, you said you'd pull out.' On saying that, she hangs up.

52

ED

Being sat at Nolan's desk listening to him run through association charts and intelligence on Troy had not been part of my plan this afternoon. Ben's blanked my calls, so I've decided to leave him alone. This in turn means I can get back home on time for the first meeting with the over-eager social worker and over-eager Lucy. Paperwork completed; we were told a couple had backed out of a course being run this weekend. Our names were duly put forward as replacements. Lucy was beside herself with joy as she can see the chances of being placed with a child appearing sooner rather than later.

'What do you think?' Nolan breaks my thoughts.

'Sorry, mate, I was miles away, go again.'

'What do you think to getting your friendly to go out with you and point out all the known addresses associated with Troy? We'll hit them all at the same time and try to flush the gun out.' He's keen, which is refreshing.

'Yeah, that's a great idea. I'll speak to our person today and arrange it for later.' I look closer at the chart of associates and see Ben's true identity linked by a line to Troy and Troy's last known address and mobile number.

This then spirals off around the whole network. Ben has

clearly gone up in the world since we recruited him. I'd been so distracted I hadn't truly appreciated how useful he has become. It's then I notice another address linked to Ben on the chart, not the YMCA one but one that's registered to a girl. I can only think this one is his girlfriend's place.

'This address here, what's that all about?' I ask.

Nolan looks at the chart and digs out an intelligence record.

'Carl Rogers has been seen going in and out of there recently. He's one of the main players with Troy. Why?' Nolan looks up from the desk.

'That one will definitely need turning over, his name has been mentioned a few times, so it's worth considering the gun could be there.' He nods and records the address in a blue A4 book he's using to keep notes.

'Tell you what, why wait? Let's get it turned over now. I'll have a team get the warrant. We'll have the door through in no time. I'll let you know if we turn anything up.'

With that he folds up the papers and shouts his DS in from the adjoining office.

I give Sienna a ring and she agrees to meet me with the car. I know I've done the right thing. Ben has to realise he can't play both sides. Hopefully there'll be nothing there and the raid will be good for his street cred and allay any thoughts that he's an informant. I'll just have to wait and see.

Sienna and I cruise down Edgware Road taking in the different cake shops and watching people smoking outside cafes, soaking up the morning sun. I see a deli. We stop and grab a cake and coffee and join the people-watchers at an outside table, observe the world go by as we wait for the call from DI Nolan's team or Ben. My money's on Ben, Sienna's is on the team. She reckons there'll be nothing there; I hope she’s right. My phone goes. It’s Nolan. They’re through her door and searching. Ben is nowhere to be seen. She claims she hasn’t seen him in days.

53

ED

So it was an ex of Ben's. DI Nolan confirms she wasn't impressed at having a knock at the door and a horde of plain-clothes cops storming her flat. They found nothing there that could link Ben with the address. No one mentioned the real reason they were there and what or whom it was in connection with. They had a warrant and that's all she needed to know. She'd get a copy, of course. The occupant wasn't impressed with the way the spaniel up-ended her knicker drawer. She attempted to grab the dog but was suitably restrained. The reason for her change in behaviour became apparent when the dog froze indicating to the handler he'd found something of interest. That something happened to be a nine-bar of weed. A result in the end but not the one they wanted. The occupant wasn't forthcoming with any information either.

'Still a result, all good for the figures.' Sienna, as always, sees the positive in any situation.

'Shame we can't be rewarded for giving them the steer,' I joke.

'Bum steer at that,' Sienna adds.

'Let's go. I've had so much coffee I'll look like I'm pissing tar.' I get up and grab my cigarettes, phone and lighter.

All I can do is wait for Ben to call. I need a holiday: no phones, no work, no Ben. Just peace and quiet where the only decision I need to take is whether to have ice in it or not. The social worker last night had indicated it might be a good time to take a break, once the intensive weekend course is over, as placement timings varied so much but it could be quick. Lucy wasn't listening to that part. It was the only part I remembered.

I retrieve the parking ticket attached to the windscreen and get in the driver's seat. I hand the ticket to Sienna who lobs it in the glove box with all the others. I'd had an email saying I was reinstated as driving. Our Commander was appalled at the decision made by the traffic officer and my ban was overturned. I engage reverse on the auto sports box and then move out and join the flow of traffic back towards Marble Arch and Victoria. I keep my eyes on the road and the mirrors. The windscreen incident shook us both up and we were aware our tradecraft could've been better at the lights. We should have anticipated adverse action by the rider. They all look the same on these mopeds, out for what they can get like fish in a pedicure tank.

I'm thinking about how much time we had in relation to Troy and his proposed use of Ben. Meanwhile Sienna is on her phone looking at a clip on YouTube.

'What's that you're looking at?' I ask her. She looks up then carries on watching.

'It's the latest upload from the BMW boys. They're talking about a link up with London and calling the link a 'diamond geezer' in some kind of mockney accent. They're also talking about expecting a white out on the streets...oh, and if it doesn't come off, there'll be a new Trojan War and the city of Troy will fall again, peace out.' They know their history, which, for a bunch of drug-running scum, is pretty impressive.'

'How many views has that clip had?' I ask.

'Over a thousand. To be fair, it's only just gone up on the site. They don't post many though, and only when they have a message they want hearing. Kind of obvious, I know, but what I'm trying to say is that they don't just put up pictures of guns and money. All their clips have a purpose and that's to intimidate.'

'How many do you watch?' I'm curious.

'Quite a few. This is how they show their strength, by baiting each other this way. Sadly, some of the younger set see it as a call to arms. Frightening world we live in when technology influences murder and stabbing rates. It's clever though as they don't have to spell out what they want, they just leave it open to interpretation. If, and it's a big if, the clip gets taken down then it's too late. The message has been seen and is being talked about within minutes of it going up,' Sienna enlightens me.

I concentrate on the road while Sienna checks her messages. If anyone were to look, they'd just see a couple in a flash car enjoying a drive rather than two detectives desperately trying to stop a gang war on London's streets. My concentration is broken by the sound of sirens. I check my rear-view and see a fleet of Territorial Support Group officers hurtle past in vans. Behind them are two unmarked cars weaving their way through the traffic. The grill glows blue. I pull over so they can make progress. I now have the plain cars alongside me. I recognise the passenger as DI Nolan. He's screaming inside the car at the traffic to move over so they can get through. I call him.

He answers and my ears become filled with sirens and radio chatter.

'Late for breakfast?' I ask. I hear him telling the driver to take a left.

'There's been a shooting in the park on Troy's estate. A kid's been shot in the head on a ride by,' his voice is stern, professional and directed.

'Fuck. I'll ask about.' He thanks me and hangs up. Sienna had heard the conversation on speaker.

'I'll make some calls while you drive, let's see if anyone's heard anything. I'll call John first at the office and see if he can do some digging on the background.'

I nod in agreement and slowly make our way over to the vicinity of the park. We won't be overt. We will look and see the faces that are out and see if any are known to us.

John feeds back all that's known so far, and I call Ben.

He answers. 'I ain't got nothin' yet, bruv. I'll call you soon as I get summat,' he's brusque and wants rid of me.

'A kid's just been shot dead. It's on Troy's patch. I want to know who did it. Where are you?' I ask him. There's a space on the line with just the sound of traffic in the background.

'That's serious shit! I ain't nowhere near there, Ed, I swear and I ain't been for ages. I'll start askin' about, take a walk and see what's happenin' and what the word is. I'll bell you later.' He hangs up.

The kid turns out to be no more than a child, a boy who would regularly take a turn on the roundabout. Rumours were, he was a runner for Troy. Started dealing recently from a set pitch but there's no evidence of that. My work phone goes and it's John.

'I've just spoken to one of mine who lives near there and he says Ben's name's coming up. Nothing concrete just that the victim's mum said he'd been round there the night before the shooting and wanted to leave a bag but she told him to get lost. I thought you should know.'

I let what John's said sink in.

'Cheers. I appreciate the call. We're heading back to the office now then straight out.' I hang up.

'Why are we going back?' Sienna asks.

'We need different transport.' I wait for the right moment and spin the car round towards Victoria.

54

BEN

The filth are everywhere askin' questions and stoppin' everyone that moves. I'd left it a good couple of hours after Ed called before I went out. Let the shit settle a bit. The park is sealed off with tape and a tent is over a patch of grass twenty feet from the roundabout and swing set. I can make out police in those CSI suits hangin' around.

Now and then a flash of light appears from inside the tent. I need to know who the kid was who got slotted. Why has there been a shootin' on our manor? I think back to them space invaders who crashed our club. Troy's been makin' enemies, that's for certain, and now it's game on. I move closer to a crowd of people from the estate. They're bein' kettled in by the riot lot but they ain't doin' nothin' other than cryin' and watchin'.

Children are gettin' hugs by their mothers and fathers or whoever is closest to care enough to comfort them. As I get near, I see the woman from the kid's flat from last night.

I stop as the reality sinks in. She's being helped by a couple of police as she lays some flowers down at the tape along with some others that are now there. I know it's her kid now. Everyone else ain't gettin' the same treatment as her. She sees me and starts shoutin'.

'You! You! You fucking murdering bastard! Peddling your drugs with our kids, are you happy now? *Are. You. Fucking. Happy. Now*?' I can see the cops tryin' to hold her back but her legs have given way already, she's on her knees, on the ground, sobbin'.

I do what anyone else would do. I run as fast as I can. My breath is heavin' in my chest and sweat's runnin' off me and gettin' in my eyes. I reach the road that leads to the bike garage and start slowin' down. I'm lookin' all round me though, expectin' to get nicked at any moment. I was too obsessed with lookin' for Five-O to see the black van come alongside me. My back's to the road though. I knew summat was wrong when I hear a door open and my world goes black as a hood is dropped on my head and tightened at the neck. I'm grabbed up and dragged in the back. The door slams over as the van accelerates away.

I've no idea who it is. No one's sayin' nothin'. I'm laid on the floor with my hands bound behind my back in what feels like plastic. The floor smells musty and I can smell stale food. I try shoutin' but then a foot gets pushed on my neck and I think better of it.

Whoever's drivin' is throwing the van around streets. I have no idea where I am. For the first time in a long while I think I might piss myself. One thing when you're off your head, another when you ain't touched nothin.

'Look, yeah. Whoever you are, you're makin' a big mistake grabbin' me up like you did. I can tell you, you got the wrong man. I never touched the kid – that's the only reason I can think you'd have me here. So why not cut this shit out, let me go and all will be cool with me.' Still nothin'. This silence carries on for what feels like an hour. Whatever I say I gets no response. Then the van stops, the engine cuts. I hear a door open and shut. The side door opens now; I can feel a rush of fresh air.

I'm dragged out and my legs are kicked out from under me and I'm forced to kneel. I'm sweatin' good now. You only make people kneel when you're lookin' to execute them. I've seen this kinda shit for real.

They always piss themselves though and I'm fuckin' close, I can feel it. I hear a bag get unzipped and the sound of metal. The feet get nearer me now. This is it; I feel sure I'm about to get wasted like the kid in the park. It must be Troy. I hear a barrel spin. It's a handgun. Only bloke I know who could get hold of one quick would be Troy. He said he was gonna do that after the one I gave away to Ed.

He put it down to bad luck: wrong place, wrong time. Filth does regular estate sweeps now lookin' for knives and guns. I ain't got no one to say goodbye to. There'll be no one at my funeral. No Twitter or FB shout-out to get people to come along so I ain't buried alone. Most will be glad I'm gone. I know that. I know what people think about people like me. Not even Ed would turn up. He always said he'd deny ever knowin' me if he were asked.

'Look, man, please don't do it! Troy, if that's you; I don't know what I'm meant to have done wrong, bruv. I always did what you asked me. For the record though I never shot that kid. It weren't me. It weren't me.' My head is hangin' now. I've lost the will to carry on and just want it over with. Ain't no use cryin' or wailin' an' shit. Gets a man nowhere – when the time's up, it's up.

The hood's grabbed off me. I can't make out who it is as they're standin' in front of the sun. All I can see is shadow as my eyes adjust to the blindness. But then it becomes clear. Clear as day.

'The fuck you on, man?'

55

ED

I was hoping to have gained a bit more information, but I feel reassured. Ben hadn't pulled the trigger on the boy. He could have been faking of course but by his behaviour he seemed legit. Not his style. He's very pissed off though, so I leave the plasticuffs on. We're alone in an abandoned lorry park.

'You fuckin' fools! What's your problem, Ed? And you, bitch face? I'd never have put summat like this with your name on it.' Sienna shakes her head and tuts.

'Language please, there may be children listening. Not that you have a great deal of time for kids,' she tells him.

'Look here! I may be many things you lot don't like but I ain't no kiddie killer. Anyways, think on what'll be happenin' to youse two when your lot find out I was kidnapped off the street, hooded and threatened to be shot in the head? Huh? Big pay day for me on that day. Now who's gonna be shittin' themselves, you pair of pussies.' He spits into the dust and tries to get up. I kick him back down again.

'Shot in the head…a gun you say?' I play him a YouTube clip from the USA of someone unzipping a bag then taking out a Magnum handgun.

'Amazing what your mind tells you is going on when you're being left in the dark, eh, Ben?' I tell him.

He shakes his head and starts laughing. 'Man, I thought I was about to die. I might use that one day, can you send me it?' he says. I laugh. He still thinks it's all a joke, or he's just relieved he's alive. He's calming down though.

'How can you have a go at me, Ed? You talk about sticking to the law when you lot are breakin' it all the time! You just kidnapped me and made me believe my life was over!' He has a point.

'We conducted a covert street extraction. You'd said how you felt under fear from Troy, so after the shooting we thought we'd make you safe. Reduce the heat and stop him sending you to a certain death by the hands of a gang named after a German vehicle manufacturer. If you prefer, we can make it known that you've been happily talking to police and providing us with a safe house, guns, drugs…' I've finally managed to make him see sense.

'OK, I get it,' he says. His head's low as he kicks at the road dust. 'Shame you don't trust me though after all we've been through. I've given you top drawer info and yet here we are with me trussed up like a Christmas turkey waitin' to be carved up and served by the rich and mighty.' He looks back up at me. His eyes lock on mine from under his mop of hair. I sit him down on the van's footplate.

'We needed to be certain in our own minds whether we could carry on working with you or just nick you. I'm still not one hundred per cent on that score. That aside, this was always going to be more fun. Keeps our skills sharp,' I explain to him while he remains sat, squinting at the sun.

'Look, take these cuffs off man and let's chill can we? You got any water?'

'Who shot the kid, Ben? He was ten, he didn't deserve to die.' Ben turns away from me.

'Honest? I don't know but I'll find out. I can't do that here though can I? I need to be back where you picked me up. The mother of the kid thinks it were me 'cause I was at hers last night tryin' to speak to the kid, see how he was after he got a kickin' from Troy. I didn't see the kickin' or nothin'. The kid never reported it to your lot either. She knows I hang with Troy and got the wrong end of the stick. On my baby's life, Ed, I never shot him, never.' I pick him up off the footplate and steady him as he gains balance.

'See this site? Take it all in as this is where you're going to tell Troy to conduct his business with the BMW boys. If you don't make this happen, then I'll assume you've chosen where your loyalties lie. With a guy who kills kids. It could have been your baby in the park getting ripped apart by random gunfire. Think about it,' I tell him as I cut the cuffs.

Sienna's sat in the driver's seat of the Observation Van. I remove the duct tape from the index plates. I'm hoping the Fraud Squad won't have had need of it or realise it's an open secret that they keep it unlocked with the keys in the sun visor. I jump in the back. Ben tries to follow but I place a hand on his chest.

'Use the walking time to think through your decision.'

He steps back off the running board, shouts, 'Fuck you,' and kicks the door as it shuts. I tap the interior and the van moves off covering him in road dust. Am I proud of what I've just done? I have no real thoughts on that. All I do know is that a child has been slain in a playground meant for kids to be kids, not be forced to deal drugs by adults who exploit every ounce of their youth until they become indoctrinated into a lifestyle they cannot leave.

I'd told Sienna she didn't need to come. I'm glad she did though. She needed to see from me that I wasn't all about Ben, his welfare, and his life. I needed that reassurance too.

It's very easy to concentrate on the damage caused to the source and lose sight of the cruelty and heartbreak these gangs cause. The younger recruits see this as the best route on the get-rich-quick scheme. Their only career path as that's what they've grown up with, pushing drugs on corners. The gangs are like a cancer that eats away from the middle, then takes more as it expands and devours everything in its path.

It will stop at nothing as it uses the host to feed off, to grow and maximise its strength and survival.

The cancer knows treatment is futile. It may take a hit but will come back stronger; all-consuming, until eventually it wipes itself out. Sated from greed, lust, and lack of competition.

I call DI Nolan. He's calmer now he's been to the scene. His team have their investigative paths to follow but he knows the community fear the gangs. Talk will be tight and not for his ears. My band of police will look to maximise what we can from where we can. You'd hope when a child dies the community would speak up and flush out the trigger-man. It doesn't always work that way though, and who can blame them? I don't live in fear of being shot when I next leave my flat, go to my car, or simply walk to my work.

Sienna turns into a McDonald's drive through. 'We need to eat, it's going to be a long day,' she says.

'I'm not hungry but you carry on. I think I've blown our only link. He didn't appear to want to think things through when we left him spitting out road dust.' I turn to her as she places her hand on my shoulder.

'He's one of many and who knows what will come out of this enquiry. The Ops team may come up with someone willing to talk off-paper or we go pro-active, infiltrate and recruit like we always do. I'll give my new one a bell later see how she is, you never know.' She takes her hand away and all of a sudden I feel cold. Am I losing the plot with everything going on both in and out of work? Irregular hours, lack of sleep, being in a constant state of alert in case the phone goes and I'm needed to respond.

'Can I take your order?' The speaker near Sienna's open window crackles into life and wakes me from my morbidity. Sienna finishes ordering and I shout out for a Big Mac large meal, diet coke and apple pie. 'I knew you couldn't resist.' Sienna smiles.

56

BEN

I'm on time for once. The shutter is down on the barbers I've been called on to. I'm round the back as the door opens and Troy's driver lets me in. He nods and indicates I should step over the threshold and go through to the cuttin' area. When I get in the lights are low and Troy's in one of the barber chairs. Ghost's with him and another fella I ain't seen before. The guy's a Jamaican. He has a basketball vest on, combat shorts that come below the knee. He's finished in Nike trainers.

'Come in, sit down.' Troy is cool so I'm guessin' he knows the brother. Ghost nods and I sit. 'So, why we here?' Troy kicks things off.

'We're here because someone has been rippin' up my manor and causin' bloodshed on my streets.' I catch a glance at Ghost, he ain't reactin' so I'm thinkin' him and me are cool here. This meetin' ain't about us being in the frame for going rogue. The Jamaican remains withdrawn right now. His time will come though else he wouldn't be here. Troy carries on.

'So, I'm thinkin' who have I upset so badly that they'd waste a kid for just doin' his job? So, I put two and two together and came up with you two. Bill and Ben.' Shit, shit, shit. He knows the name Ed gave me. He must know I'm talkin' to the filth. My palms are sweatin' now. This shit just got real.

I try not to look suss and wipe my hands on my hat as I take it off. Troy's swivellin' the barber seat from side to side and using a hairdryer to point at us both as he's speakin'. Kinda eases the tension as he looks a prick as he could've used his gun. But we all know that gun's history now as it's just been used for murder.

'Only messin'!' He swerves about in laughter and the Jamaican springs a grin revealin' a gold front tooth that matches his chain. I'm kinda sick of this theatre now, if I'm honest. Once is bad enough, but this is becomin' a habit with him.

'Chill boys chill. This here's my man from the Ham, Birmingham. The kid's mouth was a loose cannon that needed fillin'. Word got back to me it was him that was mouthin' off about what we was up to, where we laid down our belongings, and that's how the filth came about knowin' through "Community Policing". I ain't here to make them lives easy and them policies work. I'm here because I was born here. I own this manor and all youse in it. My man's here because his firm want a piece of the action and the exchange rate's gone up for the rock. The heat's about to go from simmer to flamin' hot now the kid's dead, so the job's been brought forward. After it's done, we can lie low for a while then come back stronger once all leads have dried up.'

The Jamaican's still sayin' nothin', just lettin' Troy run the show and respectin' it's his turf right now and he's just a guest on the soil.

'Two days' time you're off up north. It's too manic to do the deal down here. You're grounded until I bell you and then you roll. No questions. Just do what's instructed on time, on the day. You cool?' I look at Ghost who just shrugs his shoulders. I take his lead and say nothin'. Troy nods to the door. Our part in the meet-and-greet is over.

As we leave, the night air grips my face. It's tellin' me I'm alive, for now. My phone goes, it's Troy on WhatsApp, *All sweet.* It's a question not a statement. He doesn't do grammar. I reply with the same words. He now knows I still have the rock and the gun. Why'd he leave the rock with me? He trusts me.

He's the only one that does. The diamond's safe with the shooter but in a separate place.

Word is that the main family who run this part of London got to hear the kid was talkin' way too much. A representative visited Troy and told him to deal with it properly. At the same time they told him they'd heard about his trips to Birmingham too. They know his every move. Troy's being left to manage the BMW boys and get the situation resolved quick. That's why he's keen to get this trade done and dusted. Troy can feel his grip slippin' and he needs to get a hold of this and make good.

The hit on the jeweller ain't gone down pretty with the upper tier as this has caused extra filth on the streets and that's bad for business.

I just go where I'm needed. Rumours are being spread how Ghost and me ain't to be messed with after the guy lost his hand. That's why I reckon Troy is keen to get me doin' the run. He knows we'll get the job done proper. I have to say though the Yardie lookin' guy in the barbers looked like he don't fuck about either. Proper fella they sent.

A clear message is comin' across. Let's not be stupid over this business so we can all go home safe. Screw that. No one messes with a north London posse dictatin' how things will go down. Whether you're south of the river in a county or up country, it's our way or the highway.

I ain't forgotten the little trip earlier today neither. Ed and the bitch with an itch can go fuck themselves if I'm gonna suggest some poxy lorry park miles from nowhere. Who do they think they are? When this is done then they're next. The pair of 'em is dead. Screw the goodwill parcels, the money, food and nonsense like that. Screw all that.

Ed showed his true colours today. He's actin' like a criminal, so he can take some street justice. If he thinks he can slap me about one day, then kidnap and threaten to kill me the next he's a bigger prick than I first thought.

His girl could do with cuttin' loose from him and go work elsewhere. She's all right, minds her business while he screws everythin' up demandin' shit. I check my phone, there ain't been no messages or missed calls from him since. I put the phone back in my pocket. Credit's gettin' low but it'll have to do. I need to save it for when the call comes to roll. Ghost will have dough. He's always flush.

I know I promised Maria I'd bring round a takeout but in truth I don't wanna go near hers right now. Doors have been flyin' in today and my ex got hold of Ghost yellin' and screamin' that I'd given her address some time when I got stopped or nicked and she just got lifted with a nine-bar. Made me laugh though. She shouldn't have agreed to store it for me. Troy don't know it were his either.

I'm back in the garage now, hungry but good. Ghost is on his way over with a carry-out and Chinese. We settle down for the night, gettin' pissed. I get the Spray 'n' Pray out the roof and Ghost starts messin' around with it, posin' like a gangsta, wavin' money in one hand and pointin' the gun down at the ground across his chest with the other. I have the magazine though and I ain't told him where that is. I wouldn't put it past him to try an' rob me; he's been on a weird high since the diamond job.

Says he had a dream the other night where he was bein' strangled. When he went to try to break the lock on his neck, he couldn't find the arm, just a hand with fingers locked round his throat. He put it down to a line of coke he'd done.

I check my phone again. Just calls I've blanked, lookin' for a hit. Nothin' from Ed. I ain't bothered. Troy's told me I'm in for a good wedge of money from this drop, a real good cut he said.

I believe him. He may be as violent as hell but he ain't

disrespected me like Ed did. How could he think I'd shoot a kid? Yeah, I've given him a slap and got him taught a life lesson but that were for his own good, his own survival. Plus, Troy never asked me to kill him. I'm not sayin' I would have done though. There was something about the youth that reminded me of myself at his age.

I'm tired now and grab a sleepin' bag that was here and crash on the floor. Ghost's out of it too, just lyin' on the ground in his clothes, wasted. Troy were never goin' to call tonight. Tomorrow or the day after will be the time. Once the BMW lot have sent word, the parcel is good for collectin'. I sleep with the Mac-10 tonight. I've attached the magazine now Ghost's drugged up. I don't trust who could be the next one through the door despite me thinkin' no one other than Ghost knows where we're at, I don't wanna be ill-prepared if I'm wrong.

57

ED

Twenty-four hours. Still had no contact from Ben. The Trident Murder Investigation Team has been on the phone asking for an update. I lie and tell them our friendly is out and about and I'm waiting on a call. They'll be getting impatient now. They need an identity for the shooter and where the weapon is.

They are busy working up intelligence on where the weapon may be and I've already had to tell DI Nolan things have gone dry as far as my friendly is concerned. He doesn't ask the reasons why, he's too professional for that.

A knock on the office door breaks my thoughts. I get up and walk over and open it slightly. It's DI Nolan.

'What brings you to darken this door?' I enquire while letting him in and showing him through to our meeting room away from the main office. He sits down and opens up a folder while I put the kettle on and dispense dark grit into two mugs. Kettle boiled; I return with the drinks and sit.

'I thought I'd come over and give you a heads-up as to where we are around Troy.' I'm all ears and hope it's good news.

'We've had him under surveillance. Last night he linked up with one of the BMW boys at a services off the M6. We followed him back to London and into this barber shop in Dalston, where these two turn up.'

He shoves a couple of surveillance images across the table. I take a look and immediately see one is Ben with another male I know who goes by the street name of Ghost. I say nothing and wait for Nolan to confirm who he thinks they are, or if he needs them identifying and that's why he's here.

'We've identified them as Carl Rogers aka *Bam Bam* and Denzel Yates aka *Ghost*. Both known gang members and close trusted foot soldiers of Troy. Our concern is they're looking to progress a job and quickly with the BMW boys. Birmingham have shared intelligence that a firm from London are looking to exchange a diamond for four kilos of cocaine. Truth is there'll be no exchange. The BMW boys are planning to rob the firm and if necessary, kill them.' He pauses.

'That's not all. There was an incident in a club recently where police shut it down. A group of mopeds turned up, pissed off that a rival gang had hustled in on their club. It was nothing to do with London. It was the BMW boys flexing their wings. Troy has been dealing with them for a while and they want control of the London line. Troy is the messenger. The real firm behind it all are a leading crime syndicate who own that club along with many others. They didn't sanction Troy's excursion and now he has to sort it out. The death of the kid was the last message from Birmingham. Give them the line or more will lose their lives.' He sits back and takes a sip of coffee.

'So, what's this diamond robbery got to do with it?' I ask him.

'It's all bollocks. Yes, the guy was robbed; he was a long-time crook in the jewellery trade and the rock's worth money. The gem is all Troy has to trade and he's got no choice. Our fear is that he's using the two in the photos to do the exchange and rob the BMW boys of the cocaine. In short, it's a right mess being brought to my table. I need you to see if your friendly has heard anything and when they plan to move. I've got a surveillance team on them as I think it's close but I can't keep them employed twenty-four seven, I haven't got the budget. It's a shame "The Family" don't put the squeeze on the BMW lot and tell them to back off. It would solve many of my resource problems,' Nolan says as he closes the file.

'The family won't get their hands dirty while they have these two to do the work. Keeps the chain weak until they really need to show force. They have an empire to maintain way bigger than Birmingham could imagine. Leave it with me. Where's the intelligence strand in Birmingham? Who have they got feeding it back?'

'They're not saying, at this stage. They're being all cloak-and-dagger, which doesn't help much at all. Our Commander is liaising at a higher level to ascertain how we can work closer together. This could be open warfare unless we disrupt it,' Nolan finishes. We shake hands and he leaves. I get a refill and contemplate my next move. I don't have the time to go out and recruit. It's an intensive process and time isn't on my side. I'm also left with the fact that there's a belief that Ben and his mate are the team to put in the hit. They will kill or be killed.

I open up the secure server and find Ben's intelligence record. I find the application to revoke his use and conduct, open the document and start typing. Sienna was right, his time's up. He has become unmanageable despite my best efforts to get him to see beyond his greed.

On completion of the paperwork I hit save, hover over the send button, and then press it.

I don't feel relief. I feel sadness at my failure to turn a young life away from crime.

Many come and go in this game, and some come along who you know could be better but in the end you're powerless to effect change on the person's behaviour and beliefs. Ben's traits are engrained with the grime of the streets and the ethics of the gang code of survival. Darwin would be pleased.

He knew it was a dog-eat-dog world when all aspects of life fight for the right to remain and get stronger.

It's Friday afternoon, the sun's out; all out. I get my coat, pocket my cigarettes and leave, grabbing the car keys to the covert vehicle. Something tells me I'll need this at the weekend and I'm on-call anyway, as I am every day of the week. It's the adoption course too, which I'm looking forward to like a hole in the head. It's not the subject that bothers me, it's the idea of disclosing aspects of our personal life in front of strangers.

Ben has the opportunity to parent but doesn't care enough to see it as something to look forward to. His idea of a stroll in the park with a buggy would involve using the baby as a form of subterfuge to hide drugs and who knows what else, so he can carry on life as only he knows. That's if he remains alive to see the baby born.

58

BEN

My head's fine but Ghost looks like death. He's alive as he's snorin'. I carry on layin' where I am, just starin' at the ceilin', scratchin' my bollocks and hoping it ain't today that we need to roll as my energy's low. I sit up. Pushing myself up with my hand on the makeshift pillow of old towels from the kitchen, they all feel smooth. I throw 'em up and stop. The gun ain't there, it's gone. I kick Ghost awake.

'What are you on, man? I'm awake, I'm awake, where's the fire?' He's pushed up on one arm now and rubs his head with his other hand.

'The joke's done. Hand back the Spray 'n' Pray. I ain't got time for no games around that, just hand it back now.' He's lookin' at me like I'm talkin' Japanese.

'I ain't got the piece. You had the piece last night? So where'd you put it?' Ghost looks confused.

I grab him up and he gets to his feet. I slam him into a locker. 'Give me the piece now an' stop playin' games!'

He headbutts me on the nose and I let him go. Blood pools in my hands as I try to control the flow.

'What were you on last night, man? I know what I was on, but you've lost the plot. Have you checked the roof space, see if you didn't put it back there?' Ghost says pointing at the ceiling. I look at the table and hop up. I push open the ceilin' tile and feel about, my hand touches the bag and I pull it. It's heavy. I pull it all the way out and check in it. It's all there as last night, magazine in. I don't recall doin' it.

I didn't feel that wasted but maybe I was? I can't remember as my brain is screwed up. 'See! You prick! You coulda checked first before you started getting heavy with me. Next time I'll break your neck if you try any of that shit on again.'

I don't say nothin'. I was doin' weed last night and hit the booze but normally I'm good on it. I just put it down to one of them things. Move on, no harm done apart from a busted nose.

'I need to get some tissue paper to block this,' I say. Ghost shrugs, leaves, and returns with some. 'What time is it?' I ask him.

'It's three-thirty in the afternoon. We must have been off our heads to sleep that long.'

I check my phone. No calls from Troy. But there's a text from my Maria:

Do what he wants. I've no idea what she's sayin'. Then my phone rings. It's her.

'Yo, what's with the text? I just got it? Do what who wants?' There's a pause then a familiar voice comes on the line.

'Do what I want. I ain't so certain you got the balls for the job, so I've taken summat of yours till you tell me it's done. All I need is a photo sent to this phone of them BMW lot dead and then you get her back after I get the coke. You start rolling now, they waitin' for you. Nine o'clock tonight. NEC, Birmingham. You'll know where to go when you get there. Don't be late else she goes the same way as the kid in the park. Laters.' Troy's voice fades out.

'Who was that? You look even worse, man,' Ghost says as I flop my head down on the desk. This has to be a dream.

'Troy. He's got Maria and he's keepin' her 'till this job's

done and we get back with the coke. I don't know what he's on as I told him I'd do it, I told him,' I say. Ghost says nothin', he just leans against a bench. His head's up and his eyes are shut, like he's in prayer.

'We gotta go now. He'll text the exact place for the drop from her phone. He's gonna fuckin' kill her, ya know? She knows way too much now and he won't like that. He's gonna get us all killed. After all we've fuckin' done for the man, he's sendin' us to our death,' I say, lookin' at my man who is shakin' his head. 'He says I have to send a photo when we've killed them then bring him the coke before he'll let her go. We gotta get the motor and get rollin' man,' I say. Ghost snaps out of his trance.

'I'll go get the motor. You get the shooter and we'll go get this shit done and get your missus back. If that means Troy dies too then I'm fucking game for that. We're gonna have to save on ammo though,' he says. He comes close and grabs my hair each side and looks me in the eyes. 'Don't worry, bruv, I've got your back.' He lets go of me. He grabs his stuff then he's away under the shuttered door and off. My mind's racin'. I get the gun and the diamond and wait for him to get back with our motor.

59

ED

Today's been one I could have missed. The start of the fast-track course for fostering and adoption is nearly over. Death by PowerPoint, stories shared and dissected, all of me now wishing for the final whistle and the pub. I check my watch. It's 3.30 p.m. Still thirty minutes left on the clock. Lucy has loved it. It's been a safe space for her to share her feelings about not being able to have children naturally, and if I'm honest, it has made me aware that it isn't just us in the same position.

I feel my phone vibrate in my pocket. I step out of the main room and into a small, empty side room. As I look at the screen, I see Ben's name. My first thought is not to answer it. He's no longer my responsibility as far as I'm concerned. But it's unusual he's calling rather than texting. I answer.

'What's up?'

'Bell me back now, Ed, please, it's urgent, man.' The line goes dead. His voice was quick, garbled and tense. I press *call return* and he replies immediately.

'I ain't got long, but it's all gone mad here. They've got my bird and they're gonna kill her and the baby unless I do what they want, you gotta help me, man, you gotta help me!' He's serious.

'Calm down and take a breath. Who's they?' I ask.

'Troy. Troy's got my bird and he's holding her hostage. I've gotta drive with a mate to Birmingham and meet with some proper gangsters and pick up some coke. If I don't do it, then I'm dead and so is she. It's serious, Ed. I'm desperate and I ain't got no one else I can turn to,' he pleads.

'Look. You can't go anywhere do you understand? You have no authority from me to do anything...'

'I ain't askin' for any authority, I'm tellin' you what I'm gonna do 'cause he'll kill 'em both if I don't do it. You're gonna have to nick me to stop me, man. Just get her safe, Ed, just get her safe,' he responds quickly.

'Who else knows she's being held?'

'No one else does, just Troy and probably one of his goons who's driving.'

'It could be a ploy for Troy to flush you out as the one speaking to police. Only you would have called us. He'll know. Then he'll know who has been responsible for doors going in.'

'I ain't got long. My ride will be here, my credit's going and my battery's low. I'm tellin' you to do what you have to do. I'll survive but she won't. I'll text you her address and number. You won't hear from me again. I ain't got no choice, Ed. I gotta go and do what he wants...I ...' There's a beep on the line as the message arrives, then it goes dead. I finish writing down all he said and get on the phone to Sienna. She answers on the fourth ring.

'This must be grief if you're calling me on a Saturday.' She's not wrong.

'I've had a call from Ben. I need to meet you in thirty minutes. Are you at home?' There's a pause.

'No. Here's the postcode, house number eight. See you in thirty.' She asks no more. She's professional. She knows I'll be rushed off my feet with calls before I can get to her. I ring our DI. The phone rings out then goes to answer machine. I leave a message and hang up.

The tea break's over now and they're all filing back in. I compose a text to Lucy and press send. She has her own car here and can get home. I'd brought the work car separately. I must have known the weekend wouldn't go well and I was right. If I'm honest, I'm glad to be getting away. I exit the building, find my car and get in.

The door to the covert car shuts with a firm suction as the engine comes to life. I link my work phone to hands-free and dial the out-of-hours Intelligence Desk or Red Desk as I know it. The speakers engage with a dial tone. It took what seemed like an eternity before it's answered by a tired-sounding female.

'Red desk,' comes the reply.

'It's DS Hunter from SC&O35 I need to speak to a supervisor.'

'This is DI Brownlow how can I help you?'

'I've a live kidnap/hostage situation and need some information sanitising and passing to the on-call kidnap team.' She immediately swings into action. By the end of the call she's contacted the on-call kidnap team and her intelligence desk have started working up the intelligence to assess its validity.

'Keep this phone active, DS Hunter. A DI from the kidnap team's been apprised of the situation and she'll make contact. Call back should you need any other assistance.' On that note she's gone. I'm close to Sienna's postcode now and put a call in to DI Nolan before picking her up.

'What do you want? Don't you know it's a Saturday?' He sounds his usual, deprecating self.

'I can't be one hundred per cent sure, but I think our Birmingham job's gone live.' I await his response and there's a pause as he tells his kid to turn the TV down.

'What makes you so sure?'

'My friendly has been back in contact and they're in deep shit.'

'How bad?'

'Drug supply, guns and kidnap. Kidnap lot are dealing

with that angle. Have you had any contact from Birmingham?' I ask him. I can hear another mobile phone going in the background.

I don't explain the full kidnap situation. I don't have time as DI Nolan cuts me off,

'I think that might be them now. Give me five and I'll call you back,' he says. I bash the horn and Sienna appears at a window and shows her index finger and disappears. Shortly she's opening the passenger door, being waved at by a female of a similar age to her.

The female's hair tied up and enthroned in a towel. As she enters the car and shuts the door DI Nolan's back on the line.

'Your friendly's right. That was Birmingham. Their asset has just made contact and the meet's been set for later his evening at a unit at the NEC.'

That fits with what Ben had told me, but I don't reveal it. I need to know just how close this Intel source is to Birmingham.

'There's another issue,' Nolan says.

'The BMW boys are sending three of their best to do the exchange. They've never left a swap over without shots being fired and gurneys loading up at the end. I've got authority to deploy my team. As far as I'm concerned, it's my target's associates rolling up and that's game on in my book.' I say nothing and let him carry on speaking.

'If the Kidnap Unit establish a substantial offence and a link with this job then happy days, we'll have the whole lot tied down. Where do you want to be?' I think about that. I've had no contact from my DI and I won't go above his head. I take an operational decision.

'Meet me at Scratchwood Services and give me a spare radio so I can monitor. I can contact you quicker by radio if I need to.'

'See you at the slip road at Scratchwood Services for a quick radio drop then you're on your own. Thirty minutes, so shift your arse.' He's gone. Sienna was in Pinner so I'm not far from Scratchwood Services.

'Buckle up. We're going on a road trip. I'll explain as we go.' Sienna gives a mock salute and I point the car north and drive.

60

BEN

'Get this crap off man. What sounds you got?' Ghost asks. I chose to drive. I'm safer behind the wheel. I stick to the speed limit as I don't want any attention from cameras or cops. Last thing we need is a tug in this motor. I fuckin' hate the M1. I hate it because it's a road outta London and I'm a London guy through an' through.

My head's bangin'. I can't call Maria 'till I've sorted this out. I can't. I'm already paranoid about the filth listenin' in on my phone. Ed says not to believe what you watch on telly, but he would say that.

'What you doin' now?' I ask Ghost as he fiddles about with the bag at his feet.

'Checkin' the shooter. We won't have time once we hit the Ham.'

'Hit the Ham? What you on about?' I say.

'The Ham, Birmingham, ya know? Like the Nam, Tottenham.'

'It ain't about Tottenham or Birmingham, you prick, it's about Vietnam, ain't you watched *Full Metal Jacket*?' He's looking at me queer like, his eyebrows up towards his forehead.

'I never knew that. See, I learn summat new every day with you. When we stoppin'?' Ghost asks.

'Stoppin? I've only just got on the motorway. We ain't stoppin' 'till we get close to the NEC. Troy left a piss bottle in the side, I saw it.'

Ghost leans to his left and dives into the side pocket and brings out a small crunched rubber container with a lid.

'What am I gonna do with this?' He's holdin' it up at me expectin' me to take proper note of it.

'You takin' the piss? You take off the lid, stick your cock in it and whizz. What's your problem?' He still looks confused despite my explanation.

'I ain't takin' a piss in front of you, bruv, no way! You're gonna have to stop at the next services.' I'm gettin' well hacked off now. Services have cameras and cop cars. We've got a full tank of diesel so we don't have to stop.

'Piss in that or hold it. Either way I ain't stoppin and that's for us both, so don't overfill it. 'You ain't got any fanny disease have ya?' It's a reasonable question in my mind.

'If I did I'd have way more than you, ya monk.'

'Monk? I'm gonna be a father, ya tool!' Ghost's smilin' now but he looks in pain.

'You still smartin' from earlier man?' I ask him.

'Nah, I need a shit real bad, bruv, and there ain't no way it'll fit in that and I ain't tryin'.' Man, he's pressin' my buttons today.

'Fuck's sake.' I see a sign for Scratchwood. At least he can bail out on his own and go do his business while I wait in the car. I swing the car over three lanes and take the exit for the services. He'd better be quick. I'm on a clock and it ain't goin' backwards.

61

ED

We're in the car park at Scratchwood Services. You won't know us, suss us, or even be thinking of us when you stop here to take a leak and refuel with coffee and diesel. That is unless you're a criminal or a cop. But that's mainly because we are always looking out for each other. Seeking out can be a positive conducted out of protection and concern for welfare. Today, it's about getting a radio so we can prevent death.

I have no idea how Sienna and I will achieve that as we sit in the covert car away from the more obvious overt cameras that survey the area twenty-four seven.

Although I have Sienna and DI Nolan on side, I feel alone. I'm in charge of my world right now, as my DI still hasn't called back. I'm not calling him back either as I want both mine and Sienna's lines free just in case the operational teams need us quickly. I'm also being obstinate if I'm being honest.

I have more experience in this situation than he does despite his rank. I know I'll make the right decision based on what I'm presented with. Whether he would agree with that when the dust settles is another thing. That all depends on whether anyone dies, or Ben is compromised.

If Ben gets nicked, then so be it. He knew the score. Ben knew the choices he made would have consequences. All his life there've been consequences. I could've helped him if he'd only listened sooner.

I have the authority to protect him but I also have the humanity to want to do so. He isn't bad. He just does bad things. Ben won't like the outcome of this. He has an experienced Operational Team targeting the people he's going to meet. It can only mean two things. He's arrested or dies. I know he's strapping a gun. He didn't have to spell it out. He'd told me that when he hung up. Actions speak louder than words in this game. Funny thing is, I'd have done the same thing if Lucy was in that situation. Cop or not, the protection of family is inherent and runs through our veins like the blood that sustains us.

From where we're parked we have a good vantage point of the main car park without being overt. Trees provide shade and we're both sat in the back. Ben won't know this car either. He's never been in it. We've been allocated a second vehicle. I'd chosen a BMW 5 Series estate. I'd made the decision to switch things up. Gut instinct kicking in plus the initials for a theme. Who am I kidding? I just wanted this for the fleet. Midnight Black. Speed when we need it. We will need it today, of that I feel certain. The wait for either a source or an Ops team rendezvous is always a tense time on a live deployment.

You don't want to be compromised. You're alert, on edge and wanting the operation to come off. You don't want to blow things by spooking anything or anyone.

I text Nolan saying where we are and he replies he's five minutes away. I glance through the centre console and out the windscreen as a pure white Audi A3 slowly comes into view in the same area we're in and reverses into a parking space opposite us. The car park has many spaces more convenient than this. The passenger door opens and I recognise the occupant as Ghost from surveillance footage. There's Ben. He's sat, hoody up, leaning back in the driver's seat.

I instinctively lean back too and use the driver's seat as

cover as I try to observe what's happening. Ghost has disappeared behind the car they arrived in. I note the index, colour and occupants. The date, time and what they're doing. I hope I don't enter any evidential chain as a result. I know I have no choice. I can't and won't ignore it. I then see what to me is an obvious surveillance vehicle enter the car park and slowly move towards us.

I get on the phone and press recall. The car is inching closer. I know the occupants' have seen me. My heart is in my mouth, chest pounding. Ghost's back round now hitching up his trousers carrying a plastic bag that looks heavy at the bottom. I get through to Nolan.

'Get the fuck out of here, it's not safe.'

'I know. Just seen the white Audi and Ghost of all people shitting in a bag behind the boot. You couldn't make it up.'

He's laughing, still on the line as his car diverts right towards the petrol area. We're both laughing and the tension temporarily abates. The bandit car's going nowhere. They're in an argument over what to do with the carrier bag. Ghost trying to get in but Ben pushes him out and gesticulates at a nearby bin and the bag.

I guess what Ghost's thinking. He doesn't want a parcel of his DNA left here. He's being rightly cautious, whereas Ben doesn't want the car stinking of Ghost's fetid shit. Nolan is away out of sight, and this distraction has meant neither Ben nor Ghost have seen him. Nolan is on the phone.

'There's a bin further up the slip road, on the left, near the traffic garage. I've put the radio in a carrier bag and will drop it there. Don't lose it! Let them run from here before you leave and we'll pick them up. There are some strokes of luck you've got to go with and I'm staying behind these two. I have the surveillance capacity to split teams. Stay in touch where you can but stay well back. I don't want you spooking them. I can cover picking them up on surveillance from here. Good luck escaping that smell,' he says as he hangs up.

They've stopped arguing now. Ben's had his way and

Ghost's back in the car as they move off. I remain stationary and wait ten minutes before setting out. We collect the radio from the bin drop and turn it on. It's set to the channel they're using, and the commentary cuts in from an unknown voice.

'Lane one, north bound, no change, no change.' They have the car in sight and it isn't deviating from its pattern or direction of travel. All of this is a good sign. We're about half a mile behind them and just enjoying the ride. The early evening sun makes shades a requirement.

We know they're not being shadowed by any more of Troy's mob and that's a welcome thing. It tells me Troy isn't keen on providing a support car to shadow Ben despite the gun he must be carrying as well as the diamond if he has it. I could be wrong though.

62

BEN

'Jesus. What did you use to wipe your arse with? I swear I can smell shit.' I've gotta bring it up. There ain't no amount of air con can kick the scent of that.

'I told you I managed it, right! How do you know it's me? Coulda been you stepped in some?'

'I stayed in here when you went out. I don't wanna see your arse.' He's laughing now and I am too. Master criminals on the way to shoot up some blood have to stop for a natural. We ain't robots after all. I look across at Ghost liftin' the sole of his trainer up.

'I must have stepped in it. It's all over the bottom.'

'You coulda gone in the service station? Now we've got to put up with this for the whole journey,' I tell him.

I pull my neck bandana up around my nose. It blocks out some of the smell but it ain't perfect. I check my mirrors for Five-O but there ain't nothin' obvious.

We're well out of London now. Ain't no copper gonna know us out here. I start to calm down a bit but I really need to know what's happenin' with my girl. I can't phone Troy, it would wind him up and he could just do her there and then. Plus none of us know if the filth have our numbers and are listenin' in. I need to phone Ed. But Ghost can't know.

'I've gotta call Troy. Find out whether she's still alive or not. He nods like it's cool. My dirty line ain't linked up to the open phone system in the car. I have Ed on speed dial and press 1. He answers so quick I didn't reckon I was through.

'Yo, what's happenin' with her?' I say.

'Where in the fuck are you? I thought you had no credit left?' Ed says. I hung up on him to save some but he don't need to know that.

'Don't mind that. I wanna know how she is and if she's alive or not?'

'Look we have things in motion. We have to assume she's alive until I know otherwise. Plus, I'm sure Troy will give you the chance to do whatever it is you're doing,' Ed says all cocky sounding.

'I ain't doin' nothing, I told you.' Ghost's wide eyed now thinkin' I'm baitin' Troy.

'I can tell you're in a vehicle, Ben. I can hear the fucking traffic noise. You need to think through what you're doing and fast. We can both resolve this and keep you out of it.'

'No way, man, this has gone way beyond that. It's personal now. Especially when you bring another man's family into it without givin' the dude a chance. You know that and you'd do the same.' He's not so quick to respond to that one.

He knows I'm tellin' the truth. He'd do the same if it were him. He showed his true colours roughing me up like he did. I've had time to dwell on those things and I know he ain't a bad person. I know he's helped me try to get on the right path, done right by me when he didn't need to.

He was tryin' to talk my language but he ain't part of my world.

'Do what you wish. I can't stop you and I have no idea where you are. Remember the compromise strategy regardless but you're no longer working with me. It's a shame as we had a few laughs along the way and we made a good team. Your choice, your funeral.'

He's hung up. I try diallin' back. Now I really ain't got no credit. Ghost's the same. I know where I've got to go though, and Troy said he would bell me at nine on the dot to make sure I'm there. Then he'll call the BMW boys on to the meet-and-greet. I'm all fired up now. I'll be greetin' them with 9mm rounds that'll rip 'em to pieces. Right now, I just want my girl back and to make sure my baby ain't harmed.

'What did Troy say?' Ghost asks.

'He told me to shut the fuck up and get on with the job. That's what.' We settle back into the drive. I can still smell shit.

'We got anymore bags?' I say.

'What for?'

'For you to put over your shoes and block the smell, that's what for,' I tell him.

'No, we ain't. I used the only one I could find in here. It was one of those thick jobs and not a thin throw away. My shit would've rotted that through for sure.' I can tell Ghost's not finished.

'Besides, if this all goes tits up I ain't bein' dragged out the car by the cops with carrier bags on my feet. They'll be thinkin' I'm coverin' my trainer soles against marks not that I'm tryin' to stop the smell of my own turd,' he says while I'm laughin' again.

'It ain't that funny. Hey, we gotta turn off here accordin' to the screen. Troy must've set this up before I got the car.' I check the screen. Ghost's right. It's tellin' us to come off left towards the NEC. I've always wanted to see that place.

63

ED

The road is eating me up. Every mile we progress towards the end goal just gets quicker and quicker. I have no idea where we'll end up but I do know it won't be a five-star hotel. My phone screen lights up. It's my DI.

'Ed, just got your message, I was swimming. What's happening?'

'Ben's en route to Birmingham with DI Nolan's team behind him. He has an associate called Ghost with him. There's every chance they're armed, but that's not been confirmed. Ben's girlfriend has allegedly been kidnapped or taken hostage by Troy. The BMW boys are not going to play ball according to DI Nolan. There's going to be a shoot-out between the two gangs.' I pause and let him take it in. He's silent and I can hear the scratch of a pen nib on paper.

'Do the kidnap team know?'

'Yes.'

'I'll deal with them and keep you updated. Are you in contact with DI Nolan?'

'By phone.' I won't tell him I have a radio as he'll only freak out about me being part and parcel of the surveillance, which in my mind I'm not.

'I saw the revocation of his authority as CHIS on the

system, Friday. I'm aware of all the circumstances you've been managing. You've done what I would have done. He's acting way outside the parameters of any agreement we had. Stay in touch and say hi to Sienna for me. I'll update you with the Kidnap Unit's progress.' He's gone. I cancel the hands-free call and Sienna turns towards me.

'He's settled in well, I think,' she says.

'Yeah, you could be right there,' I agree.

The radio comes to life again, *'Subject vehicle left, left, left towards the NEC.'*

It's all flowing too well and the cop in me wants the result to be good. No enquiry for a police shooting just arrests all round and a case that stands up in court. I also want Ben back out on the streets. My wandering mind is brought back to the real world by the sounds of Sienna's phone.

'Hello,' Sienna answers and sets it to speaker.

'Is that Sienna?'

'Who's this?'

'It's me. We met at the club the other week.'

'Hey, how are you? I'm glad you called back?'

'Yeah, I'm good. I don't know if this is any use to you but there's rumours going round that Troy has gone and kidnapped a girl. It's bollocks,' she says.

'Why do you say that?' Sienna asks, cautiously.

'I've seen him with a bird and she looked like she was having a right laugh. You know, she didn't look like she was being forced anywhere,' she replies.

'Let's say you're right about the kidnap, it could be a different woman?' Sienna enquires.

'Nah, but I can see why you'd think that. I asked him outright. He just laughed and says it's a load of crap and that he's off to Birmingham tonight clubbin'.'

'How long ago was this?'

'Three hours ago. I never called you because I didn't know what to do or if you'd be interested. Anyway, you can make your mind up now. I'd like to meet up again soon, I'm well up for it, if you get my drift.'

Sienna agrees a future meeting then ends the call.

I call our DI and explain what Sienna's been told.

'I was about to call you back. The Kidnap Unit is behind Troy on the M1 towards Birmingham. From what they can see the occupants of the car are smiling, happy, and nobody is being held against their will. The DI on the kidnap team has spoken to DI Nolan and they're letting the vehicle run. If it's all linked with Ben, and this transaction, then we'll soon uncover the truth behind what's going on.'

DI Ashworth hangs up. Time will tell and very soon we'll find out. We're headed towards the NEC now and very close to the car parks. It won't be long. Surveillance officers are already covering the area and a different voice comes over the radio.

'Subject vehicle approaching a loading bay in Perimeter Road. They're parked on the right before the bend…wait…doors opening to a main loading terminal – subject vehicle has entered. Doors now closing. Visual lost, visual lost.'

Ben is out of view. The Ops team won't know if anyone else is in there. What's certain is that the job hasn't been called off.

I take our car well away from the venue and don't take the obvious route Ben took. We need to be out of sight. Our role is done. Ben's only way out is in custody or in a body bag.

64

BEN

The engine cuts out in an echo. The guy who opened the hangar doors has left. He's done what he was asked and fucked off. Can't say I blame him. The inside is one massive empty space. If we end up doin' the job here, then it will sound like major warfare. I stay in the motor, as does Ghost. He's got the piece out now, fiddlin' about with it at his feet so he doesn't inadvertently show it to outside eyes.

I don't reckon he's gotta clue how to work it beyond pullin' the trigger and hopin' it goes off in the right direction. I just hope he can hang on to it when it kicks.

I'm sittin' back, waitin' for the next person to come through the doors. It don't make sense why they'd choose here. There's cameras everywhere for a start but I'm guessin' the boys have control of them somehow. They must have an inside man.

I power the window down and listen. I suss out any fire exits and check where the outside doors are. There's good choice for gettin' out of here on foot. I say on foot because the main doors will be shut tight when those boys roll up. That could be a problem.

'Hey, Ghost. What say we do the exchange then rob 'em once we leave here? We're sittin' ducks, man, nowhere to run.

The filth will get their arses down here quicker than we can get out when you start firin' that.'

'You gotta point there, bruv. This is all sorted with them BMW boys in mind and not us.' I hear another engine. The little guy's reappeared and is opening the main doors again. Headlights blind me and I close my eyes a second. When I open them I see two motors: A Porsche Cayenne I ain't seen before, beams still on full, and the other I'd know anywhere; it's Troy.

This just ain't right. What is he doin' here? Rollin' in with them wide boys at the same time? Maybe he's brought my girl here to do an exchange once I've done the dirty work. I kinda relax with that. I just need to make sure the firepower doesn't go off in the direction of his motor. Troy stays in his car. My phone goes.

'Yo, they're ready to deal. Take the rock over and get the coke,' Troy says.

'Whoa, man, that ain't how we do things and you know it. They ain't gonna have the coke in that motor! Same way they don't expect me to have the rock in mine. Who they callin' on with the coke once they seen the rock? They can see a photo of it then we'll sort out somewhere to do the swap. Otherwise they'll suss they're bein' set up!' He just carries on breathin' down the phone.

'Do as I tell you if you want to see your girl again.'

'I need to speak with her first, man.'

'I guarantee her safety. Now hurry up so we can get away from here. Ghost will handle the firepower once you're away from the motor.' He hangs up. I can see the Jamaican dude I saw with Troy at the barbers. He's got a baseball cap on and his dreads hang out the back. He's wearin' a loose black basketball top with the Jamaican flag on, same shorts and shoes he was in before.

His clothes are meant to show me he ain't carryin' but I don't believe that for a minute. He raises his top and turns around as he walks towards me. Bare skin's all I can see around the waistband. I don't know who else is in the motor and what they're strappin'. I have no choice though. My palms are sweatin'. I don't turn my head but speak to Ghost.

'You better be ready on that piece, man. You're the only person got my back in the whole world and I'm relyin' on you now, bruv.' He says nothin' but nods and pats the gun at his feet.

'Just don't turn back. Promise me you won't?' He's lookin' kinda weird now but I ain't got time to chat. I open the driver's door and hold the pouch up and my left hand open. I start the long walk to the middle of the floor. The Jamaican can walk the long walk with me.

I ain't goin' anywhere near his car. I've been dragged into enough vehicles recently. I give it the swagger. I motion with my left hand for Ghost to up the lights. The Jamaican and his crew can get blindsided too.

He holds his arm up to his face as he gets an eye full of halogen. Now I'm pumped. He wasn't expecting that light display. We're equals now. I don't care how big those boys think they are. Ghost and me is an army and we ain't takin' no prisoners. We arrive in the middle of our arena. He sticks his chin up like he's havin' his prison mug shot taken.

'Ya, man. Let's keep this ting cool and on da level. You show me da rock and I'll show you da white.' His eyes are on mine and don't budge.

'You show me the coke and I'll show you the rock or no deal. My man's over there, he wouldn't be here but he wants to make certain it's all done good, no messin' anyone about.' The Jamaican takes a large sniff and gobs out phlegm.

'Come.' He starts walking backwards to his motor. All I can see is headlights. There's a light on in here but it's shit. The fading light through the roof windows helps. It's clear enough to make out people but if we don't do this hit quick, then I'm at a disadvantage.

As I pass the front of the BMW boy's motor my eyes are still too dazzled to make out who's inside. The rear window is down a shade and smoke comes blowin' out the top into my face. Sweet smellin'. We get to the boot and the Jamaican opens it. Inside is a black holdall. He unzips it. Sure enough the blocks are there.

'You wanna test this, wide bwoy?' It's a reasonable request.

'I'll get the test kit from Troy. If it all checks out you get the rock. His attitude immediately changes.

'No, bwoy. You ain't wanderin' aroun' 'ere wit' out me by yo side. We had a deal and yo pissin' us about now. That ain't cool, ya know.' This guy ain't gonna budge.

'Come over with me and see the rock properly. Troy can go test the shit in the boot then if he's happy, I give you the rock and he brings back the bag to the car and we all leave. How's that soundin?' He nods his approval. He leaves the boot open and walks with me towards Troy's motor. Screw Troy, he can get his hands dirty. I need to see my girl before I go any further. Once Troy's out the motor, I'll take out his minder and Ghost can let rip with the Spray 'n' Pray and we all get out of here and head back south for a white out.

I'm at Troy's motor now and Troy powers down his window.

'What's the problem?' He's all bling and attitude.

I can see there's someone in the back but they're covered in a blanket.

'I thought you'd wanna test the gear. Who else is in there?' The Jamaican starts suckin' his teeth and gettin' angsty.

'We ain't got time for reunions, ya bunch of pussys. Blood, show him his bird and let's get this done.' So he knows all about what's been goin' on. I've been played. Troy grabs the blanket and pulls it. There she is, sittin' there laughin'.

'Boo!' Maria's stoned.

'What you done to her? You said she weren't with you!'

Troy don't answer but she does.

'He's treated me like a princess which is more than you ever have. Do you think a few baby clothes is gonna make me happy and wanna stay with you, ya waster? I'll take my chances with him any day of the week. He's promised to take care of me and the baby and I'll take that, thanks very much.' She can't control her head. Her eyes are shot. Troy's out the motor now, and all I can see is a Brownin' 9mm. I start movin' back and he keeps it on me.

'This is what happens when you betray me you cock sucker.' I start steppin' back and stop as another barrel is at my head. I must have missed them gettin' out their car. I can't turn around; I'm frozen with fear but still givin' off hostility. Troy ain't finished his speech.

'Your mate told me what happened with the money and drugs that went on the missin'. You had it away and told him to tell me it weren't there. So now we're all here and you're goin' on a trip with these BMW boys. It was their cash you had away. They deserve the chance at settlin' the score. The coke? That's my gift to them, as a settlement of this owe. Now they have you, your bird and your best mate to do all my work. Don't look but he's the one behind you ready to pull the trigger on my command.

'We came all the way out here because my new associates from Birmingham needed to see I've got the balls to slay whoever I want. Especially those that cross a line like you have. Stealin' from the hand that feeds you. Very poor.' Troy's words are done for his audience.

I feel like I'm in the world's worst nightmare, but I'm not. I've been suckered into a hangar in Birmingham where I'm about to get handed over to the nastiest bastards on the planet in exchange for four keys of coke. My life's worth measured in sniff. I feel a wet heat on my legs; it gets stronger as it runs beyond my ankles. There's no stoppin' it. I should've pissed at the services but didn't wanna leave the motor with the shooter in it. Troy ain't finished.

'I know what you're thinkin' right now. You're thinkin' I ain't asked you about the rock? You still have it or so you think.' Troy's slappin' his leg now and laughin' while pointin' the 9mm about.

'I don't have no need for a fake piece of fashion paste, man. I always had the real deal. Like I'd leave that with you? You really are a tool, bruv. I'll be glad to say goodbye to a worthless, thievin' piece of scum,' he says.

Now it's my turn. I'm gonna have my last words on this earth for them to remember.

'At least when I enter hell it won't be as a kiddie killer. You're a coward slottin' a boy in the head, for what? He was doin' good for you. He brought in the most dough and he never left his patch, ever.' Troy's hand's shiftin' the piece about now but I ain't done yet.

'You say you'll look after us but you don't! Yo, Ghost! Before you go killin' me, let me know, as a dyin' man's last wish, how much he's payin' you for the privilege? C'mon, man, how much is my little life worth to a real man like you?'

The muzzle behind me lifts from my head a second then goes back. I know he don't wanna do it, but I know he will if Troy tells him.

'It's all gone quiet in the house? What's the problem, do it, go on, fuckin' do it! I ain't got nothin' left to give. I've ruined enough lives in my short years on this planet so go ahead do what you gotta do. Make sure you pay him though, Troy, you got witnesses now. What will you do about them, huh? Loose lips sink ships, Troy, and you'd know about that wouldn't ya?' That got him good.

'On your knees. Now. No one calls me a grass and lives, no one,' Troy yells as I feel the 9mm barrel firm against my temple. I ain't afraid no more though, it's like I no longer have anythin' to care about. No one cares about me. Everyone has gone out of my life, everyone. I can hear Troy breathin' like a freshly ringed bull.

'Ghost, now's the time to do what you're here for. Do him.' Troy's voice fades.

65

ED

Disorder starts playing. I reach for my source phone but quickly realise it isn't the phone. I've had to put the car radio on low as the tension is getting too much.

'You got any tablets?' I ask Sienna.

'Why would I have any? Not every woman carries tablets, Ed, some of us just take the pain and get on with life.'

'C'mon, my head feels like Ben's living in it, banging on about nothing.' She hands me two codeine and I dry swallow them.

'Cheers, that should help.'

'How much longer do you think they'll give?' she asks.

'It won't be long. Whatever that lot have planned in there they won't hang about and neither will the Ops team. I can only think they've got visual from the main NEC control room. Weird place to choose a handover, I would've never chosen here. Why not a lay-by in a country road? The bad guys must think they're covered with that one. Someone on the inside who's disabled the cameras when they let them in.'

The Ops team radio comes to life:

'All Alpha teams standby. Subjects are contained. Awaiting signal to attack.'

My adrenalin is high. I so want the job to come off. As

with all these things one shot fired by police is enough pressure on the officer but when that bullet connects and brings a death with it then he or she is in for years of stress as the investigation rolls on. All for doing their job, the job they're trained and authorised to do.

Ben doesn't deserve to die. He's more than a resource. I've come to realise that from working with him, talking to him in the early hours, because really he's lonely. He has no one in this world, never has. He wouldn't know a kind act if it hit him in the face. Violence was his only experience of kindness. The less the damage, the more the aggressor cared, and that was just his parents.

The sound of gunfire fills the air and breaks my thoughts.

The police radio comes alive: '*Attack, attack, attack.*'

The first of many explosions replaces the shots fired. We can hear the shouts from where we are situated. A police helicopter appears, and its blades cut the air as it hovers over the building, waiting for any runners.

Dogs are barking furiously outside, waiting for the same thing as the eye in the sky. Ben's game is well and truly up. It's a tight containment.

No one's going anywhere unless they're in police custody, an ambulance or a body bag.

66

BEN

There's no hidin' it now. My Converse's soaked and the smell's strong.

'Get this shit done, man.' The Jamaican has had enough and he's turned and walked away. As he does, he takes off his hat and under it's an identical small velvet pouch to the one Troy gave me. He sways away balancin' it on his head, and I see him headin' for the boot of the Porsche Cayenne.

It's all right for Mr Motivator. He knew what was gonna go down all along, as did everyone else, bar me. I feel a fool at not thinkin' it all through and realisin' summat were bait about the whole set up. What's done is done. The blade I'm carryin' ain't worth jack against the firepower here. I didn't have time to say anything. No real last words.

The main lights to the hangar suddenly flare up. Guns kick into life and my lights go out. I come to on the floor, the sound of shells fallin' around my head, jiggin' off the concrete surface. I feel like I've been punched many times but I know these weren't jabs from a fist. How I'm still here I don't know. As quick as it started, it's over. No one left to pull a trigger.

Smoke's fillin' the room. Loads of cops, guns out, shoutin' and screamin' *'Armed Police! Get down, get down.'* The voices fade in and out as they take in the scene. No need for their guns here. I can see all this from where I'm layin' on the floor. My right cheek wet from the heat of my blood that leaks from my ragged body.

A uniform cop is at my side. He's pullin' at my clothes and shoutin' for a medic. I know it's no use. I knew it as soon as I stepped out the car. I cough and my whole body wracks with pain as I feel my breathin' slow down. I'm strugglin' for air like a chronic smoker havin' an asthma attack. I've no control anymore. My ears are ringin' and I notice a weak beat at the same time.

The hangar echoes with barkin' as the smoke dies down. There are bodies everywhere. As I look under the chassis of the Porsche I see the Jamaican geezer.

He's got his arms over his head and his shoulders are pumpin' up and down. Weepin'. Weep you fuckin' waste of space, weep. Shame a bullet never found him. They must've all been for me. Sounds are fadin' now. I roll my head and look up at the skylight.

A large black bird with a huge beak stares down on me. Its head tilts to the side and its yellow eye meets my gaze. This feels like my last view of the world. A world that never accepted me, rejected me from birth and gave me a kickin' for years. My breath's gettin' shallow, the outside light's fadin' as sunset makes its move. An ambulance man is with me now, but I can tell by the way he's lookin' it ain't good. He's tryin' to get a needle in but my arm is all shot up. No vein worth a shit. His words of 'stay here with me' provide little comfort or encouragement. A fighter knows when he's beat.

I try to speak. He brings his head closer to my mouth. I whisper as best I can, 'Forget me...forget me...'

67

ED

I haven't slept well. DI Ashworth called late last night and broke the news Ben was among the dead. I hit the whisky hard, but nothing numbed the pain of his loss. I keep looking at my source phone, willing his tune to chime once more. I torture myself with where I went wrong. How I could have been a better handler to him. If he'd been paid more, would he have stopped? I'll never know.

I take solace in the fact I wouldn't be dealing with the aftermath of what was being described in the press as the worst gangland shooting in the UK. Other news feeds described it as a major sting against organised crime in the lead up to the Olympics.

Everyone was dead aside from two people whose identities weren't being revealed. Houses were being searched, more drugs and guns recovered as a result of what had been the culmination of an eight-month-long undercover operation by Birmingham Police.

My working world is one of chaos and unpredictability. When a job seems straight forward, it can just mushroom into areas you'd never imagine. I never predicted this.

There's always talk of retribution and ripping off rivals but most of the time it simmers out. Not this time though, despite how much we had prepared. Now this saga has ended, my mind will be able to turn to life outside of the criminal world. It won't last long though. Sienna's recruit has called back again. She'd heard about Birmingham.

The Jamaican that was at the final standoff was an Undercover Police Officer from the West Midlands Police. He'd given the signal to the Ops team who were watching events by camera that covered the hangar. The signal, a simple yet effective one of taking off his hat and dancing across the floor, the recovered gem in the bag on his head that Troy had given him before entering the unit. Troy had been working with him for months. No one suspected him of being police. Troy and the BMW boys had no idea they were being set up.

The UC had no indication that it would turn so quickly to a shoot-out. When the shooting started the UC collapsed behind the Porsche and prayed he'd survive as bullets danced around the hangar. He's currently off sick with stress. The eight months he was living and breathing their lifestyle has taken its toll.

68

ED

Life goes on. My work world reduced to a simmer, a much-needed simmer. Sienna has taken a holiday and John is as predictable as ever. My DI has written Sienna and me up for a commendation as a result of the way we handled the whole saga with Ben. I don't know if I can accept it though. Every emotion is still raw.

I'd underestimated the amount of pressure I was under and how that was impacting on my family life as well as my own mental and physical wellbeing. Then I think of Ben and perspective is gained. How he managed will always be beyond me.

I've agreed with Lucy to cut down the smokes to five a day, and so far it's working. We're both enjoying some free time this weekend. John has my source phone and the DI has my work phone. I am free. We see the sign for the pub where we're headed for lunch. A much-needed sit down to re-energise after all life has thrown at us in recent months.

Lucy has a busy practice too, something I'd forgotten when our worlds collided.

Her phone goes. She's not the on-call vet this weekend so we both know it isn't that. It must be a cold call as the number is withheld.

'Just ignore it, it'll be a cold caller.' She never listens to me anyway and answers it.

'Hello. Who is this?'

'Yes, it's Mrs Hunter.'

'When? Now? Oh my God…yes…yes…of course. When can we go?' I have no idea who she's talking to, but she has a paper and pen out that she carries like a handler and is scribbling notes frantically on the page.

'We can meet you in the next thirty minutes…of course. See you soon and thank you for calling us.'

She's off the phone now. Her hands cover her mouth as her beautiful emerald eyes glisten with moisture. I stop the car and turn off the engine.

'What's the matter? Has someone died? Has there been an accident?' I ask as she removes her hand.

'That was the hospital social worker. They have a baby who needs immediate care and we've been called, Ed.' She throws her arms around me and I reciprocate.

At last the tide's turning in our favour and we can start our family in the way we've been chosen.

'We can go straight there. I have everything we need in the boot if we have to bring baby home today. Car seat, clothes, blanket. Oh, Ed! This is so exciting, being able to give this little one a chance in life. I know it's early days and it doesn't mean the baby's ours or staying permanently, but we can still feel as if it is, can't we?' I look into her face. A face full of compassion I only wish I possessed.

'Of course it is. Well, there's no time to waste – let's get over there,' I say. Lucy puts the seat back and tries to calm herself before we arrive at the hospital. The baby is in a Special Care Baby Unit (SCBU). I know why babies go there but in her joy, Lucy had blanked that.

I feel good. Life is on the turn in a positive direction after all the pain and grief we'd been through trying to conceive and failing. I grab the ticket for the hospital car park and we make our way to the ward, hand in hand. We don't know when the little one will be ready to leave but the social worker sounded hopeful it should be soon.

To her this is a regular part of her work but to us it's the start of a new life journey. The security at the ward reminds me of entering custody, but with a better welcome and accommodation. I press the buzzer and can see an overhead camera move in our direction. The door clicks and we enter. The unit's peaceful; I was expecting lots of crying and wailing but there's none of that.

'Hi, you must be Mr and Mrs Hunter? I'm Claudette Jones from the social work team.' She holds out her hand, which is soft to the touch and motions that we should follow her along the corridor to the nurse's station.

Murals of clouds and butterflies adorn the walls. Smiles and hellos greet us as we go towards the station. It's as though we are being treated as new parents coming to visit their child. The social worker stops a nurse and we hang back as she looks at a chart and runs through it with her. The nurse comes over to us and shows us to a private side room and shuts the door.

'Hi, I'm the ward sister. Just to let you know little one is fractious. Had a rough night and is still withdrawing, naturally, at the moment. We're of the opinion baby's not in need of any alternative drug to help this process and it's better for them to manage it.'

'Withdrawing? From what?' Lucy asks, somewhat confused.

'Toxicology results show traces of cannabis and cocaine. The mother admits using during pregnancy but how much and how often is difficult to tell. All other tests are fine and he's feeding well. You can see him very soon but he won't be allowed out of the hospital for at least a week so it would be good if you could do some feeds here.'

Lucy is beaming with joy and the sister touches her arm as tears form in Lucy's eyes. 'No name yet but Mum is still recovering after the birth and not saying much, which is understandable in these circumstances.' The sister opens the door and we follow her further down the corridor, passing tiny cots with anxious parents sitting alongside either feeding or cuddling their newborns.

We get to a sliding door and it automatically opens. The sister goes in front and Lucy and myself follow behind her.

'Here's baby. How are you, my little one? You have visitors,' the sister says.

I can't see. I'm excited to fix eyes on the child. The sister has picked him up and Lucy looks at me.

'I'm a bit nervous, Ed. Can you have the first hold?'

'Sure, sure.' Lucy steps aside and the sister is still at the cot. All I can see are his feet kicking as they're swaddled in a blanket. I can't see a face or the rest of the body. I sit down and try to get as comfortable as a man can that has only held an infant once and not in the best of circumstances. The sister turns with the tiny bundle.

My world slows as the baby comes into view. The room begins to move as it becomes blurred, and hazy. Speech slows around me as my brain takes in the visual information. I try to concentrate on my breath to maintain composure. It isn't happening though.

I try to avert my eyes from the tiny red hat on his head.

A small hand-knitted red hat with a lemon *Stone Roses* badge stitched on the side.

I hear Lucy. 'Ed, Ed? Sister is trying to give you the baby.' It's the very same hat Sienna had made. The same hat we'd given Ben along with the babygro the baby's wearing, emblazoned with 'Daddy's little Angel'.

I take him from the sister. He rests calmly in the crook of my arm, his dark eyes widen as he blinks at the dimmed lights. I draw him close and cradle his delicate head into my neck, feeling his breath. As I place my cheek against his heart, my tears flow.

END #

AUTHOR'S NOTE AND ACKNOWLEDGEMENTS

This book is a work of fiction. All characters, names and events are from my overactive imagination. Any areas of London or any other places or names mentioned are done so to provide a setting, nothing more.

There aren't many people involved to acknowledge but the ones that are mentioned played a significant part in the novel's creation:

My wife, Emma, for suggesting I write something different. I hope I've done the story the justice that you envisaged.

Jane Isaac, for your friendship and support during my journey as a writer.

Sarah Ade, for agreeing to beta read this once I'd got sick of editing it.

Jacqueline Beard for her dedication and professionalism in doing the final beta read. I don't know how you do it but I'm truly grateful for all your support.

Emma Mitchell for her editorial support. If there are any mistakes left in the final print, they are all mine.

Mark @Kidethic for the outstanding cover design.

Russell Day for agreeing to provide a quote for the paper back version.

To *everyone* working within: Child Protection Teams, all who worked in the Major Investigation Team SCD5(7) MIT West, and all in the Covert Policing Command. This book is also for you. A small token of thanks for the great times together and for the service you have given and continue to give.

On completion of the first draft of this book I lost a friend and mentor in the police. The same fate has met some I worked with on the street. They were vastly different people in their outlooks and experiences of life but all had decent qualities that only a few were privileged to witness under extremes of circumstances. I'm proud to have known and worked with them all.

To you the reader, for your continued support, I will always be indebted. Having experienced one career of service I feel privileged to have another. It wouldn't be possible without you and I'm truly grateful. Stay safe and be kind.

See you on the next one and don't be late.

Best wishes,

Ian Patrick

June 2020

ABOUT THE AUTHOR

Ian Patrick is a retired Metropolitan police DS. He served for twenty-seven years before ill health forced his retirement. A rare form of muscular dystrophy was the culprit. The majority of his service was within the Specialist Crime Directorate. Rubicon is his debut novel and is in development for a six part TV series with the BBC.

He has appeared on stage at Bloody Scotland alongside Val McDermid and Denise Mina as well as appearing at various local literature events, in Scotland, where he lives with his family. Ian has also completed a mentorship in screen writing for film with the Scottish Film Talent Network.

When Ian's not writing he enjoys photography.

Ian can be contacted through his website ianpatrick.co.uk where you can sign up to a newsletter to be updated on any future work and events.

ALSO BY IAN PATRICK

Rubicon

Stoned Love

Printed in Poland
by Amazon Fulfillment
Poland Sp. z o.o., Wrocław

60724686R00171